PAUL TEMPLE
AND THE
GILBERT CASE

Francis Durbridge

WILLIAMS & WHITING

Cover design by Timo Schroeder

9781915887030

Williams & Whiting (Publishers)
15 Chestnut Grove, Hurstpierpoint,
West Sussex, BN6 9SS

Titles by Francis Durbridge published by Williams & Whiting

1   The Scarf – tv serial
2   Paul Temple and the Curzon Case – radio serial
3   La Boutique – radio serial
4   The Broken Horseshoe – tv serial
5   Three Plays for Radio Volume 1
6   Send for Paul Temple – radio serial
7   A Time of Day – tv serial
8   Death Comes to The Hibiscus – stage play
    The Essential Heart – radio play
    (writing as Nicholas Vane)
9   Send for Paul Temple – stage play
10 The Teckman Biography – tv serial
11 Paul Temple and Steve – radio serial
12 Twenty Minutes From Rome – a teleplay
13 Portrait of Alison – tv serial
14 Paul Temple: Two Plays for Radio Volume 1
15 Three Plays for Radio Volume 2
16 The Other Man – tv serial
17 Paul Temple and the Spencer Affair – radio serial
18 Step In The Dark – film script
19 My Friend Charles – tv serial
20 A Case For Paul Temple – radio serial
21 Murder In The Media – more rediscovered serials and
    stories
22 The Desperate People – tv serial
23 Paul Temple: Two Plays for Television
24 And Anthony Sherwood Laughed – radio series
25 The World of Tim Frazer – tv serial
26 Paul Temple Intervenes – radio serial
27 Passport To Danger! – radio serial
28 Bat Out of Hell – tv serial
29 Send For Paul Temple Again – radio serial

30 Mr Hartington Died Tomorrow – radio serial
31 A Man Called Harry Brent – tv serial
32 Paul Temple and the Gregory Affair – radio serial
33 The Female of the Species (contains The Girl at the
     Hibiscus and Introducing Gail Carlton) – radio series
34 The Doll – tv serial
35 Paul Temple and the Sullivan Mystery – radio serial
36 Five Minute Mysteries (contains Michael Starr
     Investigates and The Memoirs of Andre d'Arnell) – radio
     series
37 Melissa – tv serial
38 Paul Temple and the Madison Mystery – radio serial
39 Farewell Leicester Square – radio serial
40 A Game of Murder – tv serial
41 Paul Temple and the Vandyke Affair – radio serial
42 The Man From Washington – radio serial
43 Breakaway – The Family Affair – tv serial
44 Paul Temple and the Jonathan Mystery – radio serial
45 Johnny Washington Esquire – radio series
46 Breakaway – The Local Affair – tv serial

Murder At The Weekend – the rediscovered newspaper serials
and short stories

Also published by Williams & Whiting:
Francis Durbridge : The Complete Guide
By Melvyn Barnes

Titles by Francis Durbridge to be published by Williams &
Whiting

Cocktails and Crime (An anthology of the lighter side of
Francis Durbridge)
Murder On The Continent (Further re-discovered serials and
stories)
One Man To Another – a novel
Operation Diplomat
Paul Temple and the Alex Affair
Paul Temple and the Canterbury Case (film script)
Paul Temple and the Conrad Case
Paul Temple and the Geneva Mystery
Paul Temple and the Lawrence Affair
Paul Temple and the Margo Mystery
Paul Temple: Two Plays For Radio Vol 2 (Send For Paul
Temple and News of Paul Temple)
The Passenger
Tim Frazer and the Salinger Affair
Tim Frazer and the Mellin Forrest Mystery

INTRODUCTION

Francis Durbridge (1912-98) began in 1933 as a writer of sketches, stories and plays for BBC radio, mostly light entertainments, but a talent for crime fiction became evident in his early radio plays *Murder in the Midlands* (1934) and *Murder in the Embassy* (1937). The *Radio Times* (11 February 1938) mentioned that Durbridge had by then written some one hundred radio pieces, and Charles Hatton commented in *Radio Pictorial* (28 October 1938) that "He is one of the very few people in this country who have succeeded in making a living by writing for the BBC."

Although Durbridge continued to write plays and serials for BBC radio for many years, using his own name and the pseudonyms Frank Cromwell, Nicholas Vane and Lewis Middleton Harvey, his future was assured when in 1938 he created the dream team of novelist/detective Paul Temple and his wife Steve. The audience reaction to his radio serial *Send for Paul Temple* led to sequels over several decades that secured an impressive UK and European fanbase. Following *Send for Paul Temple* in 1938, Durbridge responded later the same year with *Paul Temple and the Front Page Men* and continued with many more. From 1939 to 1968 there were another twenty-six Paul Temple cases, of which seven were new productions of earlier broadcasts.

Then in 1952, while continuing to write for radio, Durbridge embarked on a run of BBC television serials that attracted huge viewing figures until 1980. And additionally, from 1971 in the UK and even earlier in Germany, he became known for intriguing stage plays that were not simply whodunits but more in the style of Frederick Knott's *Dial M for Murder* or Ira Levin's *Deathtrap*.

Paul Temple and the Gilbert Case was first broadcast in eight thirty-minute episodes from 29 March to 17 May 1954, with Temple played by Peter Coke (1913-2008) for the first time before making the role his own in ten further serials until the concluding *Paul Temple and the Alex Affair* in 1968. Marjorie Westbury (1905-89) was already established as Steve Temple, having assumed the role in 1945 opposite Barry Morse in *Send for Paul Temple Again* followed by *A Case for Paul Temple* (1946) opposite Howard Marion-Crawford. Then she partnered Kim Peacock on nine occasions before co-starring with Peter Coke on eleven, so she was Steve on twenty-two consecutive occasions until the final serial *Paul Temple and the Alex Affair* (1968) – which coincidentally was a new production of her first appearance as Steve in the 1945 *Send for Paul Temple Again*. But mention must also be made of Lester Mudditt, who appeared nineteen times as Sir Graham Forbes of Scotland Yard from the original serial in 1938 until *Paul Temple and the Spencer Affair* (1957-58).

A new production of *Paul Temple and the Gilbert Case* was broadcast in eight thirty-minute episodes on the BBC Light Programme from Sunday 22 November 1959 to Sunday 10 January 1960. Again of course it featured Coke and Westbury, but this time Richard Williams succeeded Lester Mudditt as Sir Graham Forbes for the third and last time. And incidentally Williams, a prolific radio actor, had much earlier played Paul Temple in the 1944 one-hour abridged version of *News of Paul Temple*. In fact he was already a Durbridge regular, with roles in the 1942 one-hour abridged production of *Mr Hartington Died Tomorrow* (which Durbridge wrote as "Lewis Middleton Harvey") and again in the new 1950 production of that serial; in Durbridge's short play (written as "Nicholas Vane") *The Essential Heart* (1943); in the serial *Farewell, Leicester Square* (1943), written as "Lewis Middleton Harvey"; in the series *Introducing Gail Carlton* (1943-44), again written as "Nicholas Vane"; and in the play

Over My Dead Body (1945). Richard Williams, moreover, was no stranger to the Paul Temple serials – with not only three appearances as Sir Graham Forbes but roles in *Paul Temple and Steve* (1947), *Paul Temple and the Sullivan Mystery* (1947-48), *Paul Temple and the Madison Mystery* (new production 1955) and *Paul Temple and the Lawrence Affair* (1956). He even appeared in the original production of *Paul Temple and the Gilbert Case* in 1954 – playing Lance Reynolds, one of the suspects, before in 1959 becoming Sir Graham Forbes in the new production!

Both productions of *Paul Temple and the Gilbert Case* were marketed on CDs. The 1954 original (BBC Audio, 2003) was also included in the box set *Paul Temple: The Complete Radio Collection: The Fifties 1954-1959* (BBC, 2016), and the 1959/60 new production was included in the box set *Paul Temple: The Complete Radio Collection: The Sixties 1960-1968* (BBC, 2017).

Turning to Temple's popularity on the Continent, the Dutch radio version was *Paul Vlaanderen en het Gilbert mysterie* (3 October – 21 November 1954, eight episodes), translated by Johan Bennik (pseudonym of Jan van Ees) and produced by Kommer Kleijn, with Jan van Ees as Vlaanderen and Eva Janssen as Ina; the German radio version was *Paul Temple und der Fall Gilbert* (4 January – 22 February 1957, eight episodes), translated by Elfriede Engelmann and produced by Eduard Hermann, with René Deltgen as Temple and Annemarie Cordes as Steve; and the Danish radio version was *Gilbert-mysteriet* (5 July – 23 August 1957, eight episodes), translated by Niels Locher and produced by Søren Melson, with Gunnar Lauring as Temple and Else Højgaard as Steve.

As with many of Durbridge's radio and television serials, *Paul Temple and the Gilbert Case* was novelised – but not as a straightforward adaptation. *Another Woman's Shoes*

(Hodder & Stoughton, August 1965) retains the plot of the radio serial, but the character names are changed and the Temples are replaced by crime reporter Mike Baxter and his wife Linda. This book appeared in Germany as *Die Schuhe*, in Italy as *La scarpa che mancava sempre*, in the *Netherlands as Wie de schoen past wordt vermoord*, in Spain as *Tres zapatos de mujer* and in Poland as *Buty modelki*.

Melvyn Barnes
Author of *Francis Durbridge: The Complete Guide* (Williams & Whiting, 2018)

This book reproduces Francis Durbridge's original script together with the list of characters and actors of the BBC programme on the dates mentioned, but the eventual broadcast might have edited Durbridge's script in respect of scenes, dialogue and character names.

PAUL TEMPLE
AND THE
GILBERT CASE

A serial in eight episodes
By FRANCIS DURBRIDGE
Broadcast on BBC Radio
29 March – 17 May 1954
CAST:

Paul Temple . . . . Peter Coke
Steve, his wife . . . . Marjorie Westbury
Charlie . . . . James Beattie
Wilfrid Stirling . . . . Charles Leno
Sir Graham Forbes . . . . . . .Lester Mudditt
Det. Insp. Kingston . . . . Duncan McIntyre
Betty Wayne . . . . Grizelda Hervey
Lance Reynolds . . . . . . .Richard Williams
Dick Metcalf . . . . .Cyril Shaps
Howard Gilbert . . . . David Peel
Mrs Talbot . . . . .Anne Cullen
Warder . . . . .Geoffrey Bond
Peter Galino . . . . .Robert Rietty
Lynn Ferguson . . . . .Peggy Hassard
Louis Fabian . . . . .Olaf Olsen
Waiter . . . . .Arthur Lawrence
Dan Priestley . . . . .Cyril Shaps
Det Sgt Johnson . . . . .Alec Ross
Miss White . . . . Elizabeth London

NEW PRODUCTION
Broadcast
22 November 1959 – 10 January 1960
CAST:

Paul Temple . . . . Peter Coke
Steve, his wife . . . . Marjorie Westbury
Charlie . . . . James Beattie
Sir Graham Forbes . . . . .Richard Williams
Det. Insp. Kingston . . . . Duncan McIntyre
Wilfrid Stirling . . . . .Douglas Storm
Betty Wayne . . . . Eva Stuart
Lance Reynolds . . . . Simon Lack
Dick Metcalf . . . . .Peter Wilde
A Warder . . . . .James Thomason
Howard Gilbert . . . . John Bennett
Mrs Talbot . . . . Kathleen Helme
Peter Galino . . . . David Spenser
Lynn Ferguson . . . . June Tobin
Louis Fabian . . . . .John Hollis
A Waiter . . . . .John Bennett
Miss White . . . . .Joan Matheson
Dan Priestley . . . . .Ronald Baddiley
Det Sgt Johnson . . . . George Hagan

EPISODE ONE

THE UNLUCKY ONE

OPEN TO:

The sound of a typewriter.
A door opens and the typewriter stops.

STEVE: Paul, where did you put that new cream shirt – with the collar attached?

TEMPLE: It's in the wardrobe, Steve.

STEVE: No, it's not. I've looked.

TEMPLE: Well, it was last night. I distinctly remember putting it there.

STEVE: (*Laughing*) Paul! Really!

TEMPLE: Now, what's the matter?

STEVE: You're wearing it!

TEMPLE: What! By Timothy, so I am! But don't tell me you've started to pack already!

STEVE: Well, of course I have! You don't except me to do everything at the last moment!

TEMPLE: But we don't leave till the day after tomorrow!

STEVE: You men – really! Do you know what I've got to do before we go away?

TEMPLE: No.

STEVE: I've got to see about the laundry, cancel the newspapers, phone the grocer …

TEMPLE: All right, darling! But I'm busy too you know.

TEMPLE closes the typewriter.

TEMPLE: The phone's never stopped ringing. First my publisher, then my agent, then some people called Conway and Waceys or something …

STEVE: (*Quickly*) Conway and Racys!

TEMPLE: (*Pleasantly vague*) What? Yes, that's right. Conway and Racys.

STEVE: But you know perfectly well that's the shop in Bond Street!

TEMPLE: Oh, good Lord, yes! Well, they said something about a fitting … three o'clock tomorrow afternoon.

STEVE: Three o'clock?

TEMPLE: Yes.

STEVE: Are you sure?

TEMPLE: Yes, at least I think it was three o'clock.

The door opens.

STEVE: (*Laughing*) You really are the limit, Paul!

TEMPLE: Yes – what is it, Charlie?

CHARLIE: Excuse me, sir. There's a Mr Stirling would like to see you.

TEMPLE: Mr Stirling?

CHARLIE: Yes, sir.

TEMPLE: Who is he – do you know?

CHARLIE: No, sir.

STEVE: Have you seen him before, Charlie?

CHARLIE: No, ma'am.

TEMPLE: What's he look like?

CHARLIE: Oh, he's quite a gent, grey hair, walks with a stick. Wouldn't be surprised if he hasn't got a gammy leg.

TEMPLE: Is that his card?

CHARLIE: Oh, yes, sir!

A moment's pause.

TEMPLE: (*Reading the card*) "Terrent Bros., Guildford. Mr Wilfrid Stirling. Assistant Sales Director". Terrent Bros., they're the refrigerator people.

STEVE: Yes.

TEMPLE: Where is he, Charlie?

CHARLIE: I've put him in the drawing room, sir.

TEMPLE: Yes, all right.

STEVE: Wilfrid Stirling … You know, that name's familiar, Paul.

TEMPLE:	He probably wants to sell us a fridge. I'll get rid of him.
STEVE:	Remember, we're having lunch early today, just after twelve.
TEMPLE:	All right, Steve.

FADE SCENE.

FADE IN TEMPLE speaking.

TEMPLE:	Mr Stirling?
STIRLING:	(*A softly-spoken man; early fifties*) Oh, good morning, Mr Temple. You probably think it's an impertinence my calling like this, but – I had to see you.
TEMPLE:	What do you want to see me about?
STIRLING:	(*Hesitatingly*) I – want to talk to you.
TEMPLE:	I rather gathered that. Well?
STIRLING:	(*Almost a definite announcement*) Mr Temple … I don't think Howard Gilbert murdered my daughter.
TEMPLE:	Howard Gilbert? (*A sudden realisation*) Are you Brenda Stirling's father?
STIRLING:	Yes.
TEMPLE:	But just a minute! I only know what I've read in the newspapers, of course, but – Howard Gilbert's already been convicted. Your evidence helped to convict him.
STIRLING:	Yes, I know it did, but …
TEMPLE:	Look, before you go any further, Mr Stirling. I'm not connected with Scotland Yard in any way. If you've got any fresh evidence, it's your duty …
STIRLING:	No! – No, I haven't. There's nothing new – no further development; it's just that … (*He hesitates*)

5

TEMPLE:	Yes?
STIRLING:	It's just that I don't think Howard Gilbert did murder my daughter.
TEMPLE:	Well – he was found guilty, Mr Stirling, and sentenced to death.
STIRLING:	Yes, I know …
TEMPLE:	I'm sorry, but I don't quite see why you came here? What did you expect me to do?
STIRLING:	(*Obviously distressed*) I don't know. I've made a fool of myself and wasted your time. I apologise.
TEMPLE:	(*Pleasantly*) Don't worry about wasting my time. I'm a professional time-waster – you ask my wife! (*Curious*) No, you must have had a reason for coming here. Don't you think Gilbert had a fair trial?
STIRLING:	Oh, yes, he did. He did, indeed.
TEMPLE:	Well, then –
STIRLING:	(*With obvious sincerity*) Mr Temple, have you ever had a feeling about something – an indefinable feeling that you just can't explain? Well – I've got that feeling about Howard Gilbert. I don't think he did murder Brenda. I know that all the evidence pointed towards it. I know that even my own evidence helped to condemn him, but – I still don't think he did it.
TEMPLE:	M'm. (*Pause*) Sit down for a moment.
STIRLING:	If you don't mind I'd rather stand. This leg of mine isn't too good when I'm sitting down.

A slight pause.

| TEMPLE: | Mr Stirling, tell me – were you fond of your daughter? |
| STIRLING: | (*Surprised*) Yes, of course I was. I was very fond of her. |

6

TEMPLE: Were you pleased when she became engaged to Howard Gilbert?

STIRLING: Very. He seemed a steady young fellow. I liked him enormously.

TEMPLE: Supposing you discovered that this hunch of yours …

STIRLING: It isn't exactly a hunch –

TEMPLE: Well, for want of a better word let's call it a hunch. Supposing you find there is justification for it …

STIRLING: I'm not against capital punishment, if that's what you're thinking. If Howard did murder Brenda, then – he's got to pay for it. But I don't think he did.

A moment's pause.

TEMPLE: Tell me what happened, exactly – the night your daughter was murdered?

STIRLING: Howard called for her at about six o'clock. He was taking her to the theatre. I saw him for a few moments and then went upstairs. I heard them talking; they were having a row; practically shouting at each other.

TEMPLE: What was the row about?

STIRLING: Brenda worked as a model at Conway and Racys, it's a shop in New Bond Street …

TEMPLE: Yes, I know it.

STIRLING: Well, Brenda liked her job; she was happy. She told Howard that she intended to stay on there after they were married. Howard didn't like the idea. To be frank he wasn't keen on her being a model.

TEMPLE: I see.

STIRLING: They left the house at about a quarter-to-seven and, according to all accounts, continued their

7

argument at the theatre. You know the rest of the story. Early next morning they found Brenda on a deserted bomb site near Soho Square.

TEMPLE: M'm. Did your daughter go out with anyone apart from Howard Gilbert?

STIRLING: No. (*Hesitantly*) At least, I don't think so. She was friendly with a girl called June Michael, but they very seldom went out together.

TEMPLE: Does Miss Michael work at Conway and Racys?

STIRLING: Yes, I believe she's in the hat department now. But she used to be a model, too.

TEMPLE: Well, I'm sorry, but I'm afraid there's just nothing I can do, Mr Stirling.

STIRLING: Yes, I know. I'm sorry to have bothered you, I only thought perhaps … (*Suddenly*) Mr Temple, I'm worried about something I found in a diary of Brenda's. I was going through her things shortly after it happened and I found this diary in one of her handbags.

TEMPLE: Well?

STIRLING: Well, apparently on May 12th, she had an appointment with a man called Fairfax. You can see the entry here.

TEMPLE: (*A moment: reading*) "L. Fairfax – 8.30." M'm. Is this your daughter's handwriting?

STIRLING: Yes, of course – it's her diary.

TEMPLE: I appreciate that – but is it her handwriting?

STIRLING: Oh, yes – quite definitely.

TEMPLE: Had you heard of this man before you found the diary?

STIRLING: No, never. That's the whole point … Brenda certainly never mentioned him.

TEMPLE: Did you tell the police about this?

STIRLING: Yes, of course. I also told Sir Henry Rawlinson; he was defending Gilbert.

TEMPLE: And nothing happened?

STIRLING: No – Sir Henry didn't seem to think it was very important.

TEMPLE: And the police?

STIRLING: I think the police did make some attempt to find him, but I never heard anything further. They were obviously unlucky.

TEMPLE: What about June Michael?

STIRLING: No, I spoke to June myself. She'd never heard of anyone called Fairfax.

TEMPLE: Well, you know, even if the police found this mysterious gentleman it isn't to say he'd be able to help them in any way.

STIRLING: I realise that, but …

TEMPLE: In any case, if I remember rightly a woman identified Gilbert; she saw him walking away from the bomb site.

STIRLING: Yes, that's right.

TEMPLE: Well, there you are …

STIRLING: But, somehow, I just can't believe it. Howard was such a good fellow; decent, straight-forward …

TEMPLE: Strange things happen in this world, Mr Stirling – sometimes to very decent people. (*A pause*) Is Howard appealing?

STIRLING: He has appealed; it was refused yesterday afternoon.

TEMPLE: Oh, I see. (*Kindly, dismissing STIRLING*) Well, I'm sorry – there's just nothing I can do.

FADE SCENE.

FADE IN STEVE humming to herself.

STEVE: Pass my hairbrush, darling, please. (*A moment*) Thank you.

We hear the sound of STEVE brushing her hair.

STEVE: (*Singing to herself*) One hundred strokes. What time is it?

TEMPLE: About half-past-eleven.

STEVE: Oh, that clock's right for a change.

TEMPLE: Yes. I say, Steve – these are shocking pyjamas!

STEVE: Yes, I know, but I've packed all your others.

TEMPLE: It's a wonder you haven't packed the kitchen stove!

STEVE: Don't be silly, dear. I want to get away from the kitchen stove.

TEMPLE laughs.

A pause.

STEVE continues to brush her hair.

STEVE: Paul …

TEMPLE: Yes?

STEVE: This Gilbert case isn't going to make any difference to our holiday, is it?

TEMPLE: Don't be silly, darling.

STEVE: Yes, well, I know you. You enjoy getting involved in things.

TEMPLE: Yes, well I'm not getting involved this time! Anyhow there isn't a Gilbert Case, it's finished – all over.

STEVE: Yes.

The sound of STEVE brushing her hair.

STEVE: He did it all right; there's no doubt about it.

A tiny pause.

TEMPLE: Did you ever see her, Steve?

STEVE: Who?

TEMPLE: Brenda Stirling. She worked at Conway and Racys, she was a model.

STEVE: Yes, I know, but all those models look alike to me. I didn't recognise her from the photographs.

TEMPLE: M'm.

STEVE: 97, 98, 99, 100! (*Yawning*) Oh dear, I can hardly keep my eyes open.

TEMPLE and STEVE get into their twin beds.

STEVE: (*Stretching herself*) Oh, isn't bed wonderful!

TEMPLE: (*After a moment*) Are you going to read?

STEVE: No. Are you?

TEMPLE: No. I'll switch the light out.

We hear the sound of the light switch.

A long pause.

STEVE: It's odd Wilfrid Stirling should have come to see you, isn't it?

TEMPLE: How do you mean?

STEVE: Well, if it had been Gilbert's father …

TEMPLE: Gilbert hasn't got a father – he's an orphan.

STEVE: How do you know?

TEMPLE: It was in the papers.

STEVE: M'm. Well, I still think it's pretty odd, about Stirling, I mean. After all, it was his daughter who was murdered.

TEMPLE: Yes, but he doesn't think Gilbert did it.

STEVE: M'm …

TEMPLE: Still, I see your point.

A pause.

STEVE: (*Sleepily*) What did you say, darling?

TEMPLE: I said: "I see your point".

STEVE: (*Almost asleep*) What point?

TEMPLE: Go to sleep!

STEVE: Goodnight!

TEMPLE: Goodnight, dear.

FADE SCENE.

FADE UP a few bars of music.
FADE music.
FADE IN scene.
TEMPLE: Are you awake?
STEVE: Yes.
TEMPLE: Do you mind if I switch the light on?
STEVE: No ...
TEMPLE switches the light on.
STEVE: What time is it?
TEMPLE: Quarter-to-one ...
STEVE: Can't you sleep?
TEMPLE: I keep thinking of that name all the time ...
STEVE: What name?
TEMPLE: The one I told you about that was in Brenda
          Stirling's diary.
STEVE: ... Fairfax ...
TEMPLE: Yes, you know, there's something familiar about
          that name. I've seen it before somewhere.
STEVE: You mean – you've heard it before?
TEMPLE: Yes ... (*Suddenly*) No – what did I say?
STEVE: You said you'd seen it before.
TEMPLE: (*Intrigued*) Yes – and that's what I meant. I've
          seen it – I've read it somewhere. (*Sitting up*) You
          know, it's a funny thing. I was half asleep just now
          and I kept thinking of that confounded name and
          saying to myself ... (*A little laugh*) ... You'll think
          this is ridiculous, Steve ... Fairfax – Oliver
          Cromwell – Charles the Second ...
STEVE: Charles the Second!
TEMPLE: Yes.
STEVE: Why Charles the Second?
TEMPLE: Don't ask me, darling!

12

STEVE: I'm beginning to think it's a jolly good job we're going on holiday!

TEMPLE: But there must be a reason for … (*He stops*) I've got it! Lord Fairfax – was the character who tried to get the King back on the throne after Oliver Cromwell died.

STEVE: Well?

TEMPLE: Association of ideas! Lord Fairfax – Oliver Cromwell – Charles the Second –

STEVE: Paul, what has this got to do with Brenda Stirling?

TEMPLE: I told you – the name in her diary. Don't you remember? May 12th, 8.30 – L. Fairfax …

STEVE: My dear Paul, if Lord Fairfax was a buddy of Oliver Cromwell's he's been dead for years!

TEMPLE: Don't you see? Brenda Stirling didn't have a date with a man called Fairfax, she had it at a place called – The Lord Fairfax …

STEVE: I wonder if you're right?

TEMPLE: (*With enthusiasm*) Of course I'm right! Pass the telephone.

STEVE: Who are you going to phone at this time of night?

TEMPLE: Sir Graham Forbes. I want to know if there's a pub, or an inn, or a hotel within fifty miles of London called The Lord Fairfax.

STEVE: But he's in bed!

TEMPLE: Well, I'm in bed! Come on, Steve – give me the telephone!

STEVE: Here we go! Here we go again!

FADE IN music.

FADE DOWN music.

FADE IN SIR GRAHAM FORBES.

FORBES: I just don't see why you should interest yourself in the Gilbert affair. The case is closed; it's finished.

TEMPLE:	I've told you why I'm interested, Sir Graham. Stirling came to see me; he was obviously upset because Gilbert's appeal had been refused and he told me about the diary.
KINGSTON:	But we know all about the diary, Temple.
TEMPLE:	Really, Inspector?
KINGSTON:	Yes.
TEMPLE:	Did you know that Brenda Stirling's appointment was at a place called The Lord Fairfax and not with a person called L. Fairfax?
KINGSTON:	(*Puzzled*) … No … This is news to me, Sir Graham.
FORBES:	Temple's got a theory, Kingston. He thinks that the L. Fairfax in the diary refers to Lord Fairfax and it's the name of an inn or a public house.
KINGSTON:	Yes, I suppose that's possible.
FORBES:	Well, so far it's only a theory; it hasn't been proved that there is a place called The Lord Fairfax.
KINGSTON:	Are we checking on it, sir?
FORBES:	(*Acidly*) We started checking on it at a quarter-past-one this morning, Inspector.
TEMPLE:	Inspector, were you in charge of the Gilbert case?
KINGSTON:	I was.
TEMPLE:	From the beginning?
KINGSTON:	Yes.
TEMPLE:	Well, I've only heard part of the story. I know they had a row and went to the theatre. I'd like to hear the rest of the story.
KINGSTON:	Well they left together before the show finished, at about ten o'clock. Now, according

to Gilbert's first statement, the row came to a climax outside the theatre and Brenda turned her back on him and walked away. Gilbert got into his car and drove home. He said – mark you, this was his first statement – that he arrived home at about half-past-ten.

FORBES: Gilbert has a flat in New Cavendish Street that he shared with a man called Lance Reynolds.

TEMPLE: Lance Reynolds. Go on, Inspector.

KINGSTON: Well, Reynolds didn't confirm Gilbert's story; he said that Gilbert arrived home at about half-past-twelve. We tackled Gilbert on this point and he changed his statement. He said he left Brenda outside the theatre at about ten o'clock, drove round the West End, parked his car in St James's Square and then went for a walk. He says he got back to the Square at about a quarter-past-twelve, picked up his car, drove home. No one saw him; or the car.

FORBES: In short: he couldn't account for his movements between ten o'clock – when he left the theatre and twelve-thirty.

KINGSTON: And we know that it was during that period that the murder was committed.

TEMPLE: I see.

KINGSTON: Two days after the murder, Gilbert sent a suit to be sponged and pressed. I went to see the cleaners and found a handkerchief in one of the pockets; it had blood on it. The blood belonged to that same group as the murdered woman. Gilbert admitted it was his

	handkerchief, but – couldn't account for the blood.
TEMPLE:	I thought the girl was strangled?
FORBES:	She was but there was a bad scratch down the side of her face. That accounted for the blood.
TEMPLE:	Who discovered the body?
FORBES:	A woman called Talbot; she has a flat in Soho Square and she was taking a short cut across the bomb site.
TEMPLE:	What time was that?
FORBES:	Just after midnight.
KINGSTON:	As she reached the bomb site a man pushed past her and started running down Greek Street. She gave us a description of the man and she picked him out at an identity parade. It was Howard Gilbert.
TEMPLE:	I see. I believe you found Gilbert's fingerprints on Miss Stirling's handbag.
FORBES:	Yes, we did.
KINGSTON:	There were five pounds in the handbag and a gold powder compact. Also, she was wearing a very nice little diamond clip. The clip alone must have been worth quite a bit.
TEMPLE:	Was anything missing?
KINGSTON:	No, nothing.
FORBES:	(*Casually*) Except her shoe.
TEMPLE:	What do you mean?
KINGSTON:	She was only wearing one shoe, on her right foot – the other must have fallen off during the struggle.
TEMPLE:	I see.
KINGSTON:	(*Quite casual*) Oddly enough we never found it.

TEMPLE: Well, thank you, Inspector. I'm grateful to you for giving me all the details.

FADE SCENE.

FADE IN a background of chatter of the dress department of a large, but somewhat exclusive, Bond Street store.

BETTY: (*A pleasant, well-spoken woman in her forties*) I'm sure you'll be pleased with the dress, Mrs Temple. It really does look awfully nice on you.

STEVE: It's not the dress I'm worried about – it's the hat. I can't make up my mind whether I like it or not.

BETTY: But it's so smart. I'm sure your husband will like it.

STEVE: Well – I hope so! He's paying for it!

BETTY laughs.

TEMPLE: Hello, Steve! Are you ready?

STEVE: I'm just waiting for my dress – they're packing it for me.

BETTY: Good afternoon, Mr Temple.

STEVE: You remember Miss Wayne, darling …

TEMPLE: Yes, of course.

BETTY: If you'll excuse me, I'll see if your dress is ready, Mrs Temple.

A moment's pause.

STEVE: How did you get on at Scotland Yard?

TEMPLE: So-so.

STEVE: Did you see Sir Graham?

TEMPLE: Yes.

STEVE: You look depressed.

TEMPLE: That wasn't such a good idea of mine, after all, Steve.

STEVE: Isn't there a place called The Lord Fairfax?

TEMPLE: Well, if there is – they haven't found it.

BETTY: Here you are, Mrs Temple.

TEMPLE: I'll take it. Miss Wayne, I believe you have a young lady working here called June Michael?

BETTY: That's right – she's in the hat department.

TEMPLE: Do you think I could have a word with her?

BETTY: She's not here today, I'm afraid.

STEVE: Is she ill?

BETTY: No, I don't think so. She was here last night – we were stocktaking.

TEMPLE: Where does she live, do you know?

BETTY: She's got a flat in Plymouth Mansions – just off Baker Street.

TEMPLE: Have you telephoned?

BETTY: The Supervisor has – apparently there's no reply. Knowing June she's probably gone to the races.

TEMPLE: I understand she was a friend of Brenda Stirling's?

BETTY: Yes, I believe they were close friends. That was a dreadful business, wasn't it?

The phone rings.

BETTY: Oh, there's the phone! Excuse me. Goodbye, Mrs Temple! See you again soon!

STEVE: Yes, of course!

TEMPLE: (*Aside to STEVE*) Not too soon, I hope.

STEVE: (*Laughs*) Are we going straight home?

TEMPLE: Yes. Via Baker Street.

FADE SCENE.

FADE IN of a door bell ringing.

A slight pause.

STEVE: Are you sure this is the right flat?

TEMPLE: It said so downstairs – Number 14: June Michael.

STEVE: Well, this is 14 all right.

TEMPLE: Yes.

STEVE: She's obviously not in.

TEMPLE: Doesn't look like it.

STEVE: Why did you want to see her, Paul?

TEMPLE: Well, we know she was friendly with Brenda Stirling and yet apparently Inspector Kingston only question … (*He sniffs*)

STEVE: What is it, Paul?

TEMPLE: Do you smell gas?

STEVE: Yes …

TEMPLE: Wait a minute!

STEVE: What is it?

TEMPLE: There's something at the bottom of the door and she's plugged the keyhole …

We hear the sound of the door handle being shaken.

TEMPLE: We've got to get this door open! Steve, go downstairs – see if you can find the porter. Tell him what's happened – quick!

FADE SCENE.

FADE UP the sound of TEMPLE still trying to force open the door.

STEVE arrives.

STEVE: (*Breathlessly*) I've got the pass key! I told the porter to phone the local hospital and get a doctor, just in case …

TEMPLE: Good.

The door is unlocked and thrown open.

STEVE starts to cough.

TEMPLE: Put your handkerchief over your mouth.

STEVE: Where is she?

TEMPLE: Get that window open, Steve! I'm going into the bedroom!

A door opens.

TEMPLE starts coughing.

TEMPLE: There she is!

In the background is the sound of the window being opened.

Very distant background street noises and traffic can be heard.

TEMPLE: Miss Michael! … Miss Michael! … Lift her head, Steve.

STEVE: Is she still alive, do you think?

TEMPLE: I don't know. Hold her head higher …

STEVE: She looks dreadful!

TEMPLE: I wish that doctor would come!

STEVE: He shouldn't be long; the hospital's only just round the corner.

TEMPLE: (*Shaking JUNE*) Miss Michael … June … can you hear me? June!

The sound of an approaching ambulance with its bell ringing can be heard in the distant background.

STEVE: It doesn't look as if she's going to come round …

TEMPLE: No …

STEVE: Do you think she's taken anything – aspirin – or something?

TEMPLE: June … listen to us! June, listen … (*He stops speaking*)

STEVE: What is it?

TEMPLE: One of her shoes is missing.

FADE SCENE.

FADE IN background noises of a fashionable London square. We hear the sound of a key being inserted in the lock of a front door.

STEVE: I'll hold the parcel.

TEMPLE: Thank you.

The front door opens.

TEMPLE and STEVE enter the hall of their house.

The front door closes cutting out the noise of the square.

CHARLIE:	(*Brightly*) Hello, sir!
STEVE:	Take this parcel and put it in the dressing room, Charlie.
CHARLIE:	Oke – yes, ma'am.
TEMPLE:	And telephone messages?
CHARLIE:	No, sir. (*Suddenly remembering*) Oh – there's a Mr Reynolds waiting to see you. He's in the drawing room. I asked him if he had an appointment, but …
TEMPLE:	Reynolds?
CHARLIE:	Yes.
TEMPLE:	How long has he been here?
CHARLIE:	About a quarter of an hour. He insisted on waiting. I couldn't get rid of him.
TEMPLE:	Yes, all right, Charlie.
STEVE:	Who is he, Paul? Do you know?
TEMPLE:	Yes, he's a friend of Howard Gilbert's. They shared a flat in New Cavendish Street.
STEVE:	Have you met him?
TEMPLE:	No, but Sir Graham mentioned him this morning. (*Thoughtfully*) Now what on earth does he want?

FADE SCENE.

FADE UP the opening and closing of a door.

REYNOLDS:	Mr Temple?
TEMPLE:	Yes.
REYNOLDS:	I do apologise for intruding like this. My name is Lance Reynolds. (*He has a terse manner; he treats STEVE almost with contempt, believing that women should be seen and not heard*)
TEMPLE:	What can I do for you, Mr Reynolds?
REYNOLDS:	I'll come straight to the point.

21

TEMPLE: (*Pleasantly*) Before you come to the point
                may I introduce my wife?

REYNOLDS: How d'ye do?

STEVE: Good afternoon. Shall I ring for tea, Paul?

REYNOLDS: If you don't mind, I have an appointment at a
                quarter-past-five and it's now nearly – (*He
                glances at his watch*) – ten minutes past.

TEMPLE: It's a pity you didn't make an appointment
                with me, Mr Reynolds. It would have
                simplified matters. I'm in the book.

REYNOLDS: Yes, I'm sorry. I ought to have telephoned.
                But I've had rather a tiresome day and then at
                the very last moment ... However, if you will
                allow me, I'd like to explain the reason for
                my visit.

TEMPLE: By all means.

REYNOLDS: I believe you saw Inspector Kingston this
                morning and that you discussed the Gilbert
                case.

TEMPLE: Did Inspector Kingston tell you that?

REYNOLDS: No; not exactly. (*Glibly*) But I make a point
                of being well informed about all aspects of
                the Gilbert case.

TEMPLE: Go on.

REYNOLDS: I imagine Inspector Kingston gave you a few
                details about me – but just in case he didn't
                ...

TEMPLE: He told me that you had shared a flat with
                Howard Gilbert. That's all he told me.

REYNOLDS: I see. He didn't mention my theory?

TEMPLE: No.

REYNOLDS: (*Very sure of himself*) Well, that simplifies
                matters. We can start at the beginning. I have
                a theory about the Gilbert case, and ...

TEMPLE: You know, I'm not officially concerned with the Gilbert case so if you've got a theory the obvious person to discuss it with is Inspector Kingston.

REYNOLDS: But Inspector Kingston knows all about my theory; we've already discussed it – at great length.

TEMPLE: Well, I'm afraid I've neither the time nor the inclination to discuss it, Mr Reynolds. To be frank, the only theories I'm interested in are my own.

REYNOLDS: (*Perturbed*) Mr Temple, you saw Wilfrid Stirling last night, didn't you?

TEMPLE: Yes.

REYNOLDS: Is that why you became interested in the Gilbert case?

TEMPLE: … Partly …

REYNOLDS: He told you about the diary, didn't he? – Belonging to his daughter. It had the name Fairfax in it. L. Fairfax.

TEMPLE: Yes.

REYNOLDS: Miss Stirling had an appointment with Mr Fairfax at 8.30 on May 12th.

TEMPLE: We don't know that for certain.

REYNOLDS: But we do – it's in the diary.

TEMPLE: Just because it's in the diary …

REYNOLDS: (*Interrupting TEMPLE*) It's my belief that Brenda Stirling was having an affair with this man Fairfax; and that he followed them to the theatre that night.

TEMPLE: It's an interesting theory, but surely, rather obvious?

REYNOLDS: The truth very often is obvious.

23

TEMPLE: Anyhow I take it you don't believe that
               Howard Gilbert murdered Brenda Stirling?
REYNOLDS: (*Bluntly*) Nothing in this world will convince
               me that he committed that murder. (*Briskly;
               resorting to his previous terseness*) Now, I've
               taken up a great deal of your time and I'll
               come straight to the point. This letter arrived
               for Howard by the afternoon post; it was
               marked "Please Forward" but I opened it.
               You'll see that it was posted in Como, Italy,
               four days ago. I want you to read it.

TEMPLE takes the letter.

A pause.

REYNOLDS: Read it aloud, please.
TEMPLE: (*Reading*) "The Danilo Hotel, Como. Dear
               Howard ... So now it's all over – all over and
               they've found you guilty. I wonder whether
               you did murder Brenda Stirling? I met you
               once, a long time ago. I expect you've
               forgotten. When I heard about the murder,
               and read the reports, and saw Brenda's
               photograph in the newspapers, I said to
               myself ... there, but for the grace of God ...
               Dear Brenda ... a lovely creature; but she
               wasn't a very easy person, was she, Howard?
               I wonder whether you did murder her or
               whether you happen to be the unlucky one
               they've picked on. I wonder! Was her shoe
               missing, Howard? Ask the police – it might
               be worth your while ... L. Fairfax."
STEVE: But Paul; if this ...
TEMPLE: You say this arrived by the afternoon post?
REYNOLDS: Yes.
TEMPLE: Why haven't you taken it to Scotland Yard?

REYNOLDS: The unimaginative Inspector Kingston? He'd probably think I'd written it myself.

TEMPLE: (*Bluntly*) Did you?

REYNOLDS: (*Ignoring the remark*) I'm leaving the letter with you. Now, if you'll excuse me. I have another appointment. Good afternoon, Mrs Temple.

STEVE: Good afternoon.

REYNOLDS: (*Turning*) I'm sorry I couldn't stay to tea. Another time, perhaps.

TEMPLE: I'll see you out.

The door opens.

A pause.

TEMPLE returns.

STEVE: Well! What an objectionable man! I've met some people in my time, but –

TEMPLE: (*His thoughts elsewhere*) Wait a minute, darling! Where's that letter? Oh, here it is … (*He picks up the letter; thoughtfully reading*) "I wonder whether you did murder her or whether you happen to be the unlucky one they've picked on –" They've picked on …?

STEVE: He means the police, surely?

TEMPLE: Do you think so?

STEVE: Who else could he mean?

TEMPLE: I don't know.

STEVE: Paul, was her shoe missing – Brenda Stirling's, I mean?

TEMPLE: Yes.

STEVE: But, so was June Michael's!

TEMPLE: Yes, so was June Michael's. (*Pause*) Steve, I hate to say this, but would you be terribly disappointed if we postponed the holiday?

The telephone starts ringing.

25

STEVE: The way things are going I shall be terribly surprised if we don't!

TEMPLE lifts the telephone receiver.

TEMPLE: (*On the phone*) Hello?

KINGSTON: (*On the other end of the line*) Paul Temple?

TEMPLE: Yes …

KINGSTON: Kingston here – Scotland Yard.

TEMPLE: Oh, hello, Inspector. I was just going to ring you. I've got some news for you.

KINGSTON: I've got some news for you too, Temple.

TEMPLE: Yes?

KINGSTON: We've just had a report in from Surrey: apparently there is an inn called The Lord Fairfax. It's just outside Westerdale.

TEMPLE: (*Surprised*) Really?

KINGSTON: You sound surprised!

TEMPLE: No – no, not at all.

KINGSTON: Well, we've found the place: now it's up to you.

TEMPLE: Er – what did you say the village was called?

KINGSTON: Westerdale. It's about six miles from Farnham near the Hog's Back.

TEMPLE: Thank you, Inspector. (*Suddenly*) Oh, what about the girl – June Michael?

KINGSTON: I haven't any news; not yet. I'm waiting for the hospital to phone.

TEMPLE: All right. I'll ring you tonight. Goodbye.

KINGSTON: (*Puzzled by TEMPLE's tone*) Goodbye.

TEMPLE replaces the receiver.

TEMPLE: (*Quietly*) Steve …

STEVE: Yes?

TEMPLE: Ask Charlie to bring the car round.

FADE IN music.

FADE DOWN music.

FADE IN the sound of TEMPLE's car: it is travelling fairly slowly.

STEVE: Are you sure it's down here, Paul?

TEMPLE: Well, it must be.

STEVE: We've been down this lane twice already!

TEMPLE: The sergeant said the second turning on the right and then …

STEVE: (*Suddenly*) There it is! On the corner …

TEMPLE: Where?

STEVE: Look! The Lord Fairfax …

TEMPLE: By Timothy, no wonder we couldn't find it!

STEVE: (*Laughing*) It must be the smallest pub in England!

The car slows down; then stops.

TEMPLE: You'd better get out my side, Steve – because of the hedge.

STEVE: Yes.

TEMPLE: I want this newspaper. There's a picture of Brenda Stirling in it …

STEVE and TEMPLE climb out of the car.

FADE SCENE.

FADE IN a very slight background noise of a tiny country inn. A mere background buzz of quiet conversation.

METCALF: (*A pleasant Cockney; early fifties*) Good evening, sir.

TEMPLE: Good evening. What would you like, Steve?

STEVE: A gin and tonic, please.

TEMPLE: And I'll have a light ale.

METCALF: Gin and tonic and light ale, right sir.

STEVE: It's a nice little place.

TEMPLE: (*Looking around*) Yes, it is …

A slight pause.

METCALF: Slice of lemon, miss?

STEVE: Thank you.

A slight pause.

TEMPLE: How far are we from Guildford?

METCALF: About eight miles, that's all. Over the Hog's Back.

METCALF pours the drinks.

TEMPLE: Will you have a drink?

METCALF: Thank you, sir; that's very nice of you. I'll have a bitter if I may.

METCALF pulls the bitter.

STEVE: I like the fireplace …

TEMPLE: Yes.

STEVE: Nice the way the settles are arranged. Must be cosy in the winter.

METCALF: Here we are, sir. Your very good health – and yours, miss.

TEMPLE: Cheers!

METCALF: Cheers!

They all drink.

A pause.

TEMPLE: Are you the landlord here?

METCALF: Proprietor. Metcalf's the name, sir.

TEMPLE: Well, my name is Paul Temple and …

METCALF: I thought I recognised you! We've met before, Mr Temple!

TEMPLE: Really?

METCALF: D'you remember – right at the beginning of the war? I ran a little pub outside St Albans – The Blue Feathers. On the main road between St Albans and High Wycombe.

TEMPLE: (*He doesn't remember*) Oh, yes. Of course. Well, Mr Metcalf, I wonder if you could help me. I daresay you read about that murder – the Gilbert affair.

METCALF: Gilbert affair?

TEMPLE: Yes – a girl called Brenda Stirling was murdered. She was a model at Conway and Racys.

METCALF: (*Vaguely*) I seem to remember something about it. She was found on a bomb site –

TEMPLE: Yes, that's right. There's a picture of her in this newspaper …

METCALF: (*Looking at the newspaper*) Oh …

TEMPLE: Have you ever seen her before?

METCALF: Me? Why, no. No, never.

TEMPLE: She's never been in here, for instance?

METCALF: No – not to my knowledge.

TEMPLE: You're sure?

METCALF: Positive. (*Suddenly*) Here – who's that – the other picture?

TEMPLE: Oh, that's a girl called June Michael.

STEVE: She tried to commit suicide.

METCALF: Go on! When was that?

STEVE: This afternoon …

METCALF: Well, I've seen 'er before. She dropped in here about a month ago. Remember her well. Good looking girl; sat over there in the corner.

TEMPLE: Are you sure?

METCALF: Course I'm sure, she 'ad three pink gins.

TEMPLE: Was she alone?

METCALF: What – a girl with 'er looks? No, there was a fellow with her. Funny chap. Grey hair – walked with a stick. Looked to me as if he'd got a bit of a gammy leg …

FADE IN closing music.

END OF EPISODE ONE

EPISODE TWO

THE THIRD SHOE

OPEN TO:

FADE IN a slight background noise of a tiny country inn.

TEMPLE: Well, Mr Metcalf, I wonder if you could help me. I daresay you read about that murder – the Gilbert affair.

METCALF: Gilbert affair?

TEMPLE: Yes – a girl called Brenda Stirling was murdered. She was a model at Conway and Racys.

METCALF: (*Vaguely*) I seem to remember something about it. She was found on a bomb site –

TEMPLE: Yes, that's right. There's a picture of her in this newspaper …

METCALF: (*Looking at the newspaper*) Oh …

TEMPLE: Have you ever seen her before?

METCALF: Me? Why, no. No, never.

TEMPLE: She's never been in here, for instance?

METCALF: No – not to my knowledge.

TEMPLE: You're sure?

METCALF: Positive. (*Suddenly*) Here – who's that – the other picture?

TEMPLE: Oh, that's a girl called June Michael.

STEVE: She tried to commit suicide.

METCALF: Go on! When was that?

STEVE: This afternoon …

METCALF: Well, I've seen 'er before. She dropped in here about a month ago. Remember her well. Good looking girl; sat over there in the corner.

TEMPLE: Are you sure?

METCALF: Course I'm sure, she 'ad three pink gins.

TEMPLE: Was she alone?

METCALF: What – a girl with 'er looks? No, there was a fellow with her. Funny chap. Grey hair –

33

walked with a stick. Looked to me as if he'd got a bit of a gammy leg …

STEVE: (*Surprised*) Was his name Stirling?

METCALF: Oh, I wouldn't know. I only said about half a dozen words to him.

TEMPLE: But you're sure about the girl – Miss Michael?

METCALF: Oh, positive.

In the background we hear the sound of the door opening and closing and voices coming and going.

TEMPLE: Well – thank you, Mr Metcalf.

METCALF: Not at all. Excuse me. I must attend to that customer.

TEMPLE: Yes, of course.

METCALF leaves TEMPLE and STEVE.

STEVE: Well, I just don't understand it. If it was Wilfrid Stirling …

TEMPLE: It was Stirling all right – unless Metcalf's lying, and I don't think he is. Why should he?

STEVE: But it was Stirling who told you about the diary, about the name Lord Fairfax …

TEMPLE: (*Correcting STEVE*) No, wait a minute, Steve. Stirling didn't mention the name Lord Fairfax – he simply showed me his daughter's diary. On May 12th it said L. Fairfax 8.30. It was my guess – that the name might refer to Lord Fairfax.

STEVE: Yes, I remember. Well, I don't see how all these bits and pieces fit together.

TEMPLE: No. Let's sit down for a moment on one of those settles. (*As he goes*) Bring your glass. Now, let's take the case from the beginning. Howard Gilbert is engaged to a model called Brenda Stirling. One night they quarrel and next morning Brenda is found murdered.

	Gilbert is accused and found guilty. But the girl's father – Wilfrid Stirling – doesn't think that Gilbert did murder her and produces a diary of Brenda's to prove that she was meeting someone called L. Fairfax. But no one seems to have heard of Fairfax …
STEVE:	And you hit on the idea that possibly the name in the diary referred to an inn or public house.
TEMPLE:	Exactly. And the police discover that there is an inn called The Lord Fairfax; we come to it and find that Stirling has previously been here with a friend of Brenda's called June Michael. And that's the whole story – except for two very interesting points. First, the shoes …
STEVE:	Yes: when the police found Brenda Stirling one of her shoes was missing and when we found June Michael – one of her shoes was missing.
TEMPLE:	And then: Lance Reynolds, a friend of Gilbert's produces a letter addressed to Gilbert written by someone called Fairfax.
STEVE:	Yes. You know, when Reynolds produced that letter I thought your theory about a public house had been blown sky high.
TEMPLE:	So did I.
STEVE:	Then we find there is a pub called The Lord Fairfax and that both Stirling and June Michael have been here!
TEMPLE:	Yes, it's certainly very puzzling.
STEVE:	You know, Paul. If you're going to get involved in this case …
TEMPLE:	Get? I am involved in it!
STEVE:	I mean really involved. I think you ought to see Howard Gilbert. After all, if you … What are you smiling at?

TEMPLE: I am seeing him – tomorrow morning.

STEVE: Oh …

TEMPLE: Do you want to come?

STEVE: No. I've been in lots of places but – not Pentonville, thank you very much!

TEMPLE: I thought you'd say that! Well come along, let's go back to Town!

FADE SCENE.

FADE IN the sound of TEMPLE's car; it is travelling fairly fast.

A pause.

STEVE: Was that Esher we came through?

TEMPLE: No. That was Cobham. Esher's about three or four miles. Slow down, Steve, you're doing sixty.

STEVE: (*Amused*) It's all right, it's a good road.

TEMPLE: Um. Just as well.

A pause.

STEVE: What time are you seeing Gilbert tomorrow morning?

TEMPLE: Half-past ten.

STEVE: Is Sir Graham going with you?

TEMPLE: I hope not, although he phoned the Governor of the prison and made the arrangements. I want to see Gilbert on his own if possible.

A pause.

STEVE: (*Thoughtfully*) Paul … about that letter that was supposed to have been written by Fairfax.

TEMPLE: Yes?

STEVE: You remember what it said: "I wonder whether you did murder her or whether …" …

TEMPLE: "You happen to be the unlucky one they've picked on" …

STEVE: Yes. Well, if the 'they' doesn't refer to the police
          then obviously it must …

As STEVE speaks there is a sudden cracking of glass.

The windscreen has been struck and the glass shattered.

STEVE: What on earth was that!

TEMPLE: Brake, Steve! Brake!

STEVE: I can't see where I'm going …

TEMPLE: It's all right, I've got the handbrake.

The car comes to a standstill.

STEVE: (*Relieved*) Phew! … (*A sigh of relief*)

TEMPLE: Lord, it's made a mess of the windscreen! Can't
          see a thing through it. Switch the engine off and
          I'll have a look.

The car engine is switched off and the car door opens.

*TEMPLE crosses in front of the car and examines the
windscreen.*

STEVE: Was it a stone, do you think?

TEMPLE: (*Thoughtfully*) I don't know what it was. (*A
          moment*) Did you see anybody by the side of the
          road?

STEVE: No, I didn't … (*Suddenly*) Paul! This has
          happened before on this road!

TEMPLE: What do you mean?

STEVE: Several people have had their windscreens
          smashed; don't you remember reading about it?

TEMPLE: Yes, of course! We're between Esher and
          Cobham! This is the mysterious mile or whatever
          they call it!

STEVE: (*Rather relieved*) Well, we're not the only ones
          anyway!

TEMPLE: No …

STEVE: I thought at first … (*She stops*)

TEMPLE: What?

STEVE: Oh, nothing …

37

TEMPLE: Move over, Steve. I'll drive.

STEVE: You won't be able to see anything.

TEMPLE knocks the rest of the windscreen out; the glass falls.

TEMPLE: I shall now!

STEVE: (*Laughs*) Yes. But it's going to be a bit draughty.

TEMPLE starts the car.

TEMPLE: Why don't you sit in the back?

STEVE: No, I'm all right, if you don't drive too fast.

TEMPLE changes gear, then lets out the clutch. The car gathers speed.

A pause.

TEMPLE: Steve, what did you think it was that hit the windscreen – at first, I mean?

STEVE: The same as you, Mr Temple – a bullet.

FADE UP music.

FADE DOWN music.

A door opens.

TEMPLE: (*Brightly*) Good morning!

STEVE: Good m… Paul, what time is it?

TEMPLE: Just gone nine …

STEVE: Oh, no!

TEMPLE: Oh, yes!

STEVE: Really, it's too bad! I asked Charlie to call me at a quarter to eight.

TEMPLE: He did call you at a quarter to eight. You said "Good morning, Charlie – thank you, Charlie – I'll be down in a moment, Charlie!" Then fell asleep again.

STEVE: Is it really nine o'clock?

TEMPLE: (*Looking at his watch*) Six minutes past to be exact. Steve, I shan't be in for lunch, I'm lunching with Sir Graham.

38

STEVE: Oh. When did you arrange that?

TEMPLE: Last night. I spoke to him on the phone after we got back from Farnham.

STEVE: Did you tell him about Stirling and June Michael?

TEMPLE: Yes.

STEVE: What did he say?

TEMPLE: Well – you know Sir Graham. He can be delightfully non-committal.

STEVE: (*After a moment*) Paul … if Gilbert doesn't get a reprieve when will they …

TEMPLE: The 2nd – that's a week on Tuesday.

STEVE: So we've got just over a week?

TEMPLE: Yes.

STEVE: Are you optimistic?

TEMPLE: I'm always optimistic, Steve. Even about breakfast.

STEVE: Oh, I'm sorry. I told Charlie to make coffee and …

TEMPLE: Don't worry, darling – the tea was delicious! (*Suddenly*) I must be off. I've got to pick up the car and I'm seeing Gilbert at half-past ten.

STEVE: Oh, yes, of course. When will you be back?

TEMPLE: Well, it depends how long I'm with Sir Graham. Look – why don't you meet me at Hayters for tea, say – quarter to four?

The door opens.

STEVE: Yes, all right, dear.

CHARLIE: Excuse me, sir.

TEMPLE: What is it, Charlie?

CHARLIE: Mr Stirling's here.

TEMPLE: Oh. (*After a moment*) Is he in the drawing room?

CHARLIE: Yes, sir.

STEVE: Did you expect him?

TEMPLE:	No, but I phoned him last night and he was out. Look, if I don't see you before I go, Steve – Hayters, a quarter to four.
STEVE:	Yes, all right.
CHARLIE:	Would you like tea, Mrs Temple – or coffee?
TEMPLE:	Tea, Charlie! Definitely tea!

STEVE laughs.
FADE SCENE.

FADE IN.

TEMPLE:	Good morning, Mr Stirling.
STIRLING:	(*Worried*) Oh, good morning, Mr Temple. I'm sorry I was out when you telephoned last night.
TEMPLE:	That's all right.
STIRLING:	I'd just slipped down to the hospital.
TEMPLE:	Hospital?
STIRLING:	(*Surprised*) To see Miss Michael …
TEMPLE:	Oh, yes, of course.
STIRLING:	What a shocking business. Whatever possessed the poor girl to do such a thing?
TEMPLE:	Is Miss Michael a friend of yours?
STIRLING:	No – she was a friend of Brenda's. I told you about her. She worked at Conway and Racys.
TEMPLE:	Yes. I know she was a friend of your daughter's, but I wondered if she was a friend of yours too, by any chance?
STIRLING:	(*Puzzled*) I think I've only seen her half a dozen times.
TEMPLE:	Then why did you go to the hospital?
STIRLING:	(*Hesitating*) I wanted to talk to her.
TEMPLE:	(*Rather deliberately*) Did you talk to her?
STIRLING:	No; they wouldn't let me see her, they said she was still unconscious.

TEMPLE:	What exactly was it you wanted to talk to her about?
STIRLING:	I wanted to know why she tried to commit suicide. She was such a lively, high spirited girl. I'm sure there must have been a reason, a very good reason for doing – what she did.
TEMPLE:	There usually is a reason …
STIRLING:	I don't think you understand …
TEMPLE:	I think I do. You believe that Miss Michael's attempt at suicide was connected, in some way, with – the murder.
STIRLING:	Yes, I do.
TEMPLE:	Well, if it's any consolation to you, that's my opinion too, Mr Stirling.
STIRLING:	Is that why you telephoned me last night?
TEMPLE:	No, I wanted to ask you a question. You showed me a diary belonging to your daughter – it had the name L. Fairfax in it.
STIRLING:	Yes.
TEMPLE:	You said you'd never heard the name before.
STIRLING:	Well, I hadn't.
TEMPLE:	Does the name Lord Fairfax mean anything to you?
STIRLING:	Lord Fairfax? No.
TEMPLE:	You've never been to a public house called The Lord Fairfax?
STIRLING:	Not that I remember. I'm practically a teetotaler, so it's not very likely.
TEMPLE:	Is Miss Michael a teetotaler?
STIRLING:	(*Surprised by the question*) June? I really don't know, I've never been in her company long enough to … (*Stops: suddenly*) No, as a matter of fact she isn't. I've just remembered.

41

	We had a drink together one night – about a month ago.
TEMPLE:	In Town?
STIRLING:	No, it was while the trial was on. I wanted to talk to June and I – telephoned her. She said she was taking a dress out to Farnham and I arranged to meet her there. You see, I work at Guildford, so it was quite easy for me to get to Farnham.
TEMPLE:	Yes, go on …
STIRLING:	We met at a hotel called The White Swan.
TEMPLE:	Is that where you had the drink?
STIRLING:	No, that was on the way home. It was June's idea; we were both feeling rather depressed and she said a drink would do us good. We stopped at some pub or other, I can't remember the name.
TEMPLE:	It was called The Lord Fairfax.
STIRLING:	(*Surprised*) The Lord Fairfax?
TEMPLE:	Yes. I take it you didn't notice the name?
STIRLING:	No, I'm afraid I didn't. I'd no reason to notice it.
TEMPLE:	Had Miss Michael been there before?
STIRLING:	She didn't say; but I think she must have been, because it was right off the main road and she found it so easily. I remember thinking at the time that it was an awfully difficult place to find if you'd never been there before.

The telephone rings.

TEMPLE:	I see. Excuse me.

TEMPLE lifts the telephone receiver.

TEMPLE:	(*On the phone*) Hello? … Yes, speaking … Yes, certainly … (*A moment*) Oh, good

morning, Sir Graham ... Yes, I'm seeing him at half-past ten ... That's right ... Yes, I will of course. (*Suddenly*) Oh, I was just going to ask you ... (*A slight pause; softly*) Oh ... Oh, I see ... Poor girl ... Thank you for ringing. Goodbye!

TEMPLE replaces the receiver.

A pause.

STIRLING: Mr Temple ...

TEMPLE: (*Thoughtfully*) Yes?

STIRLING: Am I to understand that you think the name L. Fairfax – the name in Brenda's diary – referred to the place where June and I stopped for a drink that night?

TEMPLE: I think it's a possibility.

STIRLING: And you think my daughter had an appointment there?

TEMPLE: (*Guardedly*) It's a possibility.

STIRLING: But I asked June about the name Fairfax and she said she'd never heard of it. Remember – I told you that.

TEMPLE: Yes, I remember.

STIRLING: You know, it's my opinion June knows a great deal more about this affair than anybody else. I've got to talk to her, before it's too late.

TEMPLE: It's already too late.

STIRLING: What?

TEMPLE: June Michael died this morning.

FADE UP music.

FADE DOWN music.

Slow FADE IN of heavy footsteps on concrete flooring: there is a slight echo on the voices in the corridor.

WARDER: Will you come this way, please, Mr Temple?

TEMPLE: Thank you.

We hear the sound of a heavy key being inserted into a cell door; the door slowly opens.

TEMPLE: How is Gilbert?

WARDER: Well, he's behaving rather well, sir – considering. He's been doing a lot of reading. Funny enough, we don't get a lot of trouble with them you know. Not at this stage. Excuse me, sir.

We hear the sound of a second key in a steel lock: the WARDER opens a second door.

WARDER: You've got a visitor, Mr Gilbert.

GILBERT: (*Looking up from his book; surprised*) Oh?

TEMPLE: Thank you, warder.

GILBERT: (*Rather unfriendly*) Well? What do you want?

TEMPLE: My name is Temple – I'm a friend of Inspector Kingston's.

GILBERT: (*Disinterested*) Paul Temple?

TEMPLE: Yes.

GILBERT: You write books or something, don't you?

TEMPLE: Books. May I sit down?

GILBERT: If you want to.

A pause.

TEMPLE: Gilbert, I have a contract for two novels and a collection of short stories.

GILBERT: Well?

TEMPLE: (*Smiling*) I'm only trying to impress you with the fact that I didn't come here to waste my time. I'm a busy man.

GILBERT: I'm impressed. Now what happens?

TEMPLE: (*Quite simply*) Did you murder Brenda Stirling?

GILBERT: You certainly are a busy man. You haven't even read the newspapers. Of course I murdered Brenda. We went to the theatre one night – we

44

had a row – I lost my temper … I took her on to a bombsite and strangled her. Oh, it was all quite simple, nothing complicated. A woman called Mrs Talbot saw me do it – at least she saw me running away …

TEMPLE: I see.

GILBERT: Just in case there's any doubt in your mind. I hadn't an alibi and they found blood on my handkerchief. The right kind of blood. Oh, and I made two statements, both highly contradictory.

TEMPLE: Did you steal her shoe?

GILBERT: What?

TEMPLE: I said: did you steal her shoe?

GILBERT: Oh, yes, of course. I remember. One of her shoes was missing.

TEMPLE: That's right. Did you steal it?

GILBERT: But of course!

TEMPLE: Why?

GILBERT: Well, one doesn't commit a murder every day. It was an occasion. I took the shoe as a memento.

TEMPLE: (*Unperturbed*) Left or right?

GILBERT: What?

TEMPLE: Only one shoe was missing. Which did you take – the left or the right?

GILBERT: (*After a moment*) The left.

TEMPLE: Wrong.

GILBERT: (*Slightly taken aback*) What do you mean?

TEMPLE: It was the right shoe that was missing.

GILBERT: Oh.

A pause.

TEMPLE: You know, you seem to me to be rather an impetuous young man. When you left Soho Square, your best bet would have been …

GILBERT: (*Angrily*) I never went near Soho Square!

45

TEMPLE: But you must have done. That's where they
           found the body – or just round the corner.
           Besides, this Mrs Talbot we've heard so much
           about saw you running down Greek Street.

GILBERT: (*Bitterly*) Did she?

TEMPLE: Well, didn't she?

GILBERT: Look, if you've got a lot of work to do, my
           advice to you is to go home and do it.

TEMPLE: I'm not sure I want to take your advice.

A slight pause.

GILBERT: Why did you come here? What do you want?

TEMPLE: (*A moment*) Did they tell you about June
           Michael?

GILBERT: What about her?

TEMPLE: She committed suicide.

GILBERT: When?

TEMPLE: Yesterday afternoon.

GILBERT: I can't believe it.

TEMPLE: It's in all the papers. In any case, why shouldn't
           you believe it?

GILBERT: June was such a happy person; so full of life, so
           – Why should she commit suicide?

TEMPLE: Why should you murder Brenda Stirling?

GILBERT: I didn't murder her.

A slight pause.

TEMPLE: Tell me what really happened that night.

GILBERT: We had a row. Brenda left me outside the theatre
           and I walked down to the car park. I drove round
           for about an hour and then I put the car in St
           James's Square and went for a walk.

TEMPLE: Why?

GILBERT: What do you mean – why?

TEMPLE: Why did you go for a walk?

46

GILBERT: I – I was upset because of what I'd said to Brenda – and I wanted to think. I walked almost as far as the Victoria and Albert Musuem, then I retraced my steps, picked up the car, and drove home. I got home about half-past twelve.

TEMPLE: It's not a very good alibi, is it?

GILBERT: It was never meant as an alibi! If I'd wanted an alibi I could have thought up a very much better one than that.

TEMPLE: You did.

GILBERT: What do you mean?

TEMPLE: In your first statement you told Inspector Kingston that you arrived home at half-past ten.

GILBERT: Yes, I know. I don't know what made me say that. I suppose I lost my head.

TEMPLE: How do you account for the fact that Mrs Talbot recognised you?

GILBERT: She can't have recognised me.

TEMPLE: But she did – she picked you out of an identity parade.

GILBERT: Then she made a mistake.

TEMPLE: Is that your only explanation?

GILBERT: (*On the verge of losing his temper*) Look, I've told you I didn't murder Brenda. I've told you I didn't go near Soho Square that night …

TEMPLE: (*Interrupting*) I'm not suggesting you did.

GILBERT: You said Mrs Talbot recognised me!

TEMPLE: But she did.

GILBERT: Then I say she made a mistake!

TEMPLE: All right, let's look at it from another angle. Did you recognise Mrs Talbot – had you seen her before?

GILBERT: No.

TEMPLE: Are you sure?

47

GILBERT: Yes, I'm quite sure.

TEMPLE: What about Mr Stirling, Brenda's father. Did he recognise her?

GILBERT: (*Puzzled*) I don't know. I don't think he even saw her.

TEMPLE: But he must have done – they were both at the trial.

GILBERT: Well, I really don't know whether he recognised her or not. I suppose if he had done, he'd have told the police.

TEMPLE: Yes, I suppose so.

A moment.

GILBERT: I'm sorry I lost my temper. I didn't mean to be rude, but – you're only wasting your time.

TEMPLE: But if you didn't murder Brenda – and I don't think you did, Gilbert – then you were wrongly convicted. In which case, I'm most certainly not wasting my time.

GILBERT: But we've never even met before. You don't know anything at all about me. And all the evidence points towards the fact that I did murder Brenda.

TEMPLE: Well?

GILBERT: Then why are you so sure that I didn't?

TEMPLE: Did you steal the shoe?

GILBERT: No.

TEMPLE: Then who did?

GILBERT: I don't know.

TEMPLE: (*Pause*) Did you ever go to a public house called The Lord Fairfax?

GILBERT: No.

TEMPLE: Have you ever heard of it?

GILBERT: I don't think so.

TEMPLE: Have you ever heard of a person called Fairfax –
           L. Fairfax?

GILBERT: No. (*Suddenly*) Wait a minute! Mr Stirling
           mentioned someone called Fairfax. I believe he
           came across the name in a diary belonging to
           Brenda.

TEMPLE: That's right. But you'd never heard the name
           before he mentioned it?

GILBERT: No – never.

TEMPLE: (*After a moment*) Read this letter, Gilbert.

GILBERT: What is it?

TEMPLE: Read it …

GILBERT: (*Surprised: looking at the envelope*) It's
           addressed to me …

TEMPLE: Yes …

A pause.

GILBERT: (*Reading*) "Dear Howard …So now it's all over
           – all over and they've found you guilty. I wonder
           whether you did murder Brenda Stirling? I met
           you once, a long time ago. I expect you've
           forgotten. When I heard about the murder, and
           read the reports, and saw Brenda's photograph in
           the newspapers, I said to myself … 'there, but
           for the Grace of God' … Dear Brenda … a
           lovely creature; but she wasn't a very easy
           person, was she, Howard? I wonder whether you
           did murder her or whether you happen to be the
           unlucky one they've picked on. I wonder! Was
           her shoe missing, Howard? Ask the police – it
           might be worth your while … L. Fairfax." But –
           what does this mean? I just don't understand it!
           Where did you get this letter?

TEMPLE: Your friend Reynolds gave it to me; apparently it
           arrived yesterday afternoon.

49

GILBERT: But, I told you I've never heard of anyone called Fairfax until –

TEMPLE: All right, Gilbert. Don't worry about it. Give me the letter … Now listen, I shall probably see you again – perhaps at the end of the week – but if Sir Graham Forbes comes to see you, or Inspector Kingston, or anyone else – don't lose your temper and don't get facetious. You understand?

GILBERT: (*Subdued*) Yes, all right.

TEMPLE: And if they ask you about the shoe keep quiet and say nothing. (*Almost a smile*) Your guesses are too good, you know.

GILBERT: What?

TEMPLE: It was the left shoe that was missing.

FADE UP music.

CROSS FADE to a light orchestra playing a tea-time selection of music in a hotel lounge.

FADE the music to the background.

TEMPLE: (*Slightly out of breath*) I'm so sorry I'm late, dear!

STEVE: It's nearly five o'clock.

TEMPLE: Yes, I know. I'm sorry, Steve, but – (*Sitting down*) Phew! What a day!

STEVE: Did you see Gilbert?

TEMPLE: Yes.

STEVE: Well?

TEMPLE: He's a strange fellow; got a chip on his shoulder.

STEVE: That's not exactly surprising.

TEMPLE: But he didn't do it, Steve. I'm convinced he didn't.

A slight pause.

STEVE: Would you like some tea?

50

TEMPLE: (*Rising*) No, there isn't time. We must go.

STEVE: Where are we going?

TEMPLE: I want to talk to a woman called Mrs Talbot.

STEVE: Mrs Talbot?

TEMPLE: Yes. Gilbert's supposed to have bumped into her soon after it happened.

STEVE: Oh, yes, of course. She identified him.

TEMPLE: That's right.

STEVE: Why do you want to see her?

TEMPLE: Because I've got a shrewd suspicion that she was lying. I don't think she did see Gilbert.

STEVE: But, darling, she identified him! She picked him out of several people …

TEMPLE: Yes …

STEVE: Where does she live?

TEMPLE: Soho Square … I've got the address. Have you paid for the tea?

STEVE: Yes, I have. Paul, I had lunch on my own today – at the Buttery. You know – the one in Curzon Street, and just as I was finishing, Miss Wayne came in …

TEMPLE: Miss Wayne?

STEVE: Yes, you remember. She's a buyer at Conway and Racys; you were talking to her yesterday afternoon. You asked her about June Michael.

TEMPLE: Oh, yes, of course.

STEVE: Well – I don't know whether she saw me or not; if she did she didn't take any notice. Anyway, she sat at a corner table and after a few minutes she was – joined by someone else.

TEMPLE: Well go on.

STEVE: It was Lance Reynolds.

TEMPLE: (*Surprised*) Reynolds.

STEVE: Yes.

TEMPLE: Are you sure?

STEVE: I couldn't mistake Reynolds, darling. Even if I hadn't seen him I'd have recognised his voice.

TEMPLE: Reynolds and Miss Wayne ... M'm.

STEVE: (*Smiling*) I thought you'd be interested, Mr Temple.

FADE SCENE.

FADE UP the sound of the car. It draws to a standstill and the engine is switched off.

The car doors open and close.

We hear background traffic noises.

FADE traffic noises away gradually.

STEVE: I don't think this can be the place, Paul – it's a block of offices.

TEMPLE: Well, this is the address Kingston gave me. Wait a minute! (*Reading the notice board*) Yes, this is it ... They're not all offices. There are two or three flats ... Mrs Talbot! It's over here on the ground floor ... Here we are.

STEVE: I shouldn't like to live here – it isn't exactly clean.

TEMPLE presses the bell push.

The bell doesn't work.

TEMPLE: The bell's not working.

STEVE: That doesn't surprise me.

TEMPLE: (*Surprised*) The door's open.

TEMPLE pushes the door open wider.

TEMPLE: (*Calling*) Mrs Talbot! Mrs Talbot!

STEVE: She can't be in.

TEMPLE: Doesn't look like it ... funny, leaving the door open like that.

The telephone rings.

STEVE: She may have slipped out to the pillar-box or something – Paul, we can't go in!

TEMPLE and STEVE enter the flat.

TEMPLE: (*Calling*) Mrs Talbot! Anybody in?

STEVE: She's obviously out … or very deaf! She's not answering the phone. I suppose that's the bedroom over there?

TEMPLE: I should imagine so.

STEVE: What a dreadful flat! Just look at that picture!

A pause during which the telephone continues to ring.

STEVE: (*Listening to the phone ringing*) Whoever's ringing, they're very persistent!

TEMPLE: Yes.

The phone continues to ring.

A pause.

TEMPLE: (*A sudden decision*) Answer it, Steve!

STEVE: (*Surprised*) What?

TEMPLE: Answer it, but don't say who you are …

STEVE: But, Paul, we can't …

TEMPLE: (*Quickly*) Steve, please!

STEVE: Oh, all right.

A moment: STEVE lifts the receiver.

STEVE: (*On the phone*) Hello?

REYNOLDS: (*On the other end of the line*) Is that Gerard 1071?

STEVE: Er – yes.

REYNOLDS: (*Curious*) Is that Mrs Talbot?

STEVE: (*After a moment*) Yes …

REYNOLDS: (*Urgently*) What about the Hamilton affair? Do I get the third shoe? … Hello?

STEVE: Yes?

REYNOLDS: Do you understand me? Do I get the third shoe?

STEVE: (*Weakly*) Yes.

REYNOLDS replaces the receiver at the other end. STEVE replaces her receiver.

TEMPLE:	(*Tensely*) What happened?
STEVE:	Paul, it was Reynolds! I'm sure it was. I recognised his voice.
TEMPLE:	What did he say?
STEVE:	He asked me if I was Mrs Talbot and I said ...
TEMPLE:	(*Urgently*) Yes. But what did he say?
STEVE:	(*Slowly; puzzled*) He said: "What about the Hamilton affair? Do I get the third shoe?"
TEMPLE:	Do I get the third shoe?
STEVE:	Yes.
TEMPLE:	Are you sure it was Reynolds?
STEVE:	Positive. I recognised his voice immediately. He rang off rather suddenly.
TEMPLE:	I wonder if he realised you weren't Mrs Talbot?
STEVE:	Perhaps, I don't know. So long as he didn't recognise my voice. He wouldn't – surely?
TEMPLE:	(*Thoughtfully*) Well, if he did ... (*He stops*) There's someone coming!

The door is pushed open.

MRS TALBOT:	(*Very surprised: a common tough voice*) Hello? Who are you? What's going on here?
TEMPLE:	(*Politely*) Mrs Talbot?
MRS TALBOT:	Yes. (*Annoyed*) What's the idea? Did you just walk in 'ere as if ...
TEMPLE:	The door was open, Mrs Talbot ...
MRS TALBOT:	I know the door was open! I left it open. I've been upstairs to borrow something. (*Suddenly; angry*) Look here, what's the idea walking in here like this?

TEMPLE:	I apologise, Mrs Talbot, but we did ring the bell and when there was no reply …
MRS TALBOT:	You just walked in! Well, you can just walk out – both of you. Go on, get out. (*A pause*) Go on, before I send for the police.
TEMPLE:	(*Quite pleasantly*) My name is Temple. I'm a friend of Inspector Kingston's.
MRS TALBOT:	Oh …
TEMPLE:	This is my wife …
STEVE:	(*Nicely*) How do you do, Mrs Talbot?
MRS TALBOT:	What do you want?
TEMPLE:	Well, we wanted to have a little chat.
MRS TALBOT:	Oh, I see. You just dropped in for a cosy little chat. Well, you're unlucky, both of you. I'm just off!
TEMPLE:	It won't take long; three or four minutes.
MRS TALBOT:	I'm due at the café at half-past five. I'm late already.
TEMPLE:	(*Pleasantly; dismissing the matter*) All right, another time perhaps. And once again, we apologise, Mrs Talbot. (*To STEVE*) Come along, Steve.
MRS TALBOT:	(*Curious*) Just a minute. What is it you want to talk about anyway – the Gilbert case?
TEMPLE:	Yes.
MRS TALBOT:	I thought so! Howard Gilbert! Lord, am I sick an' tired of that name!
TEMPLE:	Well, you were an important witness in the Gilbert case, Mrs Talbot.
MRS TALBOT:	I certainly was. I was the only witness.
TEMPLE:	Where do you work – in Greek Street?
MRS TALBOT:	Yes, at Farnalios.

TEMPLE:	Were you coming back from Farnalios the night you saw Gilbert?
MRS TALBOT:	Yes.
TEMPLE:	It was about half-past twelve.
MRS TALBOT:	Are you asking me or telling me?
TEMPLE:	(*Smiling*) I'm asking you.
MRS TALBOT:	Yes – it was about half-past twelve. I saw him running off the bombsite. He bumped into me.
TEMPLE:	You're sure it was Gilbert?
MRS TALBOT:	O' course I'm sure.
TEMPLE:	What was he wearing, do you remember?
MRS TALBOT:	No, I don't remember. Look – I've been through all this rigmarole before. I saw Gilbert – I told the police about it, an' I picked him out. What more do you want?
TEMPLE:	Yes, you've been very co-operative.
MRS TALBOT:	Well, then for heaven's sake leave me alone!
STEVE:	You must have a very good memory for faces, Mrs Talbot – unless of course you'd seen him before.
MRS TALBOT:	What do you mean?
TEMPLE:	My wife means – had you seen Gilbert before he bumped into you that night?
MRS TALBOT:	No of course I 'and't. Look, I'm supposed to be at work at half-past five. It's a quarter to six already!
TEMPLE:	Yes, all right. We won't keep you any longer. (*Suddenly*) Oh, there's just one point. When Gilbert bumped into you, did he say anything?
MRS TALBOT:	(*Hesitating*) No.
TEMPLE:	Are you sure?

56

MRS TALBOT:	Well, if he did I didn't hear him.
TEMPLE:	But I thought you told Inspector Kingston that he did say something but you couldn't understand what it was.
MRS TALBOT:	(*Surly*) I don't remember what I told Inspector Kingston.
TEMPLE:	No? But you've a very good memory, Mrs Talbot.
MRS TALBOT:	(*Angrily*) I've got a very good memory for faces!
TEMPLE:	(*Smiling*) Ah, yes!
MRS TALBOT:	I shan't forget yours in a hurry!
TEMPLE:	(*Pleasantly*) Then, so far as you can remember, Gilbert didn't say anything. He just pushed you on one side ...
MRS TALBOT:	He did.
TEMPLE:	But, obviously, you had a good look at him.
MRS TALBOT:	I identified him, didn't I? How could I identify him if I didn't have a good look at him?
TEMPLE:	(*Resigned*) Yes, all right, Mrs Talbot.
MRS TALBOT:	Now come on – I want to lock up. (*With heavy sarcasm*) You wouldn't like a key, would you, Mr Temple? Just in case you feel like dropping in any time ...

FADE SCENE.

FADE IN the opening and closing of a door.

CHARLIE:	Oh, hello, sir.
TEMPLE:	Hello, Charlie!
CHARLIE:	Shall I take those parcels, Mrs Temple?
STEVE:	Please. Put them in the kitchen for the time being.

CHARLIE:	Oke. (*Correcting himself*) Yes, ma'am. Oh, and Inspector Kingston's here, sir. He's in the drawing room.
TEMPLE:	(*Interested*) Oh … Right, thanks, Charlie.

FADE SCENE.

FADE IN.

TEMPLE:	Hello, Inspector! Sorry to have kept you waiting.
KINGSTON:	Oh, that's all right. Good evening, Mrs Temple.
STEVE:	Good evening, Inspector.
TEMPLE:	You look worried, Kingston.
KINGSTON:	(*Very serious*) Yes. I am worried. Very worried.
TEMPLE:	Why? What's happened?
KINGSTON:	Well, early this afternoon, we had a report …
STEVE:	(*Interrupting KINGSTON*) Paul, won't the Inspector have a drink?
TEMPLE:	Oh, yes, of course! I'm sorry, Kingston. Would you like a whisky and soda?
KINGSTON:	At this moment I'd give my pension for a whisky and soda!

STEVE laughs.

TEMPLE:	You do seem to be in a bad way!
STEVE:	It's all right, Paul. I'll do it.
TEMPLE:	One for me, too, dear. Inspector, before you tell me what happened this afternoon I think you ought to know what I've been up to. I saw Howard Gilbert this morning …
KINGSTON:	Yes, I know. Sir Graham told me.
TEMPLE:	And I've just been talking to Mrs Talbot.
KINGSTON:	With Mrs Talbot?
TEMPLE:	Yes.

A moment.

KINGSTON: When did you see Mrs Talbot?

TEMPLE: About twenty minutes ago.

STEVE: We've just left her.

TEMPLE: What is it, Kingston?

KINGSTON: (*Slowly*) Mrs Talbot's dead.

STEVE: Dead!

KINGSTON: That's why I came to see you. She was found in a field about six miles from Farnham. Apparently there'd been a struggle –

TEMPLE: When was she found?

KINGSTON: This afternoon – about two o'clock.

STEVE: Two o'clock?

TEMPLE: But that's impossible! We've only just left her flat.

KINGSTON: (*Interrupting TEMPLE*) Temple!

TEMPLE: Yes?

KINGSTON: One of her shoes was missing …

FADE IN closing music.

END OF EPISODE TWO

EPISODE THREE

PETER GALINO

OPEN TO:

TEMPLE: Inspector, before you tell me what happened this afternoon I think you ought to know what I've been up to. I saw Howard Gilbert this morning …

KINGSTON: Yes, I know. Sir Graham told me.

TEMPLE: And I've just been talking to Mrs Talbot.

KINGSTON: With Mrs Talbot?

TEMPLE: Yes.

A moment.

KINGSTON: When did you see Mrs Talbot?

TEMPLE: About twenty minutes ago.

STEVE: We've just left her.

TEMPLE: What is it, Kingston?

KINGSTON: (*Slowly*) Mrs Talbot's dead.

STEVE: Dead!

KINGSTON: That's why I came to see you. She was found in a field about six miles from Farnham. Apparently there'd been a struggle –

TEMPLE: When was she found?

KINGSTON: This afternoon – about two o'clock.

STEVE: Two o'clock?

TEMPLE: But that's impossible! We've only just left her flat.

KINGSTON: (*Interrupting TEMPLE*) Temple!

TEMPLE: Yes?

KINGSTON: One of her shoes was missing …

STEVE: One of her shoes was missing?

TEMPLE: Are you sure it was Mrs Talbot?

KINGSTON: Yes, of course.

TEMPLE: Who identified her?

KINGSTON: I did.

STEVE: But, Inspector, we saw her about twenty minutes ago.

KINGSTON: No, Mrs Temple. I don't know who you saw, but I do know that she wasn't Mrs Talbot!

TEMPLE: What happened this afternoon?

KINGSTON: I was over at Farnham making inquiries. I called at the local station and they told me about a woman they'd picked up; apparently she'd been strangled. The sergeant said that one of her shoes was missing so naturally I was curious. I asked to see the body. It was Mrs Talbot.

TEMPLE: I see.

STEVE: What sort of person was she, Inspector?

KINGSTON: About thirty-five; blonde; rather a good-looking woman in a – well, rather tough sort of way.

TEMPLE: Is there a Mr Talbot?

KINGSTON: No; she was a widow. Which reminds me, she was friendly with a fellow called Galino.

TEMPLE: Italian?

KINGSTON: Yes, he's a waiter. I must have a word with him.

TEMPLE: Tell me: was Mrs Talbot a good witness – at the trial, I mean?

KINGSTON: It depends what you mean by a good witness. She was nervous of course, on the other hand who wouldn't be at a murder trial. Anyway she convinced the jury that she'd seen Howard Gilbert.

TEMPLE: Did she convince you?

KINGSTON: She picked him out at an identity parade.

TEMPLE: Are you still convinced? M'm?

KINGSTON: (*Hesitating*) Well –

TEMPLE:	There's a doubt in your mind, isn't there?
KINGSTON:	Well, frankly, yes. Quite apart from this new development – some very strange things have been happening just recently.
TEMPLE:	How dy'e mean?
KINGSTON:	Well – I'm beginning to wonder if Gilbert wasn't framed in some way or other. I'm even beginning to wonder whether he … (*Changing his mind*) Still, we can talk about that some other time. Now what happened this afternoon? You obviously didn't see Mrs Talbot so – who was it you did see?
TEMPLE:	Your guess is as good as mine. We arrived at the flat at about a quarter to six. The door was half open and – well, when we didn't get any reply, we decided to investigate. We were in the flat when a tough looking woman walked in and said she was Mrs Talbot, so I never doubted her.
KINGSTON:	What happened?
STEVE:	(*Faintly amused*) She acted as if she was very annoyed and kicked us out.
KINGSTON:	Would you recognise her if you saw her again?
STEVE:	I would, wouldn't you, Paul?
TEMPLE:	Yes, of course.
KINGSTON:	I wonder who on earth she was? Have you got your car here, Temple?
TEMPLE:	Yes.
KINGSTON:	Would you run me down to Soho Square?
TEMPLE:	Yes, certainly.
KINGSTON:	There's just a chance she may still be at the flat.
TEMPLE:	I doubt it, Inspector – still we can try. I'll see you later, Steve.

STEVE: Yes, all right, dear! Goodbye, Inspector.
KINGSTON: Goodbye, Mrs Temple.
FADE SCENE.

FADE IN.
KINGSTON: Well, whoever she was, we don't have to ask why she came here! Just look at this room!
TEMPLE: (*In the background*) By Timothy, she certainly turned the place upside down!
KINGSTON: Just look at it!
TEMPLE: (*Still in the background*) The bedroom's even worse – clothes all over the place.
KINGSTON: I wonder if she found what she was looking for?
TEMPLE: (*Joining KINGSTON*) You can see what happened. She was probably in here when we arrived. She went out through the kitchen there, down the fire escape; then she hit on the idea of pretending to be Mrs Talbot and came back …
KINGSTON: … through the front door.
TEMPLE: Exactly.
KINGSTON: Was the flat fairly tidy when you came in?
TEMPLE: I wouldn't call it tidy, but it certainly wasn't anything like this. She obviously searched the place immediately we left.
KINGSTON: Yes. (*Looking about him*) Of course we can't tell if there's anything missing.
A slight pause.
TEMPLE: No. Kingston, do you know a man called Lance Reynolds?
KINGSTON: (*Faintly surprised*) Yes, I told you about him. He shares a flat with Howard Gilbert.
TEMPLE: Yes, that's the fellow. I'm rather interested in Reynolds, Inspector.

KINGSTON:	Oh?
TEMPLE:	Do you know anything about him?
KINGSTON:	Well, he's about forty-seven; a bachelor; rather fond of the ladies; has a private income; very interested in photography; travels abroad quite a lot. That's about all. Oh, and he has a theory about the Gilbert case.
TEMPLE:	Yes – he told me about that. What does he do exactly, for a living, I mean?
KINGSTON:	I don't think he does anything. He doesn't have to. Frankly, the fellow's a bore. Keep him at a distance, Temple, or he'll make a nuisance of himself.
TEMPLE:	(*Thoughtfully*) Yes …
KINGSTON:	(*Curious*) But what made you think of Reynolds?
TEMPLE:	Well – when we were here earlier this evening the phone rang. My wife answered it. (*He hesitates*) Well, to cut a long story short, Steve said she was Mrs Talbot and the man on the other end who sounded remarkably like Reynolds – said … "What about the Hamilton affair? Do I get the third shoe?"
KINGSTON:	(*Puzzled*) Do I get the third shoe?
TEMPLE:	Yes.
KINGSTON:	What did he mean?
TEMPLE:	I don't know.
KINGSTON:	(*Thoughtfully*) What about the Hamilton affair?
TEMPLE:	Yes. Does the name Hamilton convey anything to you?
KINGSTON:	No, nothing. Are you sure it was Reynolds on the telephone?

TEMPLE:	Well, my wife's not usually mistaken about a voice.
KINGSTON:	There's someone at the door!

A slight pause.

GALINO:	(*Calling*) Mary, it's Peter! Where are you? (*Surprised*) What's happened? What are you doing here?
KINGSTON:	I'm Detective-Inspector Kingston. This is Mr Temple. Are you Peter Galino?
GALINO:	Yes. (*Quickly*) What's happened? Where's Mary?
KINGSTON:	Mrs Talbot isn't here at the moment.
GALINO:	Then where is she? She's usually here at … Has there been a burglary?
KINGSTON:	Yes.
GALINO:	When?
KINGSTON:	Early this evening …
GALINO:	But where was Mrs Talbot?
TEMPLE:	Have you an appointment with her?
GALINO:	Yes. I said I'd drop in about seven. I usually do on a Thursday. (*Alarmed*) Has something happened to Mary?
KINGSTON:	When did you last see Mrs Talbot?
GALINO:	Last night. We had supper together.
KINGSTON:	What time was that?
GALINO:	Oh – late. About half past twelve.
KINGSTON:	Where did you have it?
GALINO:	At my place. I've got a couple of rooms in Meryl Street, you know, near Euston. Look, Inspector, if something's happened please tell me …
KINGSTON:	Can you account for your movements between eleven o'clock this morning and four o'clock this afternoon?

GALINO:	Yes, I think so.
KINGSTON:	Well?
GALINO:	Well, I went to work just after ten – I'm a waiter at Leonardo's Restaurant. I stayed there until about a quarter past five.
KINGSTON:	I see.
GALINO:	What is it? What's happened?
KINGSTON:	Mrs Talbot's dead.
GALINO:	(*Softly*) Dead? Was she murdered?
KINGSTON:	Yes …
GALINO:	I see.
TEMPLE:	You don't sound very surprised, Mr Galino.
GALINO:	(*Tensely*) No, I'm not. I knew this would happen. I told her. I told her something would happen … (*Emotionally*) Oh, Mary! Why didn't you listen to me!

A tiny pause.

TEMPLE:	How well did you know her?
GALINO:	Well, when I first arrived in this country, about six months ago, I had no friends and very little money. I was lonely and very miserable. One afternoon I went into a reference library on the Tottenham Court Road. I'd been walking about all day and I just didn't know what to do with myself. Mary – Mrs Talbot – was in the library; we got talking; she invited me back here to tea. After that we became – very good friends.
TEMPLE:	Why did you think Mrs Talbot would be murdered?
GALINO:	She was mixed up in something. I don't know what it was; she never told me … but ever since the Gilbert case she seemed frightened

of something. It was almost as if she was being blackmailed by someone.

KINGSTON: Were you blackmailing her, Galino?

GALINO: Me? No, of course not?

KINGSTON: Did she ever give you any money?

GALINO: (*Hesitating*) Yes …

KINGSTON: When?

GALINO: About a week ago. I was hard up. I – borrowed ten pounds.

KINGSTON: I see.

GALINO: That's why I came here tonight. I – wanted to repay it.

TEMPLE: Galino, have you heard of a man called Hamilton?

GALINO: Hamilton? No …

TEMPLE: Mrs Temple never mentioned him?

GALINO: No … (*Shaking his head*) She wouldn't … Even if he was a friend of hers it's doubtful if she would have mentioned him to me.

TEMPLE: You say you've been over here six months?

GALINO: Yes.

TEMPLE: Are you on a permit?

GALINO: Yes, a temporary permit. I've just applied for a renewal.

KINGSTON: (*Dismissing GALINO*) All right, Galino. Report to my office tomorrow morning – nine o'clock.

A slight pause.

GALINO: (*Nervously*) Why do you want to see me tomorrow morning?

KINGSTON: You were a close friend of Mrs Talbot's. There are a great many questions we shall want to ask you.

GALINO: I've told you all I know – there's nothing else I can tell you.

KINGSTON: But you haven't told us anything. You simply said you met her in a reference library and you became very good friends. If you became "very good friends" then obviously you must know a great deal about her, who she mixed with, where she used to go …

GALINO: (*Quickly*) No, no, you don't understand. I was fond of Mary, very fond of her, but we didn't see a great deal of each other and … (*Suddenly*) I was frightened and I didn't want to get involved …

TEMPLE: (*Bluntly*) How did you know she was mixed up in something? (*Pause*) Well?

GALINO: It's difficult to explain. There were times when she just disappeared … for days … a week even … then when we met she wouldn't tell me where she'd been or who she'd been with …

TEMPLE: Did she ever talk to you about Howard Gilbert?

GALINO: No, she wouldn't talk about him. I used to ask her about Gilbert; especially when the trial was on … I was worried, because … (*He stops*)

TEMPLE: Because what? (*A moment*) Go on, Galino … why were you worried?

GALINO: Because the night she said she saw Gilbert she was with me.

KINGSTON: With you?

GALINO: Yes, she came straight to my place from the restaurant and she didn't leave until after one o'clock. When I spoke to her about it she said

71

it was half past eleven, but – I know it was later, very much later.

TEMPLE: (*To KINGSTON*) But, Inspector, I understood Mrs Talbot worked at a restaurant in Greek Street?

KINGSTON: She did.

TEMPLE: Well, either you or Sir Graham told me that on the night of the murder she left the restaurant about ten minutes before she bumped into Gilbert – about a quarter to twelve in fact.

KINGSTON: She did leave the restaurant at a quarter to twelve. We checked on it.

GALINO: But she didn't go straight home, Mr Temple.

TEMPLE: She went to your place which is nowhere near where she was supposed to have seen Gilbert.

GALINO: Yes.

KINGSTON: And you say it was after one when she left.

GALINO: Yes.

TEMPLE: In other words, she didn't bump into Howard Gilbert that night – she didn't see him in fact?

GALINO: (*Hesitating*) Well –

TEMPLE: I certainly think Mr Galino ought to make a statement, Inspector! The sooner the better!

KINGSTON: Come to my office tomorrow morning at Scotland Yard. Nine o'clock.

GALINO: Yes, sir. Nine o'clock.

FADE SCENE.

FADE UP a background of traffic noises.
We hear the opening of a car door.
GALINO rushes up to TEMPLE as he is about to enter his car.

72

GALINO:	(*From the background*) Mr Temple! Mr Temple!
TEMPLE:	(*Turning*) Hello, Galino! What is it?
GALINO:	(*Breathless*) I – I wanted to ask you something.
TEMPLE:	Well?
GALINO:	Will you be at Scotland Yard tomorrow morning?
TEMPLE:	I very much doubt it.
GALINO:	(*Nervously*) What's going to happen, Mr Temple? What will they do with me? Supposing they think I'm mixed up in this business?
TEMPLE:	But you are mixed up in it, Galino. You said so. Don't you remember?
GALINO:	… Yes.
TEMPLE:	Well?
GALINO:	No, Mr Temple, don't go yet. Please!
TEMPLE:	(*Annoyed*) What is it? What do you want?
GALINO:	You think I've behaved badly over this, don't you? You think I ought to have gone to the police the moment I suspected that – Mary wasn't telling the truth.
TEMPLE:	Why didn't you?
GALINO:	I couldn't. You see I'm a foreigner here. I'm working on a temporary permit.
TEMPLE:	What's that got to do with it?
GALINO:	Mary said that if I went to the police it wouldn't do any good – she said the police would report me to the Ministry of Labour and I'd be deported.
TEMPLE:	Nonsense! If you'd told the police the truth they'd have been on your side and nothing would have happened to you. Now, you'll be asked to make a statement and there's a doubt – a very big doubt – whether they'll believe a word of it.

GALINO: I know – that's what I'm worried about, Mr Temple.

TEMPLE: Well, what do you expect me to do?

GALINO: (*Desperately worried*) You know the police, sir – you're a friend of theirs. If you say you believe me, if you say I'm telling the truth …

TEMPLE: Listen, Galino, I think you know a great deal more about this business than you say you do.

GALINO: I don't! I swear I don't.

TEMPLE: (*Brusquely*) What was Mrs Talbot up to? Why did she say she saw Howard Gilbert the night Brenda Stirling was murdered?

GALINO: I don't know. Honestly, I don't know.

TEMPLE: (*After a moment*) All right, Galino.

GALINO: (*With obvious sincerity*) Oh, I know I've behaved stupidly. But that doesn't mean I know anything about the Stirling murder. I don't. I'd never heard of Brenda Stirling until I read about her in the newspapers. That's the truth, Mr Temple.

TEMPLE: (*Hesitating: not sure whether to believe GALINO or not*) Galino, when did you first realise that she was – mixed up in something?

GALINO: I wanted to see her one night; she said she couldn't manage it. Her sister was ill and she had to go out to Aldershot. I didn't believe her. I thought she'd got friendly with someone else; there was a night porter. I thought perhaps she'd arranged to see him, so (*He hesitates*) I followed her that night. She went out to Hampstead, to a club called La Martella. I was wrong – about the porter, I mean. Her appointment was with a woman; a woman I'd see once or twice before at the restaurant where I work.

TEMPLE: Go on …

GALINO: I couldn't understand why she wanted to see this woman; when I asked her about it the next day she lost her temper and told me to mind my own business.

TEMPLE: What sort of a place was this La Martella?

GALINO: Very expensive; it wasn't at all the kind of place that Mary was used to …

TEMPLE: You think she had a definite appointment with this woman?

GALINO: I'm sure she did. The woman was waiting for her; besides I tipped the commissionaire and he told me that they'd been there once before.

TEMPLE: Did you find out who this woman was?

GALINO: Yes, I've told you. I recognised her. She works at a dress shop called Conway and Racys. Her name's Betty Wayne.

FADE IN music.

FADE DOWN music.
FADE IN the sound of a door bell ringing.
The door opens.

STEVE: (*Surprised*) Oh, hello, Mr Reynolds!

REYNOLDS: Good evening, Mrs Temple. Is your husband in?

STEVE: No, but I'm expecting him back at any moment. Would you like to come in and wait?

REYNOLDS: (*Hesitating*) Well, I have another appointment at half past seven, I – don't think I will, thank you very much.

STEVE: Can I give him a message?

REYNOLDS: (*Vaguely*) No, I don't think so, I … (*Suddenly*) I thought Mr Temple might be

	interested to know that my flat has been burgled …
STEVE:	Oh!
REYNOLDS:	Yes. Someone apparently impersonated me over the telephone and told my housekeeper to leave the key under the mat. The stupid woman thought it was me and did as she was told.
STEVE:	How very unfortunate. When did this happen?
REYNOLDS:	This afternoon. When I got back this evening the whole place was completely upside down. Oddly enough they seem to have concentrated on Howard Gilbert's room, that's why I thought Mr Temple ought to know about it.
STEVE:	Well, I'll tell him, Mr Reynolds – but I think perhaps you ought to see him yourself in view of what's happened.
REYNOLDS:	Yes, perhaps I ought to …
STEVE:	I don't think he'll be very long.
REYNOLDS:	(*Hesitating; consulting his watch*) No; I don't think I'll wait, Mrs Temple. I'll try and telephone later tonight.
STEVE:	Yes, all right. Have you lost much?
REYNOLDS:	No, they appear to have taken hardly anything. I have a theory that … Well, I'll discuss that with your husband. I'm sorry to have disturbed you.
STEVE:	Not at all.
REYNOLDS:	(*Pleasantly*) We – saw one another at lunch, didn't we?
STEVE:	Yes.
REYNOLDS:	I wasn't sure at first if it was you or not.
STEVE:	It was.

REYNOLDS: Miss Wayne's an old friend of mine. I gather you know each other.

STEVE: Slightly.

A moment.

REYNOLDS: Well – I'll, er – phone later. Goodnight, Mrs Temple.

STEVE: Goodnight, Mr Reynolds.

FADE SCENE.

FADE IN TEMPLE speaking.

TEMPLE: When did Reynolds call?

STEVE: About five minutes before you arrived. You only just missed him.

TEMPLE: Well, he certainly told you an interesting story.

STEVE: I don't believe him, Paul.

TEMPLE: You think he made it up, about the man phoning and the flat being burgled?

STEVE: I'm sure he did. He was simply trying to cover up that phone call to Mrs Talbot.

TEMPLE: You mean, he knew that you'd recognised his voice and he was hoping to convince you that it was an impersonation.

STEVE: Yes.

TEMPLE: (*Hesitating*) You don't think he was impersonated, Steve?

STEVE: Look, dear, that was Reynolds on the telephone, I'm sure of it. I recognised his voice the moment he spoke.

TEMPLE: M'm. And he must have recognised yours.

A pause.

STEVE: Yes. More coffee?

TEMPLE: Please.

STEVE pours the coffee.

TEMPLE: (*Thoughtfully*) Reynolds said: Is that you, Mrs Talbot? You said, yes. Then he said …

STEVE: What about the Hamilton affair? Do I get the third shoe?

TEMPLE: (*Quietly*) Yes.

STEVE: Did you tell Inspector Kingston about the call?

TEMPLE: I did.

STEVE: What did he say?

TEMPLE: He seemed interested.

STEVE: He's rather a curious man, isn't he, Paul? I can't quite make him out.

TEMPLE: (*Rather surprised*) Kingston?

STEVE: Yes.

TEMPLE: Why do you say that?

STEVE: (*Vaguely*) Oh, I don't know. I don't care for him terribly. I think he's a bit of a bully.

TEMPLE: Yes, I think he is rather. Don't tell me you suspect Kingston!

STEVE: No, of course not, but – (*Changing her mind; dogmatically*) Well, I don't know.

TEMPLE: (*Laughing*) That good old intuition, eh, Steve?

STEVE: Here's your coffee.

TEMPLE: Thanks.

STEVE: (*A moment*) Paul, will Galino's statement make any difference to Howard Gilbert?

TEMPLE: I wouldn't like to say. I expect the Home Secretary will consider it, but just how much importance he'll attach to it remains to be seen.

STEVE: But so many things have happened since Gilbert was arrested. June Michael committed suicide; Mrs Talbot was murdered …

TEMPLE: Yes, I know. But they don't prove that Howard Gilbert didn't murder Brenda Stirling.

STEVE: But, surely the person who murdered Brenda Stirling also murdered Mrs Talbot – and that couldn't have been Gilbert.

TEMPLE: That's what I think, Steve – but I'm not the Home Secretary. Galino's statement may make a difference – we shall just have to wait and see.

STEVE: And supposing it doesn't?

TEMPLE: What do you mean?

STEVE: Will you still go on with the case?

TEMPLE: Yes of course. I'm not only interested in Howard Gilbert. I'm interested in the case generally. There are certain aspects of this affair which … (*Suddenly, changing his line of thought*) Steve, I know you disagree with me, but I think there's a chance – an outside chance – that Reynolds was telling the truth.

STEVE: Well, of course there's always an outside chance, but …

TEMPLE: No, look, Steve, I don't think you understand. I know you're convinced it was Reynolds that phoned Mrs Talbot and I think you're right, but – supposing it wasn't?

STEVE: Well, if it wasn't then it was someone with a voice exactly like Reynolds or someone who impersonated him.

TEMPLE: Yes – and they might do it again. They might impersonate someone else.

STEVE: What are you getting at?

TEMPLE: Well, I don't want to frighten you, Steve, but – we're up against a pretty ruthless individual.

STEVE: Well?

TEMPLE: Obviously he knows I'm interested in the case, so …

STEVE: Are you worried about me?

TEMPLE: Of course I'm worried about you! First Brenda Stirling, then Mrs Talbot …

STEVE: Don't be silly, dear! I can look after myself.

TEMPLE: Yes, I know, famous last words! Now, Steve, listen – I'm serious. If ever I phone you and ask you to meet me somewhere I want you to say to me – over the phone – "Where's Charlie fishing?"

STEVE: (*Amused*) Where's Charlie fishing?

TEMPLE: Yes and I'll reply – "In the Thames". If I don't say "In the Thames," don't meet me, Steve. It doesn't matter whether you're convinced it's me or not – don't meet me.

STEVE: (*Amused*) Yes, all right, Paul!

TEMPLE: It doesn't matter what I say or how urgent I sound, if I …

STEVE: (*Laughing*) Yes, dear, I understand. I say "Where's Charlie fishing?" – and you say, "In the Thames".

TEMPLE: That's right.

STEVE: (*Highly amused*) Darling, I think you're very sweet. (*Pulling TEMPLE's leg*) And clever too!

TEMPLE: (*Realising what STEVE is doing*) All right, Mrs Temple! All right!

STEVE laughs.

TEMPLE: No, but, Steve. I'm serious.

STEVE: Yes, I know, dear – don't worry, I'll remember. (*Changing the subject*) Paul, this Italian fellow Galinos or Galino.

TEMPLE: Galino – yes?

STEVE: He told you that Betty Wayne met Mrs Talbot at a club called La Martella?

TEMPLE: Yes.

STEVE: But what would a woman like Mrs Talbot want with Betty Wayne? Miss Wayne's the smart, sophisticated type – well, you know, you've met her.

TEMPLE: (*Thoughtfully*) Yes.

STEVE: I can understand Betty Wayne being friends with Reynolds, but Mrs Talbot – that's very hard to believe.

TEMPLE: Galino didn't say that they were friends, he simply said that they'd met. (*Curious*) Steve, how well do you know Miss Wayne?

STEVE: I hardly know her at all. I've bought two or three dresses from her, that's all. I usually ask for her when I'm in Conway and Racys. She's awfully good about alterations.

TEMPLE: I know she calls herself Miss Wayne, but is that just a business thing or …

STEVE: No, I don't think she is married – in fact I'm sure she isn't.

TEMPLE: Where does she live, do you know?

STEVE: I believe she's got a flat in Chelsea somewhere. Why? Are you going to see her?

TEMPLE: I wasn't but – that might be quite an idea.

START FADE.

TEMPLE: I wonder if she's in the phone book.

STEVE: It's all right, dear – I'll get it.

FADE SCENE.

FADE IN the sound of a car; it is travelling rather slowly.
A pause.

STEVE: We've just passed two hundred and six …

TEMPLE: What was the address in the phone book?

STEVE: Four hundred and twelve … Reigate House.

TEMPLE: This road seems to go on for ever …

STEVE: Three hundred and twelve … that's on the other side … Is that an odd number?

TEMPLE: Very odd.

STEVE: (*Laughing*) I don't think we shall ever find it – you should have telephoned her.

TEMPLE: Wait a minute! Three eighty-two – that's better!

STEVE: Let's park the car here and walk down the road.

TEMPLE applies the brakes: the car slows down.

STEVE: Paul! Look! Isn't that Mr Stirling?

TEMPLE: Where?

STEVE: On the other side ... Quick, darling – he's just going round the corner.

TEMPLE: Oh, the man with the stick!

STEVE: Yes!

A moment.

TEMPLE: (*Slowly*) Do you know, I think it is! Yes, that's Stirling all right ... That's curious, isn't it?

STEVE: I wonder if he's just left Miss Wayne?

TEMPLE: Yes – that's what I was thinking. I'll bet a fiver that's Reigate House on the corner. Come on, Steve – let's cross over.

FADE SCENE.

FADE IN the sound of a door bell ringing.

STEVE: There's someone coming!

The door is unlatched; a chain removed and the door opens.

STEVE: (*Pleasantly*) Good evening, Miss Wayne.

BETTY: (*Surprised*) Oh, good evening, Mrs Temple!

STEVE: I think you've met my husband?

BETTY: Yes, of course, we – met two or three days ago.

TEMPLE: Miss Wayne, I'm awfully sorry to bother you, but I rather wanted to talk to you about a friend of yours.

BETTY: (*Embarrassed*) Well, I'm afraid you've caught me at a very awkward moment. I'm just dressing for a dinner date and I'm terribly late already. Do you think we could talk tomorrow morning, Mr Temple?

TEMPLE: Well –

BETTY: I'm not due at Conways until twelve so if we could meet sometime before then – that would do splendidly.

TEMPLE: Yes, all right, Miss Wayne. I'll phone you tomorrow morning.

BETTY: Would you? I do apologise for not asking you in but I really am in the most frightful hurry.

TEMPLE: All right, I'll phone you about ten. (*Smiling*) It's not terribly urgent, I simply want to have a word with you about Mrs Talbot.

BETTY: (*Surprised*) Mrs Talbot?

TEMPLE: Yes.

BETTY: (*Unsure of herself; nervously*) Who's Mrs Talbot?

STEVE: She's the woman who identified Howard Gilbert.

BETTY: But – why should you want to see me about her?

TEMPLE: Wasn't she a friend of yours?

BETTY: Good gracious, no. I've – never even seen the woman.

TEMPLE: (*Dismissing the matter*) All right, Miss Wayne, I'll phone you tomorrow.

STEVE: (*Pleasantly*) By the way, my husband and I had a little bet. He said that was Mr Stirling who left here just now and I said it wasn't.

BETTY: (*Genuinely surprised*) Mr Stirling?

TEMPLE: Yes. I'm sure I saw him leave just as we arrived.

BETTY: You mean Brenda Stirling's father?

TEMPLE: Yes.

BETTY: I'm afraid Mrs Temple's right, Mr Temple. You didn't see him leave here.

STEVE: There you are, darling!

TEMPLE: I could have sworn it was Wilfrid Stirling.

83

BETTY: (*Amused*) I'm beginning to think you imagine things, Mr Temple – no wonder you write novels.

START FADE.

BETTY: Give me a ring tomorrow morning. Goodbye, Mrs Temple.

STEVE: Goodbye.

FADE SCENE.

FADE IN the sound of footsteps on a pavement followed by the opening of a car door.

STEVE: Shall I drive?

TEMPLE: No, it's all right, dear, I'll drive. Jump in.

STEVE and TEMPLE get into the car. We hear the sound of the car doors closing.

STEVE: Do you think she was going out, or was it just an excuse to get rid of us?

TEMPLE: I don't know.

STEVE: I don't think she was telling the truth about Mrs Talbot.

TEMPLE: No, neither do I. But you know, I think she was telling the truth about Stirling.

STEVE: She certainly seemed very surprised when you mentioned him.

TEMPLE: In fact I thought she seemed rather frightened. Have you got the key, Steve?

STEVE: It's in the pocket.

TEMPLE: Oh, yes.

STEVE: Of course we might have been mistaken – perhaps it wasn't Stirling we saw.

There is a sound from the back of the car: a moan: someone is obviously in pain.

TEMPLE: It was Stirling all right and I'm pretty sure he came out of that house because … (*He stops speaking; surprised*) Listen.

84

STEVE: What?

TEMPLE: I thought I heard someone …

STEVE: (*Frightened*) Paul, there's someone in the back of the car on the floor! Look!

TEMPLE: (*Turning and leaning over the seat*) Good Lord, it's Peter Galino! Galino, what's happened?

GALINO: (*He is badly hurt and in obvious pain. Almost indistinct; in pain*) It's … my head … He … hit … my … head …

STEVE: Just look at his face, he …

TEMPLE: This must have happened while we were talking to Miss Wayne …

GALINO mutters something.

STEVE: He's trying to say something!

TEMPLE: (*Bending down*) Yes, what is it, Galino?

GALINO: Mr Temple …

TEMPLE: Yes.

GALINO: I – I lied to you … Hamilton is … the man you want. You'll find him … at … La Martella …

STEVE: Hamilton! That's the name that Reynolds mentioned.

TEMPLE: Yes. (*Suddenly*) Steve, listen – there's a call box on the corner of the street. Get through to the operator and tell her we need an ambulance, straight away –

STEVE: Yes, all right.

TEMPLE: And Steve …

STEVE: Yes?

TEMPLE: When you've made the call don't come back here, pick up a cab and go home.

STEVE: But, Paul, surely …

TEMPLE: (*Quickly*) Now, please – don't argue, darling, do as I tell you! Phone for an ambulance then go home. I'll see you later.

85

STEVE: Yes, all right.

GALINO starts to moan. He is still in pain.

TEMPLE: It's all right, Galino, we'll get you to a hospital.

FADE SCENE.

FADE IN STEVE playing the piano: something fairly quiet – not too gay.

A clock chimes the half hour.

A door opens.

CHARLIE: I've just made some coffee, Mrs Temple. Would you like some?

STEVE: No, thank you, Charlie. Was that half past ten?

CHARLIE: Yes, but that clock's a bit on the slow side. It's about twenty to eleven.

STEVE: Oh.

CHARLIE: Has Mr Temple got his key?

STEVE: Yes, I think so – but I shall wait up anyway.

CHARLIE: Yes, all right, Mrs Temple. Goodnight.

STEVE: Goodnight.

CHARLIE: (*Suddenly*) Oh, I forgot to tell you. Mr Stirling telephoned.

STEVE: When was that?

CHARLIE: It was just after you and Mr Temple went out.

STEVE: Did he leave any message?

CHARLIE: No, he said he'd probably ring later.

STEVE: (*Thoughtfully*) Yes, all right.

CHARLIE: You sure you wouldn't like some coffee?

STEVE: No, thank you, Charlie. Goodnight.

CHARLIE: Goodnight, Mrs Temple.

The door closes.

The piano starts again.

The telephone rings.

The piano stops.

STEVE crosses to the telephone.

STEVE: (*On the phone*) Hello?

We hear the sound of Button A being pressed followed by coins dropping.

TEMPLE: (*On the other end of the line*) Hello? Is that you, Steve?

STEVE: Hello? Hello? … Hello?

TEMPLE: Is that you, Steve?

STEVE: Oh, hello, Paul! I can hardly hear you.

TEMPLE: It's a shocking line … Darling, listen! I want you to do something … Can you hear?

STEVE: Yes, I can hear, now.

TEMPLE: (*Briskly*) Well, listen – I want you to change into a long frock, get a taxi and meet me in Sloane Square. I'll be waiting for you outside the stationers – you know, facing the square …

STEVE: Yes, all right. I'll be there in about thirty minutes.

TEMPLE: Fine …

STEVE: (*Suddenly*) How's Galino?

TEMPLE: He's pretty bad; I'll tell you all the news when I see you.

STEVE: Yes, all right.

TEMPLE: Be as quick as you can, Steve.

STEVE: Yes, of course … (*Suddenly remembering*) Oh, Paul …

TEMPLE: (*A little impatient*) Yes?

STEVE: (*Quite simply*) Where's Charlie fishing?

TEMPLE: (*After a slight hesitation*) What's that? What did you say?

STEVE: I said: Where's Charley fishing?

FADE IN music.

END OF EPISODE THREE

EPISODE FOUR

LA MARTELLA

OPEN TO:

STEVE: (*On the phone*) Hello?
We hear the sound of Button A being pressed followed by coins dropping.
TEMPLE: (*On the other end of the line*) Hello? Is that you, Steve?
STEVE: Hello? Hello? … Hello?
TEMPLE: Is that you, Steve?
STEVE: Oh, hello, Paul! I can hardly hear you.
TEMPLE: It's a shocking line … Darling, listen! I want you to do something … Can you hear?
STEVE: Yes, I can hear, now.
TEMPLE: (*Briskly*) Well, listen – I want you to change into a long frock, get a taxi and meet me in Sloane Square. I'll be waiting for you outside the stationers – you know, facing the square …
STEVE: Yes, all right. I'll be there in about thirty minutes.
TEMPLE: Fine …
STEVE: (*Suddenly*) How's Galino?
TEMPLE: He's pretty bad; I'll tell you all the news when I see you.
STEVE: Yes, all right.
TEMPLE: Be as quick as you can, Steve.
STEVE: Yes, of course … (*Suddenly remembering*) Oh, Paul …
TEMPLE: (*A little impatient*) Yes?
STEVE: (*Quite simply*) Where's Charlie fishing?
TEMPLE: (*After a slight hesitation*) What's that? What did you say?
STEVE: I said: Where's Charley fishing? (*Click*) Hello?
TEMPLE: It's all right. I'm still here. (*A moment*) In the Thames!

91

STEVE: (*With a little laugh*) Yes, all right, Paul! I shan't be long.

FADE IN music.

FADE IN a background of traffic noises in Sloane Square followed by the sound of a car door opening.

TEMPLE: By Timothy, you've been quick!

STEVE: I was lucky. I caught a cab straight away.

The car door shuts.

STEVE: What happened to Galino?

TEMPLE: He's in a pretty bad way, but I think he'll pull through all right.

STEVE: Where is he?

TEMPLE: St Mathews Hospital; the ambulance picked him up about ten minutes after you left.

STEVE: Did he say anything?

TEMPLE: Only what you heard. The poor chap passed out just after.

STEVE: Have you seen Sir Graham?

TEMPLE: No, but I phoned him and I've seen Kingston. Kingston's at the hospital; he's staying there in case Galino comes round.

STEVE: I see. Well – where are we going? Why did you want me to change?

TEMPLE: You remember what Galino said: Hamilton's the man you want, you'll find him at La Martella …

STEVE: Yes?

TEMPLE: Well, I told Sir Graham about it; apparently they've had their eye on La Martella for some time.

STEVE: What is it, a night club?

TEMPLE: Yes, but curiously enough it's not in the West End. It's in Hampstead of all places.

STEVE: Didn't Galino mention it once before?

TEMPLE: Yes. That's the place he followed Mrs Talbot to, the night she met Betty Wayne.

STEVE: Oh, yes, of course. Paul, do you think that this man Hamilton – that Galino mentioned – is the person behind all this?

TEMPLE: Galino must think so or he wouldn't have said what he did. We'd better be making a move. I promised to pick Miss Ferguson up at eleven ...

STEVE: Who's Miss Ferguson?

TEMPLE: (*Laughing*) Don't worry, Steve – she's not the girl friend. La Martella's a club. Miss Ferguson happens to be a member, that's all.

STEVE: Yes, but you still haven't told me who she is!

TEMPLE: She's one of Sir Graham's young ladies. I believe she's a Canadian.

STEVE: You mean – she's from Scotland Yard?

TEMPLE: Yes. (*Amused*) You know the type. Flat heel shoes – 48 hips!

STEVE: (*Laughing*) Oh, have a heart, dear. Make it 46!

FADE SCENE.

FADE IN the sound of the car: it is travelling fairly slowly.

STEVE: I don't see any sign of your Miss Ferguson. Where did you arrange to meet her?

TEMPLE: Sir Graham made the arrangements. He said she'd wait for me at the entrance to Baker ... (*He stops*) Oh, there's Sir Graham.

STEVE: Yes, and do you see the girl he's talking to?

TEMPLE: Where? Oh!

STEVE: (*Significantly*) Is that your idea of 48 hips?

TEMPLE: But that can't be the girl. It's impossible. Look at the dress she's wearing, and look at her shoes ...

STEVE: I am looking!

TEMPLE: She's extremely smart, isn't she?

STEVE: Who wouldn't be in that outfit! The sooner I join Scotland Yard the better. They've spotted us. You'd better pull in, dear.

The car draws up to the kerb; TEMPLE switches off the engine.

The car door opens.

FORBES: Hello, Temple! (*Surprised*) Why, hello, Steve! I didn't expect to see you.

STEVE: I'll bet you didn't! How are you, Sir Graham?

FORBES: Oh, I'm all right – a little harassed as usual! Temple, may I introduce Miss Ferguson?

TEMPLE: Good evening, Miss Ferguson!

LYNN: Good evening.

TEMPLE: Jump in!

LYNN: Thank you.

TEMPLE: Oh – this is my wife.

LYNN: How do you do, Mrs Temple? This is a pleasant surprise … (*She has a slight Canadian accent*)

STEVE: It is indeed.

FORBES: Temple, I've talked to Lynn – Miss Ferguson – and she's completely in the picture so far as the Gilbert case is concerned – so you can speak quite freely.

TEMPLE: Good. Can we drop you anywhere?

FORBES: No, I've got my car round the corner. Ring me tomorrow morning, Lynn – about eleven.

LYNN: Yes, sir.

FORBES: Well, goodbye, and enjoy yourselves!

TEMPLE: Goodbye, Sir Graham!

STEVE: Goodnight, Sir Graham!

The car door closes.

TEMPLE: How long will it take us to get to this place?

LYNN: About a quarter of an hour; but I think we ought to have a talk before we start, Mr Temple.

TEMPLE: Yes, I agree. Miss Ferguson, tell me … By the way, I think we'd better make it Lynn if we're supposed to be old friends.

LYNN: (*Laughing*) Yes, it would be better.

STEVE: (*Drily*) Yes!

TEMPLE: Tell me all you know about La Martella; when did you first go there?

LYNN: About three months ago. There was nothing wrong with the club itself but we heard a rumour that certain people were frequenting it and – well, we thought we'd better keep an eye on things.

TEMPLE: I see.

STEVE: Who runs the place?

LYNN: A man called Fabian, Louis Fabian.

STEVE: Fabian? Rather an odd name …

LYNN: Yes. Quite frankly, Fabian is La Martella: without him the place would close over night.

TEMPLE: Well – what's the attraction exactly? Is it the food or the floor show or …

LYNN: (*Amused*) No, the food's very ordinary and there just isn't a floor show. The attraction's Fabian. He's an extremely handsome young man and a very good dancer.

STEVE: But does he dance with the guests?

LYNN: He never stops! Big women, fat women, thin women, little women, tall women, he dances with them all.

TEMPLE: I gather he works for a living.

LYNN: (*Laughing*) He certainly does!

STEVE: And does this go on all night?

LYNN: Until about two o'clock and then he disappears: and disappear is the word. He doesn't say he's going, he doesn't say goodnight, he just disappears. Ten minutes later the place is as dead as a door nail.

TEMPLE: He sounds a remarkable young man.

LYNN: He certainly is. Of course there are all sorts of rumours about him. Most of them, I suspect, spread by Fabian himself.

STEVE: What sort of rumours?

LYNN: Well, some people say he's a Prince – an Austrian Prince of some kind. Maybe he is – he's certainly the Prince of dancers.

TEMPLE: You still haven't told me why you're keeping an eye on the place?

LYNN: (*Vaguely*) Well, we just thought it was one of those night spots we ought to keep an eye on, that's all.

TEMPLE: (*Unconvinced*) I see.

LYNN: I gather from Sir Graham that you're looking for a man called Hamilton.

TEMPLE: Yes.

LYNN: What makes you think he might be at La Martella?

TEMPLE: I've no particular reason for thinking so, I just – (*Imitating LYNN's vagueness*) thought he might be there, that's all.

There is a moment's pause then LYNN laughs.

LYNN: Okay, Mr Temple! Okay! We're both cagey by instinct.

TEMPLE: There's just one point: does this fellow Fabian know that you're attached to Scotland Yard?

LYNN: Good heavens no! He thinks I'm a good time gal; the daughter of an American oil magnate.

TEMPLE: I see.

LYNN: By the way, I'll have to sign you in of course. What do you want me to put?

TEMPLE:	I think we'd better play safe and put Mr and Mrs Temple – he might recognise us anyway.
LYNN:	Yes, I agree. After all, there's no reason why you shouldn't be a friend of mine, is there, Mr Temple?
TEMPLE:	None at all.
STEVE:	(*Drily*) No, none at all!
TEMPLE:	Well, we'd better make a start.

FADE UP the sound of the car starting.

FADE DOWN.

FADE IN the sound of a dance orchestra: it is in the near background.

LYNN:	We'll join you in a few minutes, Paul. Come along, Steve.
TEMPLE:	Have you signed the book?
LYNN:	Yes, I've just done it. (*To STEVE; as they cross the hall*) Have you a lipstick I can borrow? I've done my usual trick!
STEVE:	(*Laughs*) I know, you've changed your handbag!
LYNN:	Yes, and left everything behind!

STEVE laughs.

FADE IN a background of new arrivals and the general atmosphere of the main hall of a fashionable night club.

REYNOLDS:	Good evening.
TEMPLE:	(*Turning; surprised*) Hello, Reynolds! I didn't recognise you at first.
REYNOLDS:	I didn't recognise you either. It was my friend here who spotted you.
BETTY:	Good evening, Mr Temple.
REYNOLDS:	I think you know Miss Wayne?
TEMPLE:	Yes, of course. We've already met this evening.

97

REYNOLDS: (*Curious*) Indeed?

BETTY: Mrs Temple called round about a dress I sold her, she – wanted to see me about an alteration.

REYNOLDS: Wasn't that a little unusual, after business hours?

BETTY: Yes, but I was rather worried about the alteration and I gave Mrs Temple my card.

REYNOLDS: (*Unconvinced*) I see.

TEMPLE: You don't know my wife, when it comes to alterations, Reynolds!

BETTY gives a little laugh.

BETTY: I'll see you in a few minutes, Lance.

REYNOLDS: Yes, all right.

A moment.

TEMPLE: Cigarette?

REYNOLDS: Er – thank you. (*He takes a cigarette*) I didn't know you were a member here?

TEMPLE: I'm not. I'm with a friend of mine.

REYNOLDS: Oh, I see.

TEMPLE lights the cigarettes.

REYNOLDS: Thank you.

TEMPLE: I understand from my wife that you wanted to see me about something?

REYNOLDS: Yes. I called round earlier but you were out. My flat was burgled this afternoon. Someone impersonated my voice over the telephone and told my housekeeper to leave her key under the mat.

TEMPLE: But, surely, that's a matter for the police – it doesn't concern me. Did you report it?

REYNOLDS: Yes, of course. (*Curtly*) I thought you'd be interested, that's all.

TEMPLE: Why?

REYNOLDS: Look, Temple, I'm quite convinced that the burglary this afternoon had something to do with the Gilbert case. Howard's room was an absolute shambles. They even stripped the fittings off the front of the wardrobe.

TEMPLE: (*Humouring REYNOLDS*) I wonder what they wanted?

REYNOLDS: I just don't know.

TEMPLE: Would you like to know, Reynolds?

REYNOLDS: What do you mean?

A moment.

TEMPLE: Yours wasn't the only flat that was broken into this afternoon.

REYNOLDS: No?

TEMPLE: No … You remember Mrs Talbot, the woman who identified Howard Gilbert?

REYNOLDS: (*After a moment's hesitation*) Yes …

TEMPLE: Her flat was broken into …

REYNOLDS: When?

TEMPLE: Late this afternoon; about half past five.

REYNOLDS: How do you know? Who told you?

TEMPLE: Inspector Kingston.

REYNOLDS: Was anything taken?

TEMPLE: Not that we know of …

REYNOLDS: (*Hesitantly*) Did the Inspector see Mrs Talbot?

TEMPLE: Yes.

REYNOLDS: Oh!

TEMPLE: But – not at the flat.

REYNOLDS: Not at the flat?

TEMPLE: No. Mrs Talbot's dead.

REYNOLDS: What!

TEMPLE: She was found early this afternoon – near Farnham.

REYNOLDS: (*Taken aback*) I – can't believe it.

TEMPLE: It's true, Reynolds. You seem very perturbed. Was Mrs Talbot a friend of yours?

REYNOLDS: No, no, of course not. I never met the woman. I saw her at the trial of course, but – that was all.

TEMPLE: Well, she's dead. They found her in a field. Apparently there'd been a struggle.

REYNOLDS: (*Uncertain of himself*) I wonder what she was doing down at Farnham? Didn't she live in Greek Street?

TEMPLE: Soho Square. We don't know what she was doing in Farnham.

REYNOLDS: (*A moment*) Well, if you'll excuse me – there's Miss Wayne.

TEMPLE: Yes, of course. (*Suddenly; casually*) Oh, by the way …

REYNOLDS: (*Turning*) Yes?

TEMPLE: One of her shoes was missing.

REYNOLDS: (*Puzzled*) What?

TEMPLE: When they found Mrs Talbot, one of her shoes was missing.

REYNOLDS: (*Vaguely; non-committally*) Oh. (*A moment*) That's very odd.

TEMPLE: Very.

REYNOLDS: Well, I'll probably see you later.

TEMPLE: I hope so.

FADE UP background noises slightly: the orchestra playing.
A pause.
FABIAN arrives: he has an Austrian accent: a pleasant, if somewhat smooth personality.

FABIAN: Mr Temple?

TEMPLE: Yes.

FABIAN: Oh, good evening, sir. Welcome to La Martella. My name is Fabian.

TEMPLE: Oh, Mr Fabian! I've heard a great deal about you.

FABIAN: I've heard a great deal about you, too, Mr Temple. I noticed your name in the book so I thought I'd better introduce myself. Have you reserved a table?

TEMPLE: Well – I think my friend has. Miss Ferguson.

FABIAN: Yes, of course. There's always a table for Miss Ferguson. Well, I hope you enjoy yourself.

TEMPLE: Thank you. I hope so too. Ah, here she is with my wife.

STEVE and LYNN arrive.

STEVE: I'm afraid we've been rather a long time, darling.

LYNN: It was my fault, Paul, this face of mine takes an awful lot of fixing. (*A shade too 'girlish'*) Why hello, Mr Fabian!

FABIAN: Hello, Miss Ferguson! Nice to meet you again.

LYNN: You look very handsome tonight; what have you been doing to yourself?

FABIAN: (*Amused*) I'll bet you say that to all the boys!

They all laugh.

TEMPLE: (*To FABIAN*) I don't think you know my wife. Steve – this is Louis Fabian.

FABIAN: How do you do, Mrs Temple?

STEVE: How do you do?

FABIAN: I'm delighted to meet you. I hope you like our little club.

STEVE: Well, it's certainly – different. I love the décor.

LYNN: Aren't those cherubs cute?

FABIAN: Let me show you to your table. (*Leading the way*) Miss Ferguson …

LYNN: (*Coyly*) Oh, thank you …

FABIAN leads LYNN across the hall, followed by TEMPLE and STEVE.

TEMPLE: (*Softly, to STEVE, puzzled*) Do you really like the décor?

STEVE: Don't be silly, the whole place looks exactly like a
…

TEMPLE: Exactly.

FADE SCENE.

FADE IN of the dance orchestra and a background of people dancing.

STEVE: (*Watching LYNN and FABIAN on the dance floor*) Yes, he is awfully good looking, isn't he?

TEMPLE: Who?

STEVE: Fabian.

TEMPLE: I suppose he is in a slick sort of way.

STEVE: Well, I think he's good looking – and he certainly is the Prince of dancers.

TEMPLE: I should say it's about the only thing he is Prince of. If he wasn't christened Willi Schritzenbounder or something like that I'll eat my hat.

STEVE laughs.

TEMPLE: I don't see any sign of our friend Reynolds.

STEVE: They were on the floor a moment ago.

TEMPLE: I've got a feeling they've left.

STEVE: It looks like it.

The dance orchestra stops: there is a smattering of applause.

STEVE: Was he surprised when you told him about Mrs Talbot?

TEMPLE: He was more than surprised: he was distinctly rattled.

STEVE: I'm convinced it was Reynolds who telephoned her.

TEMPLE: Yes. I've got to find out about Hamilton. I'm sure
Galino was telling the truth when … (*He stops*)
Here's Fabian. If he asks you to dance don't forget
what I told you.

STEVE: I won't forget.

FABIAN and LYNN arrive at the table.

LYNN: Hello, there! Are you two enjoying yourselves?

STEVE: We certainly are!

TEMPLE: I didn't know you could dance like that, Lynn!

STEVE: You've been holding out on us.

FABIAN: Miss Ferguson's a beautiful dancer …

LYNN: Now, Louis!

FABIAN: No, no, really, I'm quite sincere. I mean it. It's so
unusual too, for a Canadian.

LYNN: Them's fighting words, partner!

They laugh.

The orchestra starts again.

FABIAN: (*Amused*) Would you like to dance, Mrs Temple?

STEVE: Oh, thank you. Will you look after my bag, Lynn?

LYNN: Yes, of course.

TEMPLE: What would you like to drink, Lynn?

LYNN: Well – that champagne looks awfully good to me!

FADE SCENE.

FADE UP of orchestra and people dancing.

FABIAN and STEVE are dancing.

STEVE: It's a lovely floor.

FABIAN: Yes, it is. How long have you known Miss
Ferguson, Mrs Temple?

STEVE: Oh – she's a very old friend of my husband's.

FABIAN: She seems an awfully nice person.

STEVE: Yes, she is.

FABIAN: I'll never forget the first night she came here. She
was wearing a white dress and quite the nicest pair

of earrings I've ever seen. She came with a young fellow called Deakin. The Hon. Toby Deakin, terribly tall and rather shy.

STEVE: Oh, yes, we all know Toby. (*A pause*) You seem awfully busy tonight; is it always like this?

FABIAN: Most nights. Sometimes it's so crowded you can hardly dance. (*A little laugh*) But we enjoy ourselves.

STEVE: It's a very good orchestra.

FABIAN: Of course. If you are going to dance well you must have a good orchestra. (*A pause*) Mrs Temple …

STEVE: Yes?

FABIAN: Why did you come to La Martella?

STEVE: (*Vaguely*) Well, we heard a great deal about it and we thought we'd like to come here.

FABIAN: Was that your only reason?

STEVE: (*Slowly*) No … My husband wanted to meet one of your members; a man called Hamilton.

FABIAN: (*After a moment*) Hamilton?

STEVE: Yes.

FABIAN: I know most of our members, but – Hamilton, you say? Does Miss Ferguson know him?

STEVE: No, I don't think she does.

FABIAN: Your husband must be mistaken, Mrs Temple. I'm sure there's no one of that name here. However, I'll ask my secretary for you, just to make certain.

STEVE: Thank you.

A pause.

FABIAN: I saw your husband talking to Lance Reynolds.

STEVE: Yes.

FABIAN: He's a very old friend of ours; one of our original members.

STEVE: Oh, really? I didn't know that … (*A pause*) Was Howard Gilbert a member?

FABIAN: No! That was an unpleasant business. It was a great shock to Mr Reynolds. They were very good friends, you know.

STEVE: Yes, so I believe.

FABIAN: Was your husband interested in the Gilbert case?

STEVE: He still is.

FABIAN: But the case is over, surely – Gilbert was convicted.

STEVE: It's only since he was convicted that my husband became interested. It's curious you should mention Howard Gilbert because …

FABIAN: (*Correcting STEVE*) No, you mentioned him, Mrs Temple.

STEVE: Did I? Well, it's curious we should talk about him because that's why my husband wanted to meet this man Hamilton.

FABIAN: Oh?

STEVE: Apparently Hamilton was a friend of Mrs Talbot's.

FABIAN: Mrs Talbot?

STEVE: She was an important witness in the Gilbert case.

FABIAN: Oh, of course! She saw Gilbert just after the murder was committed.

STEVE: That's right. (*A pause*) Did you ever meet her?

FABIAN: Why, no. Why should I?

STEVE: She came here one night.

FABIAN: I'm quite sure she didn't.

STEVE: I'm sorry, but she did.

FABIAN: Mrs Temple, you don't think I'd allow a woman like that to come to the Martella.

STEVE: But I think she came with Miss Wayne.

FABIAN: Miss Wayne?

STEVE: Yes.

FABIAN: How very curious.

The orchestra stops: there is a smattering of applause.

105

FABIAN: (*Smiling*) Shall we go back to the table?

STEVE: Please …

The orchestra starts again.

FADE the orchestra to the background.

STEVE and FABIAN return to the table.

LYNN: Well, wasn't I right, Steve – doesn't he dance like an angel?

STEVE: An archangel.

TEMPLE: You'll have to sit the next one out, darling – I'm taking no chances, not after that exhibition.

STEVE: I doubt whether I'll ever dance with you again, Paul!

They laugh.

FABIAN: (*Pleasantly*) Will you excuse me, please? I may see you all later …

STEVE: Yes, of course – and thank you.

FABIAN: Thank you. Mrs Temple.

A pause.

LYNN: What time is it?

TEMPLE: It's nearly two o'clock.

LYNN: He'll probably have one more dance with somebody and then disappear – you watch.

TEMPLE: Does he live here?

LYNN: No, I believe he's got a flat in South Audley Street.

TEMPLE: You've never been there?

LYNN: Not me; I'm allergic to etchings.

They laugh.

STEVE: Lynn, the first time you came here – did you come with a man called Toby Deacon?

LYNN: (*Surprised*) Toby Deacon – who's he?

STEVE: (*Annoyed*) Oh, dear …

TEMPLE: What's the matter, Steve?

STEVE: I wonder if he was trying to catch me? He asked me how long we'd known Lynn and I said she was an old friend of yours. Then he said the first time she came here was with a man called Deacon …

TEMPLE: And you said you knew him.

STEVE: Yes.

LYNN: Oh, dear.

TEMPLE: Did you ask him about Hamilton?

STEVE: Yes. He said he felt sure he wasn't a member here but he'd ask his secretary.

TEMPLE: How did he react?

STEVE: He didn't seem unduly perturbed; but he was certainly surprised when I asked him if he knew Mrs Talbot.

LYNN: (*Quietly; a warning*) Here's a waiter!

A moment.

WAITER: Mr Temple?

TEMPLE: Yes?

WAITER: I was asked to give you this note, sir.

TEMPLE: Oh, thank you.

TEMPLE takes the note.

TEMPLE: (*To LYNN and STEVE*) Excuse me.

TEMPLE opens the note.

STEVE: Cigarette, Lynn?

LYNN: No, thanks. I've just put one out.

A slight pause.

TEMPLE: (*To the WAITER*) The answer's yes …

WAITER: Thank you, sir.

The WAITER departs.

STEVE: Who's it from, Paul?

TEMPLE: From Fabian. He wants to see me.

STEVE: What do you mean?

TEMPLE: Read it …

STEVE takes the note.

STEVE: (*Reading*) "Dear Temple … I want to talk to you. My address is 27B South Audley Street. I suggest you call tomorrow afternoon, anytime between four o'clock and five. Yours sincerely, Louis Fabian. P.S. Don't bring your friend from Scotland Yard."

FADE IN music.

FADE IN the sound of a car; it is travelling on a main road.

LYNN: I guess you haven't had a very successful evening, Mr Temple.

TEMPLE: I wouldn't say that.

LYNN: No?

STEVE: Well – did you find out anything?

TEMPLE: Only that you dance very much better with Mr Fabian than you do with anyone else.

LYNN: Give the devil his due, he can certainly dance.

STEVE: He certainly can.

LYNN: (*A moment*) I wonder how he found out that I was attached to Scotland Yard?

TEMPLE: I'll ask him.

LYNN: (*Amused*) I wish you would. You can drop me on the corner, Mr Temple.

TEMPLE: Are you sure?

LYNN: Yes, this'll do fine.

TEMPLE: As we started with Christian names can't we continue?

LYNN: Well, if you don't mind.

The car comes to a standstill.

TEMPLE: Of course not. Is that all right?

LYNN: Yes, dandy. My flat's just round the corner.

STEVE: Goodnight, Lynn!

LYNN: Goodnight, Steve!

TEMPLE: Goodnight, Lynn!

LYNN: Goodnight, Paul.

The car door slams.

TEMPLE changes gear and the car gathers speed.

STEVE: What a very nice girl.

TEMPLE: Yes, isn't she.

STEVE: Slow up, dear – traffic lights.

The car slows down.

TEMPLE: Would you like to drive?

STEVE: No – why?

TEMPLE: I wondered, that's all.

STEVE: (*Laughing*) Darling, don't be silly! (*Suddenly*) It's
          gone red!

TEMPLE: Really? I thought it was pale blue. I've had two
          small sherries, Steve, and a glass of wine. I'm
          quite capable of seeing the traffic lights. I might
          even spot an odd pedestrian.

The car slows to a standstill at the traffic lights.

*During the following dialogue a taxi draws level with the
TEMPLE's car and waits for the lights to change.*

STEVE: (*Amused*) Yes, well pull over to the left – there's a
          taxi trying to nose past you.

TEMPLE: He's got to wait the same as everybody else …

As the taxi draws level.

TEMPLE: By Timothy, he's cutting it fine, isn't he? He
          couldn't get closer if he tried …

STEVE: (*Amused*) Serves you right …

TEMPLE: These taxi drivers really are the limit! I think they
          could drive through the eye of a needle. (*A slight
          pause*) Good Lord! …

STEVE: What is it?

TEMPLE: The woman in that taxi.

STEVE: Well?

TEMPLE: Take a good look, but don't let her see you …

STEVE: It's the woman who said she was Mrs Talbot!

TEMPLE: Yes. Did she see you?

STEVE: I don't think so. The lights are changing. What are you going to do?

TEMPLE: (*Changing gear*) I'm going to follow the taxi. Sit back, Steve, in case she turns round …

The taxi draws away from the lights followed by TEMPLE's car.

FADE UP the sound of the taxi, followed by TEMPLE's car.

FADE SCENE.

FADE IN the sound of TEMPLE's car travelling at cruising speed.

STEVE: Where are we? What is this place?

TEMPLE: I think it's Belton Gardens …

STEVE: Slow down – he's going round the corner.

TEMPLE: I believe that's Darlington Street.

TEMPLE's car slows down and turns the corner.

STEVE: Yes, you're right – it is Darlington Street …

TEMPLE: Hello, he's pulling up …

TEMPLE's car slows down; almost to a standstill.

STEVE: Don't get too near.

TEMPLE: No, I'm going to stop here …

The car stops.

STEVE: I wonder which house she's going into?

TEMPLE switches the engine off.

TEMPLE: She's going to cross the road I think.

A pause.

A car approaches from the background and drives past TEMPLE's car; it is travelling fairly fast.

STEVE: What are you going to do?

TEMPLE: I'm going to make a note of the address and then … (*Suddenly*) Wait a minute! Do you know, I believe Wilfrid Stirling lives in Darlington Street. I remember he gave me his address and telephone number. I'm almost sure it was a Bayswater number ... Yes, that would be right, wouldn't it – Bayswater.

STEVE: She's crossing over, Paul!

TEMPLE: Watch the house ... We'll check the number when we drive past ...

A pause.

STEVE: She's obviously got a key – she's letting herself in ...

TEMPLE: There's a telephone box across the road. I'm going to look the address up.

TEMPLE opens the car door.

TEMPLE: I shan't be a minute, Steve.

STEVE: Yes, all right.

The car door closes.

FADE SCENE.

FADE IN the opening of a telephone booth door.

STEVE: Paul!

TEMPLE: (*Amused*) What's the matter? Don't you think I'm capable of finding the address on my own?

STEVE: It didn't look a very good light so I've brought you this torch ...

TEMPLE: (*Laughing*) Oh! Well, you'd better come inside.

TEMPLE and STEVE enter the telephone box.

TEMPLE: As a matter of fact you're right. It isn't a very good light! Give me the torch. Thanks. Now, which book ...

STEVE: This is it. S – Z.

FADE UP the sound of an approaching car; it is travelling very fast.

TEMPLE opens the book and flicks the pages.

TEMPLE: Stiles ... Still ... Stilling ... Stimson ... Stirling –
here we are – (*A moment*) By Timothy, I was
right! Wilfrid Stirling ... 292 Darlington Street.

STEVE: But, Paul, if Wilfrid Stirling's a friend of the
woman who impersonated Mrs Talbot, then
obviously ...

*During the above speech there is the sound of rapid gun fire:
someone is spraying TEMPLE's car with bullets. They are
firing from the passing car.*

The car roars down the road and fades out of hearing.

STEVE: (*Alarmed*) What's happening?

TEMPLE: Steve, look at our car! ... Just look at it!

STEVE: Oh, Paul!

TEMPLE: They thought we were still sitting in it ... they
passed us once, drove round the Square, then came
down Darlington Street. Look at the bullet holes!
They certainly weren't taking any chances! Thank
Heavens you brought me that torch, Steve ...

FADE IN music.

FADE DOWN music.

TEMPLE: What time do you make it, Steve?

STEVE: It's about half past three.

TEMPLE: When is your appointment at Conway and Racys?

STEVE: Oh, anytime.

TEMPLE: I'll pick you up about five.

STEVE: Yes, all right. It's funny you couldn't get Betty
Wayne this morning.

TEMPLE: The operator said the number was out of order, but
it's my bet she left the receiver off.

STEVE: Yes. (*After a tiny pause*) What time are you seeing
Fabian?

TEMPLE:	The note said between four and five. I'll probably leave in about twenty minutes. Pass me that paper, Steve.
STEVE:	You're not going to look at that picture of the car again?
TEMPLE:	Darling, pass me the paper!

STEVE passes the newspaper.

STEVE:	You must have looked at that photograph twenty times.
TEMPLE:	Yes – and every time I look at it I think how lucky we were to be in that telephone box. Just look at it, Steve!
STEVE:	I don't want to look at it. It terrifies me to even think about it. (*After a moment*) Paul, why didn't you tell the police the truth?
TEMPLE:	I did tell them the truth.
STEVE:	The Sergeant asked you what we were doing in Darlington Street and you said …
TEMPLE:	I said we were using the telephone. Well, it's perfectly true, we were using the telephone.
STEVE:	Now don't be silly, Paul! You know perfectly well that if we hadn't followed that taxi we shouldn't … (*She breaks off*)

There is a knock on the door and CHARLIE enters.

STEVE:	Yes – what is it, Charlie?
CHARLIE:	Sir Graham Forbes would like to see you, sir.
TEMPLE:	Oh – bring him in, Charlie.
CHARLIE:	Yes, sir. (*To SIR GRAHAM, who is in the hall*) Will you come in please, Sir Graham?
FORBES:	Thank you. Hello, Steve!
STEVE:	Come in, Sir Graham!
FORBES:	Good afternoon, Temple!
TEMPLE:	How are you, Sir Graham?
STEVE:	Would you like some tea?

113

FORBES: No, thank you, my dear.

TEMPLE: You look worried. Is anything wrong?

FORBES: (*Seriously*) Temple … What time did you leave Lynn Ferguson last night?

TEMPLE: About half past two – this morning. We dropped her in Baker Street.

STEVE: Why? What's happened, Sir Graham?

FORBES: Whereabouts in Baker Street?

TEMPLE: Not far from where we picked her up: she said her flat was just round the corner.

FORBES: Yes, that's right.

STEVE: Has anything happened to her?

FORBES: I hope not, Steve, only – she was supposed to phone me this morning, and she didn't. I told my secretary to get in touch with her, but – well, to cut a long story short, she never went back to the flat last night.

STEVE: But she said … Are you sure?

FORBES: Absolutely positive. There's a night porter at the flats who's on duty till seven in the morning and he didn't leave his desk.

TEMPLE: Oh, dear.

FORBES: What time was it when you left Hampstead?

TEMPLE: About two fifteen: it took about a quarter of an hour to Baker Street.

FORBES: I see. And then you came back here?

TEMPLE: Yes.

FORBES: Well – what were you doing in Darlington Street?

TEMPLE: I told you – or rather I told the Sergeant. The car went wrong and I went into a telephone box to phone a garage.

FORBES: Yes, but just a minute! Darlington Street was miles out of your way. If you were coming here from Baker Street …

114

STEVE: Paul!

FORBES: (*Looks at STEVE then across at TEMPLE*) What happened last night, Temple?

TEMPLE: We dropped Lynn Ferguson at Baker Street; when we got round the corner we were waiting for the lights to change when a taxi pulled up, with a woman in it.

FORBES: Well?

TEMPLE: It was the woman who impersonated Mrs Talbot.

FORBES: Go on …

TEMPLE: We followed the taxi and eventually it stopped in Darlington Street. We saw the woman get out and go into one of the houses. I had a feeling, although I wasn't sure, that the house belonged to Wilfrid Stirling. Steve and I went into a telephone box to check the address and while we were in the box – well, you know what happened.

FORBES: Yes, but why didn't you tell this to the Sergeant instead of making up a stupid story about your car breaking down?

TEMPLE: Frankly, I didn't want to go into details. Also I … (*Hesitates; vaguely*) I didn't want to go into details.

FORBES: Did you see the man in the car – the man who fired the shots?

TEMPLE: No; we were both in the telephone booth – fortunately.

FORBES: I see.

STEVE: Sir Graham, are you worried about Lynn?

FORBES: Well, I don't like it, Steve. She's a very capable girl; she never takes unnecessary risks. I'm quite sure that if she could have telephoned she would have done so.

TEMPLE: How long has she been working for you?

FORBES: About three years. Her position's rather a peculiar one; although she's attached to the Yard she's not on what we call the established staff.

TEMPLE: Does she work for Kingston?

FORBES: No; she doesn't work for any of the regular C.I.D. people. She's answerable to me, personally, or – in certain instances – to Major Fletcher of M.I.5.

TEMPLE: I see. What was she doing at La Martella?

FORBES: I told you. We were keeping our eye on Fabian because … (*He breaks off*)

The door opens and CHARLIE enters.

TEMPLE: (*Irritated*) Yes – what is it, Charlie?

CHARLIE: I found this parcel near the kitchen door. It must have been left there.

STEVE: Well – what is it?

CHARLIE: I don't know. It wasn't there at two o'clock when I put the milk bottles out.

TEMPLE: Let me have it, Charlie.

CHARLIE: Yes, sir.

TEMPLE takes the parcel.

A pause.

STEVE: What is it, Paul?

TEMPLE: (*Quietly*) It's a box of some sort. Have you no idea who delivered it?

CHARLIE: No, sir. Whoever it was he didn't ring the bell.

TEMPLE: Yes, all right, Charlie. (*A moment*) It's addressed to you, Steve. Shall I open it?

STEVE: Yes, of course.

TEMPLE unties the parcel; removes the brown paper wrapping.

STEVE: (*Surprised*) Paul! It's a shoe!

FORBES: A shoe? (*Puzzled*) Is it one of yours, Steve?

116

STEVE: No!

FORBES: Well, if it isn't one of yours why should anyone …
              (*Suddenly; serious*) Temple, what is it?

TEMPLE: (*Quietly*) Don't you recognise it, Steve?

STEVE: (*Staring at the shoe*) Yes … it's Lynn Ferguson's.

FADE IN closing music.

END OF EPISODE FOUR

EPISODE FIVE

THAT GOOD OLD INTUITION

OPEN TO:

CHARLIE: Excuse me, Mr Temple. I found this parcel near the kitchen door. It must have been left there.

STEVE: Well – what is it?

CHARLIE: I don't know. It wasn't there at two o'clock when I put the milk bottles out.

TEMPLE: Let me have it, Charlie.

CHARLIE: Yes, sir.

TEMPLE takes the parcel.

A pause.

STEVE: What is it, Paul?

TEMPLE: (*Quietly*) It's a box of some sort. Have you no idea who delivered it?

CHARLIE: No, sir. Whoever it was he didn't ring the bell.

TEMPLE: Yes, all right, Charlie. (*A moment*) It's addressed to you, Steve. Shall I open it?

STEVE: Yes, of course.

TEMPLE unties the parcel; removes the brown paper wrapping.

STEVE: (*Surprised*) Paul! It's a shoe!

FORBES: A shoe? (*Puzzled*) Is it one of yours, Steve?

STEVE: No!

FORBES: Well, if it isn't one of yours why should anyone … (*Suddenly; serious*) Temple, what is it?

TEMPLE: (*Quietly*) Don't you recognise it, Steve?

STEVE: (*After a moment; staring at the shoe*) Yes … it's Lynn Ferguson's.

FORBES: Miss Ferguson's? Are you sure?

TEMPLE: Yes, I'm absolutely sure.

FORBES: But I don't understand. If the shoe belonged to Lynn then surely … (*He stops; hesitates*) Temple, you don't think she's dead and they've sent Steve the shoe as a warning?

121

STEVE: Oh, Paul!

TEMPLE: (*Quietly*) No. No, I don't think so. I think the shoe was sent as a warning, yes – but curiously enough I don't think anything's happened to Miss Ferguson.

STEVE: Sir Graham, a few moments ago Paul asked you why Lynn went to La Martella. You said you wanted to keep an eye on Fabian.

FORBES: Yes, that's true.

TEMPLE: Why? Why did you want to keep an eye on Fabian?

FORBES: (*Evading the question*) We were pursuing a special investigation; it was necessary for one of us to – well – keep an eye on him.

TEMPLE: You still haven't answered the question, Sir Graham. What was Lynn Ferguson doing at La Martella?

A pause.

FORBES: We suspected that Fabian was mixed up in a drug smuggling racket and that he was using the club as a coverup. We decided to investigate and put Miss Ferguson on the job.

STEVE: Did she discover anything?

FORBES: Not a thing. As a matter of fact, on her last report she said she thought the club was a genuine profit making concern and that Fabian was perfectly straight.

TEMPLE: M'm.

FORBES: Was that your impression?

TEMPLE: Well, I've only been there once, Sir Graham: I wouldn't like to venture an opinion. I'll tell you more when I've had a chat to Fabian.

FORBES: Are you seeing him?

TEMPLE: Yes, this afternoon. He sent me a note just before he left the club. I've got it here somewhere – Oh, here we are. You'd better read it.

FORBES takes the note.

FORBES: Thank you. (*A slight pause. Reading*) "I suggest you call tomorrow afternoon, anytime between four o'clock and five. Don't bring your friend from Scotland Yard" … (*Surprised; looking up*) Then he knew about Lynn.

TEMPLE: Apparently.

FORBES: Did you show Lynn the note?

TEMPLE: Yes.

FORBES: Was she surprised?

TEMPLE: (*Smiling*) A little. Sir Graham, tell me – did anyone know about Miss Ferguson?

FORBES: What do you mean?

TEMPLE: Did anyone else – any of your colleagues for instance – know that she was investigating La Martella?

FORBES: No, I've told you. Lynn was completely independent.

TEMPLE: I see.

FORBES: Temple, you told me you wanted to go to La Martella because Galino said that's where you'd find Mr Hamilton.

TEMPLE: Galino did say that, Sir Graham, but that wasn't my only reason for wanting to visit La Martella. I believe that Mrs Talbot went there one night and that she had an appointment with a woman called Betty Wayne.

FORBES: Betty Wayne?

TEMPLE: Yes. Miss Wayne works at Conway and Racys; so did Brenda Stirling, so did June Michael. Now, to say the least I find that rather a strange

123

coincidence. Mrs Talbot, as we know, was the principal witness in the Gilbert case.

FORBES: That is a coincidence. Did you ask Fabian about Mrs Talbot?

TEMPLE: Steve did.

STEVE: He said he'd never heard of her.

FORBES: And Miss Wayne?

STEVE: He knew Miss Wayne of course; she's a member.

TEMPLE: Apparently Miss Wayne frequently goes to La Martella; she was there last night with Mr Reynolds.

FORBES: You mean Lance Reynolds?

TEMPLE: Yes.

FORBES: But he shares a flat with Howard Gilbert – or rather he did.

TEMPLE: Yes, I know. Another interesting coincidence, Sir Graham.

FORBES: You know, Temple, I'm very worried about the Gilbert case. I saw the Home Secretary this morning; in view of what's happened there's almost bound to be a stay of execution.

TEMPLE: I hope so, Sir Graham.

FORBES: You don't think Gilbert did murder Brenda Stirling?

TEMPLE: I'm quite sure he didn't.

FORBES: I must confess I'm rather doubtful. This Galino business has shaken me. According to Kingston, Galino said that he was with Mrs Talbot the night she was supposed to have seen Gilbert.

TEMPLE: That's what he said.

STEVE: Has he made an official statement, Sir Graham?

FORBES: Yes, I believe so. Kingston saw him this morning.

STEVE: How is Galino?

FORBES: I gather he's still pretty bad, Steve.

TEMPLE: Have you any objections to my seeing him?

FORBES: (*Faintly surprised*) No, of course not. Why do you ask?

TEMPLE: (*Casually*) I telephoned the hospital this morning and was told he wasn't receiving visitors.

FORBES: Oh, I expect that's a precautionary measure; it doesn't apply to you, Temple.

TEMPLE: I'd like to see him; I'm rather curious about a remark he made.

STEVE: You mean, the one about finding Hamilton at La Martella?

TEMPLE: No, no, something quite different. He said he first met Mrs Talbot in a reference library. (*Vaguely*) I wondered which library it was, that's all.

The door opens.

CHARLIE: Excuse me, sir. Mr Stirling's called; he says he'd like to have a word with you.

TEMPLE: Did you tell him I was in?

CHARLIE: Yes, I'm afraid I did, sir. (*Innocently*) Did I make a bloomer?

TEMPLE: Show him into the study, Charlie.

CHARLIE: Yes, sir.

STEVE: What do you think Stirling wants?

FORBES: He's probably read about last night and wonders what you were doing in Darlington Street.

TEMPLE: Yes.

FORBES: I've got a hunch Mr Stirling knows a great deal more about this business than we think. I've a

	jolly good mind to send Kingston to pick him up.
TEMPLE:	No, no, don't do that, Sir Graham, please. Stirling's mixed up in this affair all right, but just which particular piece of the jigsaw he represents we don't know – not yet – and we won't find out by taking him down to Scotland Yard.
STEVE:	But if Stirling's mixed up in this business – and he obviously must be – then why did he call Paul in the first place? After all, it's entirely through Stirling that Paul intervened in the Gilbert case.
FORBES:	That's true.
TEMPLE:	(*Smiling*) You know, it's a curious coincidence but in a case of this kind there always seems to be a Mr Stirling.
FORBES:	What do you mean?
STEVE:	I think I know what you mean, darling. You mean a mysterious figure you just can't quite weigh up.
FORBES:	Well, I can weigh Mr Stirling up all right and if I had my way I'd take him down to the Yard.
STEVE:	Then why don't you?
FORBES:	Because Inspector Kingston's in charge of the case and I make a point of never interfering. In any case, he agrees with your husband.
TEMPLE:	Supposing, for argument's sake, you questioned Stirling. What would you hope to find out?
FORBES:	I'd expect an explanation as to why he visited Miss Wayne, why he took June Michael to an inn called The Lord Fairfax, and why that woman visited him last night.

TEMPLE: All right, I'm Mr Stirling. Question one: I visited Miss Wayne because my daughter used to work for her and I thought perhaps she might have some useful information about Brenda's activities. Question two: I didn't take June Michael to an inn called The Lord Fairfax; she took me. And in any case I didn't know it was called The Lord Fairfax, I'd never been in it before. Question three: What woman are you talking about? I certainly didn't see anyone last night. Mrs Temple must have been mistaken.

FORBES: M'm.

TEMPLE: Now where do we go from there, Sir Graham?

FORBES: Well, you still haven't answered Steve's question.

TEMPLE: What question?

FORBES: Why did Stirling come to see you in the first place?

TEMPLE: He came to see me because – (*Smiling*) he didn't think Gilbert committed the murder.

FORBES: If you had a daughter and she was murdered would you try to get the convicted man acquitted?

TEMPLE: That depends on whether I thought he was guilty or not. And don't forget, Sir Graham, Stirling came to me after the trial, after he'd given evidence against Gilbert, after he had been convicted and after the appeal had been turned down.

FORBES: Yes, but he told you about the entry in his daughter's diary; the reference to Lord Fairfax; so far as you were concerned that started the ball rolling.

TEMPLE: Yes, but how was he to know that? Remember, there was nothing new about that information, Sir Graham – it had already been given to Scotland Yard.

FORBES: (*Thoughtfully*) Yes … Yes, I suppose so.

A pause.

TEMPLE: Sir Graham, would you do something for me?

FORBES: Of course.

TEMPLE opens a drawer.

TEMPLE: I've got a photograph here. I found it in June Michael's flat the afternoon she – (*Significantly*) committed suicide. I'd like you to check it for me.

FORBES: Yes, of course.

FORBES take the photograph.

FORBES: (*Faintly surprised*) Hello!

TEMPLE: Do you recognise him?

FORBES: Yes, I think I do …

TEMPLE: Is it a man called Larry Boardman?

FORBES: Well – if it isn't, it's certainly very much like him.

TEMPLE: Boardman's dead, isn't he?

FORBES: (*Thoughtfully*) Yes, he died some little time ago.

STEVE: Larry Boardman? The name's familiar …

TEMPLE: No, I doubt whether you've heard of him, darling.

FORBES: He was a jewel thief; confidence man; trickster. Quite a charmer in his way. The crook with a heart of gold – chiefly other people's. (*Almost a sigh*) Still – we never caught him … Was he a friend of June Michael's?

TEMPLE: I should imagine so. I found the photograph in her bedroom.

FORBES: M'm. I'm pretty sure it's Boardman. Still, I'll
            check on it. Well, I'd better be making a move.

START FADE.

FORBES: I'll let you know if there's any news about Miss
            Ferguson.

TEMPLE: Would you like to have a word with Stirling
            before you go, Sir Graham?

FORBES: No, no, you see what it's all about, Temple. If
            it's important give me a ring.

COMPLETE FADE.

FADE IN the opening of a door.
TEMPLE has entered the study.

TEMPLE: Sorry to have kept you waiting, Stirling.

STIRLING: That's all right, sir. I apologise for intruding
            like this but – Mr Temple, what happened last
            night?

TEMPLE: Haven't you read the papers?

STIRLING: Yes, but – they've got the most extraordinary
            story. They say you parked your car in
            Darlington Street and that someone took shots
            at it.

TEMPLE: That's correct, Mr Stirling.

STIRLING: But why should anyone want to do that?

TEMPLE: Presumably because they were under the
            impression that we were sitting in it.

STIRLING: You mean – someone deliberately tried to kill
            you?

TEMPLE: That was my impression.

STIRLING: But – but that's fantastic. People don't do that
            sort of thing.

TEMPLE: On the contrary, so far as I'm concerned they
            seem to make quite a habit of it. (*Smiling*)
            Nowadays life is very much stranger than

fiction, Mr Stirling, you only have to read the newspapers to discover that. However, we're none the worse for the experience. It was very nice of you to call …

STIRLING: Have you any idea who was responsible?

TEMPLE: Not the slightest. I had a spot of trouble with the car; parked it in Darlington Street and went into a telephone box. Whilst I was telephoning someone peppered my car with bullets. Unfortunately I didn't see them.

STIRLING: I see.

TEMPLE: (*Pleasantly*) You live in Darlington Street, don't you, Stirling?

STIRLING: Yes, I do. I do indeed. That's why I was so curious about what happened.

TEMPLE: Why should you be curious?

STIRLING: (*Hesitantly*) Well, I wondered if, by any chance, you thought that what happened last night had anything to do with me.

TEMPLE: Why should I think that?

STIRLING: Because I live in Darlington Street.

TEMPLE: A great many people live in Darlington Street, Mr Stirling.

STIRLING: Yes, I know, but – they haven't all been questioned by the police.

TEMPLE: When were you questioned?

STIRLING: This morning.

TEMPLE: By Inspector Kingston?

STIRLING: No. One of the local people called round. He wanted to know if I'd heard the shots.

TEMPLE: Did you?

STIRLING: No, I was fast asleep.

TEMPLE: Did you receive any visitors last night?

STIRLING: No – I listened to the radio until about ten o'clock then I had a bath and went to bed.

TEMPLE: I see. (*Suddenly; quite pleasantly*) Mr Stirling, I'm glad you called round this morning because there's something I wanted to ask you. Did you ever hear your daughter mention the name Hamilton?

STIRLING: No.

TEMPLE: She wasn't friendly with a man called Hamilton, by any chance?

STIRLING: Not to my knowledge. I don't think she was friendly with anyone except Howard Gilbert. Oh, and Miss Wayne of course.

TEMPLE: Oh, she was a friend of Miss Wayne's?

STIRLING: Yes, yes, they were very good friends. I thought I told you that?

TEMPLE: I don't remember. Are you a friend of Miss Wayne's?

STIRLING: No; I don't think I've spoken more than half a dozen times to her.

TEMPLE: I see. (*Suddenly; pleasantly*) You haven't a car by any chance, have you, Mr Stirling?

STIRLING: (*Surprised*) Er – yes.

TEMPLE: Is it outside?

STIRLING: Yes, as a matter of fact it is.

TEMPLE: I wonder if you could drop me somewhere? I have an appointment at four o'clock in South Audley Street …

STIRLING: Yes, of course.

TEMPLE: I don't want to take you out of your way.

STIRLING: No, no, that's quite all right.

TEMPLE: Oh, splendid! Excuse me!

TEMPLE crosses the room, opens the door and calls out.

TEMPLE: Steve! Steve!

STEVE: (*From the drawing room*) Yes, darling?

TEMPLE: (*Calling*) Here a moment! (*To STIRLING*) Are you sure I'm not taking you out of your way?

STIRLING: No, that's quite all right, Mr Temple. I'm on my way to Oxford Street.

TEMPLE: Oh, good.

STEVE enters.

STEVE: What is it, Paul?

TEMPLE: Steve, Mr Stirling's very kindly offered to drop me. (*To STIRLING*) Oh, I don't think you've met my wife.

STIRLING: No, I haven't had that pleasure. How do you do, Mrs Temple?

STEVE: How do you do, Mr Stirling?

TEMPLE: Darling, Mr Stirling's giving me a lift as far as South Audley Street. I'll meet you later – about four o'clock where we arranged.

STEVE: Yes, all right, Paul.

TEMPLE: I may be a little late, Steve – I'm going to try and get hold of a car.

STEVE: I'll wait. I'll be at the front entrance.

START FADE.

TEMPLE: Yes, all right. Are you ready, Mr Stirling?

STIRLING: Yes, certainly! Goodbye, Mrs Temple! I'm very glad to have met you.

STEVE: Goodbye, Mr Stirling.

COMPLETE FADE.

FADE UP the chimes of an elaborate door bell.
There is a pause.
The door is opened.

FABIAN: Ah, come in, Mr Temple! Come in!

TEMPLE: I'm afraid I'm rather late, Fabian.

FABIAN: Not at all. I said between four and five. Let me take your hat.

TEMPLE: Thank you.

FABIAN: Go straight through, Temple – through the wrought iron gates and turn right.

TEMPLE walks through the hall followed by FABIAN.

TEMPLE: By Timothy, you've got quite a place here.

FABIAN: Yes, it was specially designed for me, by the same man that did La Martella.

TEMPLE: Yes, I can see that.

FABIAN: Would you like a drink?

TEMPLE: No, I don't think I would, thank you very much.

FABIAN: (*Faintly amused*) Are you sure?

TEMPLE: Yes, quite sure.

FABIAN: Do you mind if I have one?

TEMPLE: No, of course not.

FABIAN mixes himself a drink.

FABIAN: You know why I wanted to see you, don't you?

TEMPLE: I haven't the slightest idea.

FABIAN: Oh, come on, my dear fellow! I should have thought it was obvious.

TEMPLE: It probably is – to you.

FABIAN: You got my note?

TEMPLE: Of course – that's why I'm here.

FABIAN: I made a reference to your friend from Scotland Yard. I meant Miss Ferguson.

TEMPLE: I rather gathered that.

FABIAN: (*Smiling*) Well, that's what I want to talk to you about, Mr Temple. Miss Ferguson.

TEMPLE: What about Miss Ferguson?

FABIAN: (*No longer smiling*) Why is she watching La Martella?

TEMPLE: Surely that's a question for Miss Ferguson – not me.

FABIAN: You're a friend of hers, you know perfectly well what's going on, so obviously …

TEMPLE: (*Interrupting FABIAN*) On the contrary, Mr Fabian – I haven't the slightest idea what's going on. And I find it rather disturbing.

FABIAN: What do you mean?

TEMPLE: My wife and I met Miss Ferguson for the first time last night when we were introduced by a mutual friend. I was anxious to meet her because I'd heard that she was a member of your club and both Mrs Temple and I wanted to visit La Martella.

FABIAN: Why?

TEMPLE: We'd heard a great deal about it, and – my wife wanted to dance with you.

FABIAN: Mr Temple, it's half past four in the afternoon. There's no soft light, no music. (*A shade annoyed*) I'm a businessman. Let's put our cards on the table. Why did you come to the club last night? Why have Scotland Yard suddenly decided to keep an eye on the place?

TEMPLE: You know, Fabian, I'm always a little perturbed when someone says "lets put our cards on the table." It usually means they simply want me to put my cards on the table. Nothing more.

FABIAN: (*A shrug*) If we're not going to trust each other, Mr Temple, there seems to be very little point in continuing the conversation. I asked you to call here because I thought it might be to our mutual advantage if we had a frank talk together.

TEMPLE: All right, Fabian. I went to your club last night because I wanted to meet a man called Hamilton. I was told that I should find him at La Martella.

FABIAN: Did you?

134

TEMPLE: No.

FABIAN: That doesn't surprise me. I've never heard of him. Why do you want to meet this man Hamilton?

TEMPLE: Because I believe he's mixed up in the Gilbert case and as you probably know, I'm investigating the case.

FABIAN: And that was your only reason for coming to La Martella?

TEMPLE: No, not my only reason. I was told that several weeks ago a woman called Mrs Talbot had an appointment at your club with Betty Wayne.

FABIAN: Who told you that?

TEMPLE: The same man that told me about Hamilton.

FABIAN: Well, I don't know who your friend is but he doesn't seem to be very well informed. Believe me, I know everything that goes on at La Martella and I know nothing about a Mr Hamilton and I certainly didn't permit Miss Wayne to introduce a woman like Mrs Talbot. (*Annoyed*) I won't have that type of person in the club. Not at any price.

TEMPLE: Then you knew about Mrs Talbot?

FABIAN: No, but I read about her when the case was on. She was a very disreputable person.

TEMPLE: She was considered a very good witness, Mr Fabian.

FABIAN: That may be …

TEMPLE: However, I'm not suggesting that Mrs Talbot was one of your members. I'm simply suggesting that she met Miss Wayne and they had a conversation together there.

FABIAN: Not to my knowledge.

A pause.

135

TEMPLE: Fabian, have you heard of a man called Peter Galino?

FABIAN: No.

TEMPLE: Well, he was the person who first told me about La Martella; he told me about the meeting between Mrs Talbot and Miss Wayne.

FABIAN: Well, you can tell Mr Gali – Galino, did you say?

TEMPLE: Yes.

FABIAN: Well, you can tell Mr Galino from me that if he starts any more malicious rumours I shall consult my lawyer and take immediate action.

TEMPLE: (*Watching FABIAN*) I doubt whether Galino will be very impressed. You see, he's in hospital; he was beaten up shortly after he gave me the information about Mrs Talbot.

FABIAN: (*Astonished*) Beaten up?

TEMPLE: Yes.

FABIAN: But that's impossible!

TEMPLE: Unpleasant, but not impossible – it happened.

FABIAN: But look here, are you inferring that he was beaten up because he told you about my club and the supposed meeting between Betty Wayne and Mrs Talbot?

TEMPLE: I'm not inferring anything, Mr Fabian, I'm simply giving you the facts. And the facts, so far as you are concerned are not very pleasant.

FABIAN: (*Angrily*) What do you mean?

TEMPLE: Galino tells me about La Martella; shortly afterwards he is attacked and very nearly murdered. Miss Ferguson's a special investigator from Scotland Yard, is told to watch the club and make periodical reports to Sir Graham Forbes and follows out her instructions and then suddenly – disappears.

FABIAN: Disappears? You mean Miss Ferguson's disappeared?

TEMPLE: That's what I mean, Mr Fabian.

FABIAN: But when did this happen?

TEMPLE: Last night.

FABIAN: But that's impossible! I don't believe you! You're lying ...

TEMPLE: Pick the telephone up and get Scotland Yard – they'll confirm it.

FABIAN: But I can hardly believe it, why ... Temple, you don't think I had anything to do with Miss Ferguson's disappearance? Surely to God you don't think that ...

TEMPLE: (*Interrupting FABIAN*) You knew that she was from Scotland Yard?

FABIAN: (*Worried; trying to 'cover' himself*) Well, I'd heard something. I wasn't sure of course ...

TEMPLE: You seemed very sure last night when you sent me that note. Incidentally, how did you know she was from Scotland Yard? Who told you?

FABIAN: No one told me. I became suspicious so I asked Inspector Kingston about her; he was non-committal of course but I felt sure I was right.

TEMPLE: When did you see Inspector Kingston?

FABIAN: He came to the club two or three weeks ago. One of our members lost a diamond ring and the insurance people reported it to Scotland Yard. It was just a routine inquiry.

TEMPLE: But you took the opportunity of asking him about Miss Ferguson?

FABIAN: Yes.

TEMPLE: Because you'd heard rumours.

FABIAN: (*Slightly confused*) What do you mean?

TEMPLE: You'd heard a rumour about Miss Ferguson so you asked Kingston about her.

FABIAN: No, I hadn't heard a rumour. It was just a feel I had … a sort of …

TEMPLE: (*Interrupting FABIAN*) But you said you had, Fabian. A moment ago I said you knew she was from Scotland Yard and you said – well, I'd heard a rumour.

FABIAN: I – I didn't mean that.

TEMPLE: In other words you just had a 'hunch' about Miss Ferguson and it turned out to be right.

FABIAN: (*Irritated*) Yes. Yes, that's about it.

TEMPLE: (*Unconvinced; quietly*) It doesn't seem very convincing, does it?

FABIAN: (*Angrily*) I don't care whether it's convincing or not, it happens to be the truth.

TEMPLE: And is that what you're going to tell the police when they ask you how you knew that Miss Ferguson was watching the club, how you knew she was a special investigator from Scotland Yard?

FABIAN: (*Still angry*) I shan't tell the police anything. I'm not interested in the police. And if they're friends of yours, Mr Temple, I'd be very grateful if you'd tell them to keep away from La Martella. I'm running a perfectly respectable nightclub and I don't want any interference. I want to be left strictly alone.

TEMPLE: I'll deliver your message.

FABIAN: (*Brusquely*) Now, if you'll excuse me, I have another appointment.

TEMPLE: There's no need to show me out, I can find my own way. (*After a moment; turning; quite pleasantly*) Oh, my wife got the shoe all right, Mr Fabian – thank you.

FABIAN: (*Puzzled*) The shoe?

TEMPLE: Yes.

FABIAN: What do you mean?

A moment.

TEMPLE: Miss Ferguson must have lost one of her shoes last night, and it was sent to my wife. I assumed that she lost it at the club and not knowing her address you sent it to my wife.

FABIAN: (*Confused*) No, I never heard anything about it. But one can't lose a shoe! That's ridiculous!

TEMPLE: (*Quite casually*) Apparently Miss Ferguson did. Well, I'd better say goodbye.

FABIAN: (*Suddenly*) Mr Temple – one moment, please!

TEMPLE: (*Turning*) Yes?

FABIAN: You didn't believe what I said – about Miss Ferguson, did you? You think someone told me about her.

TEMPLE: On the face of it I would say that was the most likely explanation.

FABIAN: Well, it isn't true. I simply had a hunch. People have hunches you know.

TEMPLE: My wife frequently gets them; I even get them myself on occasions. As a matter of fact, I've got one now – about Miss Ferguson. (*Facing FABIAN*) I've got a hunch that we're going to find her in very much the same condition as Peter Galino. I hope for her sake, and for yours, that I'm wrong.

A pause.

FABIAN: (*Curtly*) Whatever happens to Miss Ferguson is no concern of mine. I'm not interested in the young lady.

139

TEMPLE: That's not what I'm getting at. She was interested in you, Mr Fabian.

FADE IN music.

FADE DOWN music.

FADE UP the sound of a car; it slows down and draws to a standstill.

There is a background of traffic noises.

TEMPLE: (*Calling from the car*) Steve! Steve!!!!

STEVE: (*Arriving at the car*) Oh, hello, darling! I didn't recognise you ... I say, this is a jolly nice car! Where did you get it from?

TEMPLE: I've hired it.

STEVE: Very, very nice.

TEMPLE: Yes, and very, very expensive. Mind the door, Steve.

STEVE: Oh, pardon me!

STEVE closes the door.

TEMPLE: I'm beginning to think it would have been cheaper to have bought a new one. Did anyone ring up after I left?

STEVE: Yes, your publisher. They want to know when they're going to get the new novel. I told them it was being typed.

TEMPLE: Good. Anyone else?

STEVE: Oh, the insurance people rang up about the car. They wanted to know what hit it.

TEMPLE: Did you tell them?

STEVE: (*Amused*) Yes. I said bullets.

TEMPLE: What's the matter?

STEVE: The man couldn't believe his ears. He thought I said pullets.

TEMPLE changes gear; the car drives away.

TEMPLE: Well, did you do what I suggested?

STEVE: Yes.

TEMPLE: What happened?

STEVE: I took the dress back and asked to see Miss Wayne.

TEMPLE: Did you see her?

STEVE: Yes, but it wasn't any use – she just wouldn't talk about anything except the alteration. I mentioned Reynolds, I mentioned Stirling, I mentioned Fabian, but I might just as well have talked about the weather.

TEMPLE: M'm.

STEVE: How did you get on with Fabian, by the way?

TEMPLE: M'm – not too badly. He's a pretty smooth customer.

STEVE: Of course he is, or he wouldn't be running La Martella.

TEMPLE: Did you tell Miss Wayne I tried to get her on the telephone?

STEVE: Yes.

TEMPLE: What did she say?

STEVE: She didn't say anything, she just went on talking about the dress. (*Suddenly*) Paul, you should have turned left.

TEMPLE: No, I'm going to St Mathews Hospital. I'm seeing Peter Galino at half past five.

STEVE: Oh.

TEMPLE: I'm afraid you'll have to sit in the car, Steve, unless you'd like to wait in the hospital.

STEVE: No, I'll be all right. You know, Betty Wayne's definitely worried, Paul.

TEMPLE: You think so.

STEVE: I'm absolutely sure. As soon as I mentioned Reynolds she coloured up and turned her back on me. There's something funny going on there, you know.

TEMPLE: Yes.

STEVE: Do you think Reynolds is the man Galino referred to, the mysterious Mr Hamilton? After all, don't forget he was at La Martella.

TEMPLE: I don't see how he can be, Steve. It was Reynolds who first mentioned Hamilton, remember – on the telephone at Mrs Talbots.

STEVE: Yes. (*Thoughtfully*) You know, I'm beginning to get a sort of intuition about this case, Paul.

TEMPLE: (*Smiling*) That good old intuition, eh, Steve?

STEVE: You can laugh, darling – but I've been right before.

TEMPLE: I'm not laughing. I've a great respect for that good old intuition of yours. Well – who do you put your money on this time? Wilfrid Stirling? Lance Reynolds? Betty Wayne? Louis Fabian? …

STEVE: You've left one out, darling.

TEMPLE: Who? (*Suddenly*) Oh, Howard Gilbert. By Timothy, it would be a terrible let down if he was guilty after all, wouldn't it?

FADE IN music.

FADE DOWN music.
A door opens and closes.

TEMPLE: Good evening, Galino.

GALINO: (*Surprised*) Oh! Oh, it's you, Mr Temple. I was with the Inspector … He said he'd call back sometime this afternoon.

TEMPLE: How are you feeling? Are you any better?

GALINO: Yes, I suppose so. My head is bad though … It's still difficult to talk sometimes.

TEMPLE: Does that mean you don't like answering questions?

GALINO: (*Surely*) I've done nothing else but answer questions ever since I've been here …

TEMPLE: Does that surprise you? You're a pretty important person, Mr Galino.

GALINO: What do you mean?

TEMPLE: Don't you remember what you said? You said Mrs Talbot was with you the night Howard Gilbert …

GALINO: (*Quietly; embarrassed*) Yes, I know. I don't know what made me say that, I must have been crazy, I …

TEMPLE: (*Slowly; interrupting GALINO*) Are you going back on that statement?

GALINO: It isn't a question of going back on what I said, just …

TEMPLE: Well, what is it?

GALINO: I was confused … It was a great shock to me when I heard that Mary – Mrs Talbot – was dead.

TEMPLE: Go on …

GALINO: I made a mistake … It wasn't that night she came to see me.

TEMPLE: (*Contemptuously*) So she might have bumped into Gilbert after all – is that it?

GALINO: (*A shrug*) She identified him; it was in all the newspapers. Isn't that enough for you?

TEMPLE: Have you seen anyone else, Galino, while you've been in hospital – besides Inspector Kingston, I mean?

GALINO: (*Hesitantly*) No …

TEMPLE: You'd better tell me the truth, you know. I can always check on it.

GALINO: I've told you the truth.

143

TEMPLE: What happened the other night, Galino? Who attacked you?

GALINO: I don't remember.

TEMPLE: You don't remember?

GALINO: (*Quickly; tensely*) No, I don't remember! I don't remember what I did, or where I went, or what I said.

TEMPLE: Well, let me refresh your memory. You told me to go to a club called La Martella, you said that if I went there I'd meet a man called Hamilton …

GALINO: I don't know anybody called Hamilton … I've never heard of La Martella … Mr Temple, forgive me, but – my head is very bad. I – I just don't want to talk.

TEMPLE: (*Quietly; after a moment*) You've changed your mind, haven't you?

GALINO: I've told you, I can't talk … My head is very bad.

TEMPLE: (*Watching GALINO*) Why?

GALINO: (*Nervously*) What do you mean?

TEMPLE: (*Standing over GALINO*) Why have you changed your mind?

GALINO: (*Hesitantly; a shade frightened*) I've told you, I can't talk …

TEMPLE: All right, Galino. I can't make you talk, if you don't want to. But before I go there's something I want to say.

GALINO is about to protest.

TEMPLE: It's all right, you needn't get excited. I'm not going to ask you about Hamilton or La Martella or anything like that. I just want you to tell me something. The other night you said the first time you met Mrs Talbot was in a reference library on the Tottenham Court Road.

144

GALINO: Well?

TEMPLE: What day was that, Galino – do you remember?

GALINO: Yes, I told you – it was a Monday … December 9th.

TEMPLE: Are you sure?

GALINO: Yes, of course I'm sure. Now I've told you, I'm not going to answer any more questions, not if …

TEMPLE: Just one moment, Galino. It's not important, but something I'd like to know. Was it raining when you went into the library?

GALINO: What are you getting at?

TEMPLE: It's a perfectly simple question. Was it raining?

GALINO: (*Surely*) No, it wasn't. As a matter of fact it was a very nice day.

TEMPLE: (*Smiling; with a friendly nod*) Thank you, Mr Galino. You've been most helpful.

FADE SCENE.

Slow FADE UP.

INSPECTOR KINGSTON is talking to STEVE; there is a background of traffic noises.

KINGSTON: … I quite agree, Mrs Temple. On the other hand if Howard Gilbert didn't commit the murder then who did? We know for a fact that Brenda Stirling … (*He breaks off*) Oh, here's your husband!

TEMPLE: (*Surprised*) Why, hello, Inspector!

KINGSTON: Hello, Mr Temple! I was just going into the hospital when I spotted your wife.

STEVE: Did you see Galino, darling?

TEMPLE: Yes, I've just left him.

KINGSTON: How is he?

TEMPLE: He's not exactly communicative.

KINGSTON: No.

TEMPLE: His memory doesn't seem to be quite as good as it was earlier.

KINGSTON: I'm worried about Galino. I saw him this morning and there seemed to me to be a distinct change. He was surly, almost insolent. Completely contradicted his original statement.

TEMPLE: Yes, I know.

STEVE: Do you think – (*Changing her mind*) No, I suppose that's impossible.

KINGSTON: What were you going to say, Mrs Temple?

STEVE: I was going to say, do you think someone's seen him perhaps …

KINGSTON: In other words – has he been got at? I wondered that.

TEMPLE: I don't think he has.

KINGSTON: No, neither do I. I told the nurse not to allow visitors under any circumstances.

TEMPLE: (*Shaking his head*) He hasn't seen anybody and he hasn't received any letters.

KINGSTON: Well, perhaps he's scared; perhaps the beating up did the trick after all.

TEMPLE: That's possible.

KINGSTON: Well, we'll have another talk to him anyway. Goodnight, Mr Temple.

TEMPLE: (*Stopping KINGSTON*) Oh, Inspector!

KINGSTON: (*Turning*) Yes?

TEMPLE: Is there any news of Miss Ferguson?

KINGSTON: No, there isn't. Sir Graham's very worried. (*Curious*) By the way, Mr Temple, did you know that Miss Ferguson was attached to Scotland Yard – that she was watching La Martella?

TEMPLE: Yes.

146

KINGSTON: (*Annoyed*) Well, it was news to me. It's a pity Sir Graham didn't mention her before; it's always nice to be kept in the picture.

TEMPLE: She wasn't investigating the Gilbert case.

KINGSTON: Well, that makes a nice change. So many people seem to be investigating the Gilbert case.

Steve coughs in embarrassment.

TEMPLE: Oh.

KINGSTON: I'm afraid there's nothing we can do about it; even if I want to.

TEMPLE: (*Changing the subject*) Inspector, you said just now that you didn't know about Miss Ferguson.

KINGSTON: I said I didn't know she was attached to Scotland Yard.

TEMPLE: Didn't Mr Fabian mention her to you at some time?

KINGSTON: Fabian? The fellow who runs La Martella?

TEMPLE: Yes.

KINGSTON: Of course he didn't. (*Amused*) Did he know about Miss Ferguson?

TEMPLE: It was the night you were making inquiries about the diamond ring.

KINGSTON: What diamond ring?

TEMPLE: I was told that a member of La Martella lost a diamond ring and that the insurance company asked you to investigate.

KINGSTON: (*Amused*) Did Fabian tell you that?

TEMPLE: Yes.

KINGSTON: And is that when I'm supposed to have heard about Miss Ferguson?

TEMPLE: Yes. Fabian said he asked you whether Miss Ferguson was attached to Scotland Yard or not.

KINGSTON: And what did I say?

TEMPLE: Apparently you were non-committal.

KINGSTON: (*Chuckling*) I'll bet I was. It's a pity Mr Fabian wasn't. You write novels, don't you, Mr Temple?

TEMPLE: Yes.

KINGSTON: Well, if you're ever hard up for a plot I should have a chat to Mr Fabian. He's certainly got the imagination. (*Still amused*) Goodbye, Mrs Temple!

STEVE: Goodbye, Inspector.

KINGSTON: Goodbye, Temple.

TEMPLE: (*Watching KINGSTON depart*) Goodbye, Kingston!

STEVE: (*After a moment; emphatically*) Paul, I don't like that man!

TEMPLE: (*Turning; pleasantly*) You said that before, Steve.

TEMPLE opens the car door.

TEMPLE: Move over, I'll drive.

STEVE: No, it's all right, I'll drive.

TEMPLE: Darling, move over! This car doesn't belong to me, I only borrowed it.

STEVE: And what do you mean by that?

TEMPLE: Look, Steve, we don't want to start an argument in front of the hospital.

STEVE: It seems an excellent place to start an argument!

TEMPLE: Oh, all right, you drive. And if you scratch it –

STEVE: I know exactly what you'll say, darling!

TEMPLE laughs and moves round and gets in the other side of the car.

STEVE starts the car engine.

STEVE: Are we going straight home?

148

TEMPLE: No, I want to call at a reference library on the Tottenham Court Road. I'm not sure of the number. You'll have to drive all the way down.

STEVE: All the way down the Tottenham Court Road?

TEMPLE: Yes, darling.

STEVE: Move over. You drive.

TEMPLE laughs.

FADE UP the noise of the car engine.

FADE DOWN the noise of the car.

FADE SCENE.

FADE UP.

MISS WHITE: Good evening, sir.

TEMPLE: Good evening. A friend of mine called here about six months ago and borrowed a book from your library …

MISS WHITE: From the reference library?

TEMPLE: (*Hesitating*) Yes, I believe so. I was wondering if you could tell me the name of the book?

MISS WHITE: (*Both puzzled and amused*) Well, that's a little difficult, Mr –

TEMPLE: Temple, Paul Temple.

MISS WHITE: Oh – well – have you the exact date, Mr Temple?

TEMPLE: Yes, it was a Monday – December 9th.

MISS WHITE: (*Thoughtfully*) I see …

STEVE: What exactly happens here when you ask for a book?

MISS WHITE: Well, you consult the catalogue, decide which book you want, then write the number of the book together with your name and address on a slip of paper. We take the slip and give you

149

the book. You can't take the book away of course, you've got to read it on the premises.

TEMPLE: I see. And what happens to the slip?

MISS WHITE: Well, we're supposed to file them, but – quite frankly, quite a lot of them get destroyed. However, we can look for Monday, December 9th, you said …

TEMPLE: Yes.

MISS WHITE: Well, I'll soon find the slip if we've got it: Monday's a pretty slack day. What did they call your friend?

TEMPLE: Talbot. Mrs Mary Talbot.

MISS WHITE: All right, Mr Temple. I'll see if I can find it. Please, take a seat. I shan't be long.

TEMPLE: Thank you.

A pause.

STEVE: Paul, why do you want to know the name of the book?

TEMPLE: I'm rather curious, that's all, Steve.

STEVE: Yes, but why? I can't see that it matters what book Mrs Talbot was reading. I expect it was a filthy day and she simply popped in here to get out of the rain.

TEMPLE: As a matter of fact it was a very nice day.

STEVE: Now how do you know, Paul? You're not going to tell me you remember what sort of a day it was over …

TEMPLE: I asked Galino. The weather was perfect, therefore Mrs Talbot must have come in here for a definite reason. Why do you usually go into a reference library? Because you want to look at a newspaper or consult a book.

STEVE: Galino didn't; he was just bored.

TEMPLE:	Galino was different; he was a foreigner; he had no money and didn't know what to do with himself. Mrs Talbot had a fairly comfortable flat and I imagine a certain amount of money.
STEVE:	Yes, but surely she wasn't the sort of woman to go to a reference library.
TEMPLE:	That makes her visit all the more curious. Ah, here's our friend!
MISS WHITE:	You've been lucky, Mr Temple. I've found the slip. (*Reading*) "Monday, December 9th. Mrs Mary Talbot, Soho Square, London, W.1." …
TEMPLE:	That's it.
MISS WHITE:	Well, apparently she asked for two books … "The Theory of the Photographic Process" – and that's a well-known book on photography, and a reference book called "Encyclopaedia of the Social Sciences" …
TEMPLE:	(*Thoughtfully*) M'm … Is that the one edited by Sir Ronald Bakerton?
MISS WHITE:	Yes, I believe it is. It's been out about eighteen months.
TEMPLE:	(*Still pondering*) Yes, that's right. (*Suddenly*) Well, thank you, Miss – ?
MISS WHITE:	White.
TEMPLE:	Thank you, Miss White – you've been most helpful.
STEVE:	(*To TEMPLE; quietly*) Satisfied, Mr Temple?
TEMPLE:	(*Quietly*) Yes, I'm satisfied.

FADE UP music.

FADE DOWN music.
FADE UP the sound of a key being inserted in a lock.

The door is suddenly opened from the inside.

STEVE: Why, hello, Charlie! I thought you were going out this afternoon.

CHARLIE: (*Perturbed and in a definite state of confusion*) Yes, I did intend to, Mrs Temple, but …

STEVE: Is anything the matter?

TEMPLE: What is it, Charlie?

CHARLIE: (*Perplexed*) There's a young lady to see you, sir. I think she's very ill, sir. I was just going out when the bell rang and – blimey, she didn't 'alf make me jump!

STEVE: What happened, Charlie?

CHARLIE: She was standing in the doorway, Mrs Temple. She was as white as a sheet; she said … "Is Mr Temple in" and then she passed out. Phew, I didn't 'alf have a job with her.

TEMPLE: Did you ring for a doctor?

CHARLIE: No, I tried to get hold of you, Mr Temple. I phoned Scotland Yard but they said you weren't there.

TEMPLE: Where is she now?

CHARLIE: She's in the sitting room, on the settee. I didn't know what to do with her, Mr Temple, I thought …

TEMPLE: That's all right, Charlie! Come along, Steve.

The door opens.

STEVE: (*Suddenly; surprised*) Paul, it's Miss Ferguson!

TEMPLE: (*Quickly; crossing to the settee*) Lynn!

FADE UP of LYNN FERGUSON; she is still dazed and in a semi-stupor, having been drugged.

LYNN: Who … is … that? Is that … you … Mr Temple?

TEMPLE: Lynn, are you all right? What happened? Where have you been?

LYNN:	(*Speaking with an effort*) They … dropped me outside your house … I was told …
STEVE:	(*Softly; kneeling beside LYNN*) Lynn, tell us what happened … What happened after we left you?
LYNN:	(*Trying to talk*) I – I walked part of the … way to … my flat and then … (*She stops speaking; dazed*)
STEVE:	(*Worried*) Paul, is she going to be all right?
TEMPLE:	(*Quickly*) Ring for Dr Lester – you'll find the number on my desk!
LYNN:	No, wait … Wait … I'll be all right … I'm beginning to feel better …
TEMPLE:	(*Softly*) What happened, Lynn?
LYNN:	They gave me something … An injection … I don't know what it was …
STEVE:	Who's they?
LYNN:	(*Quietly*) Hamilton …
TEMPLE:	(*Quickly*) Have you seen Hamilton?
LYNN:	Yes. Yes … I've seen him …

FADE IN closing music.

END OF EPISODE FIVE

EPISODE SIX

A WARNING FROM
MISS WAYNE

OPEN TO:

FADE IN voice of STEVE.

STEVE: (*Suddenly; surprised*) Paul, it's Miss Ferguson!

TEMPLE: (*Quickly; crossing to the settee*) Lynn!

FADE UP of LYNN FERGUSON; she is still dazed and in a semi-stupor, having been drugged.

LYNN: Who … is … that? Is that … you … Mr Temple?

TEMPLE: Lynn, are you all right? What happened? Where have you been?

LYNN: (*Speaking with an effort*) They … dropped me outside your house … I was told …

STEVE: (*Softly; kneeling beside LYNN*) Lynn, tell us what happened … What happened after we left you?

LYNN: (*Trying to talk*) I – I walked part of the … way to … my flat and then … (*She stops speaking; dazed*)

STEVE: (*Worried*) Paul, is she going to be all right?

TEMPLE: (*Quickly*) Ring for Dr Lester – you'll find the number on my desk!

LYNN: No, wait … Wait … I'll be all right … I'm beginning to feel better …

TEMPLE: (*Softly*) What happened, Lynn?

LYNN: They gave me something … An injection … I don't know what it was …

STEVE: Who's they?

LYNN: (*Quietly*) Hamilton …

TEMPLE: (*Quickly*) Have you seen Hamilton?

LYNN: Yes. Yes … I've seen him …

TEMPLE: Lynn, what happened?

LYNN: After you left me I walked round the corner towards my apartment … I was just about to go inside when … Mr Temple, do you think I could have a drink of water?

TEMPLE: Yes, of course! (*Turning*) Oh, Charlie – fetch me a glass of water. Quickly!

CHARLIE: Okedoke! Sir Graham Forbes is here, sir!

STEVE: Hello, Sir Graham. Come in!

FORBES: (*Surprised*) Lynn! (*Crossing to LYNN*) Lynn, are you all right?

TEMPLE: Yes, she'll be all right in a moment, Sir Graham.

FORBES: But what's happened? I got back to the Yard and my secretary said your man had just telephoned me with a sort of message about a girl being ill or something. I thought it was Steve.

TEMPLE: Charlie was just going out: he opened the door and Lynn was on the doorstep in a state of collapse.

STEVE: I'm afraid Charlie lost his head; he thought we were at the Yard and telephoned you.

FORBES: I see.

CHARLIE: (*Arriving*) Here's the glass of water, sir.

TEMPLE: Thank you. (*Taking the glass*) Here we are, Lynn …

LYNN takes the glass and drinks.

LYNN: (*After drinking*) Thank you … (*Looking up; a suggestion of a smile*) Hello, Sir Graham …

FORBES: Are you all right now?

LYNN: I still feel pretty weak, but – I guess I'd better tell you what happened in case I pass out again. After Mr and Mrs Temple dropped me I walked round the block to my apartment. I got almost as far as the entrance, then a car suddenly drew into the sidewalk and I was pushed inside it. It was all done so quickly I hadn't time to think or scream or anything. There was a man sitting in the back

158

	of the car and as soon as I was inside he dropped a sort of hood thing over my head and pressed a revolver against my ribs.
STEVE:	Oh, how horrible!
LYNN:	I was certainly frightened. I just didn't know what to do.
FORBES:	Go on, Lynn.
LYNN:	Well, to cut a long story short they took me to a country house some place. I didn't know where it was because I couldn't see anything and frankly I was too darned scared anyway to notice things.
FORBES:	How long were you in the car?
LYNN:	I should say about forty minutes.
TEMPLE:	Go on, Lynn.
LYNN:	I was in the house for about a quarter of an hour before I saw anybody. Then I was taken to a room on the top floor; it was an enormous room and in one of the corners there was a man sitting behind a desk. I couldn't see clearly because there was a light on his desk and it was shining in my face nearly the whole time. He started to ask me questions …
FORBES:	What sort of questions?
LYNN:	Well, they all more or less boiled down to the same thing. He wanted to know why I was always going to La Martella. I told him I was a member and that I liked going there because they had a very good orchestra and I was fond of dancing. He quite obviously didn't believe me. He knew I was attached to Scotland Yard and that I was making certain investigations. He wanted to know what those investigations were …
FORBES:	Did you tell him?

159

LYNN: No – at least, not at first. I stuck to my story. I
           said it was perfectly true that I was attached to
           the Yard but I went to La Martella because
           Fabian was such a wonderful dancer and – well –
           I just liked dancing.

TEMPLE: Go on ...

LYNN: They took me back to my room and left me alone
           for an hour. I was fairly optimistic; I thought I'd
           satisfied them. Then suddenly they sent for me
           again and I found myself back in the enormous
           room, facing the desk, and being asked more or
           less the same questions.

TEMPLE: By the same man?

LYNN: Yes; but this time he seemed very curious about
           the man you were interested in, Mr Temple.

TEMPLE: You mean Hamilton?

LYNN: Yes. He kept asking me time and time again if I
           knew anything about Hamilton and I kept
           repeating – "No, I've never heard of him!"
           Suddenly he lost his temper: he said I was lying
           and that I'd been sent to La Martella to try to
           find Hamilton and to investigate the Gilbert case.
           I denied this – for one thing it wasn't true, and
           secondly I couldn't see any connection between
           the Gilbert case and La Martella.

FORBES: Go on ...

LYNN: Well – when they realised that I wasn't going to
           tell them anything they ... gave me an injection.
           I don't know what it was they gave me but ... I
           felt terrible ...It was as if my mind no longer
           belonged to me ... I've never felt so strange and
           so desperately frightened ...

A pause.

STEVE: Are you all right, Miss Ferguson?

LYNN: I – I told them the truth, Sir Graham. I'm sorry – I couldn't help it. I don't know whether it was the injection or not, but – I tried ... I tried desperately hard not to tell them, but ... it wasn't any use ...

FORBES: Don't worry, my dear. Don't worry about it.

TEMPLE: (*Softly; gently*) What was it you told them?

LYNN: I told them I was investigating a drug smuggling organisation ... That I suspected that La Martella was being used as their headquarters ... I said I'd never heard of a man called Hamilton until you mentioned the name ...

TEMPLE: What did they say?

LYNN: That seemed to satisfy them; in fact oddly enough it changed the whole situation.

STEVE: (*Puzzled*) What do you mean?

FORBES: Do you mean that they were relieved when you told them, quite genuinely, that you were not investigating the case?

LYNN: Yes. It was perfectly obvious that my activities – as far as the drug investigations were concerned – didn't interest them in the slightest.

TEMPLE: (*Quietly*) Go on, Lynn – finish your story.

LYNN: After I'd told them about ... my reasons for going to La Martella ... they made me lie down ... Someone, I don't know who it was, took one of my shoes away ... I must have dozed off because ... when I woke up I was in the car again. They released me just round the corner ... As I got out of the car I heard someone say ... "You're opposite Mr and Mrs Temple's place, Miss Ferguson." ... I realised then that I was in Montpelier Square.

FORBES: (*Quietly*) I see.

161

TEMPLE: Lynn, how many people did you see – altogether, I mean?

LYNN: Four … The driver of the car, the man who actually stopped me in the street, the man who put the hood over my head, and the man I've told you about – the one that asked all the questions.

FORBES: Would you recognise them again?

LYNN: I might recognise the man who stopped me – I'm not sure.

FORBES: What about the others?

LYNN: I doubt it …

TEMPLE: I rather imagine, from what you've told us, that the important person was the man who asked the questions?

LYNN: Yes, I think so.

STEVE: And you think he was Hamilton?

LYNN: Yes, I'm sure he was.

FORBES: But you didn't recognise him?

LYNN: No, and yet, I wondered at one time whether it was …

TEMPLE: Fabian? Had he an accent?

LYNN: There was a slight suggestion of one and – well, he was so interested in my reason for going to La Martella.

FORBES: I agree. So far as I can make out that was the only reason why they picked you up. It's my bet it was Fabian.

STEVE: In other words, Fabian is Hamilton?

FORBES: Yes.

LYNN: But why did they take my shoe away? I just don't understand why they should have taken … (*Surprised*) Why, you've got it! You've got it, Mrs Temple!

STEVE: Yes.

LYNN: But where did you get it from?

FORBES: They sent it to Mrs Temple – as a warning.

LYNN: A warning?

TEMPLE: Yes. They wanted to remind us what happened to Brenda Stirling, June Michael – and Mrs Talbot.

LYNN: (*Softly*) I see. I expect you thought the same thing might happen to me?

FORBES: It did cross our minds. However, now that you're safe I'd better contact Kingston. Can I use your phone, Temple?

TEMPLE: Yes, of course.

FORBES: I shall tell the Inspector to keep a very close eye on La Martella. In my opinion, Fabian's the man we're after.

STEVE: Does that mean you now think that Gilbert's innocent and that Fabian murdered Brenda Stirling?

FORBES: I don't know about that, Steve, but – I certainly think he's the mysterious Mr Hamilton we've heard so much about.

TEMPLE: Well, if you think that, Sir Graham, we'd both better keep an eye on him. (*To STEVE*) It looks as if your dancing's going to improve, darling.

FADE IN music.

FADE DOWN music.

FADE IN background noises of the main hall of La Martella; we hear the sound of the dance orchestra.

TEMPLE: Oh, here you are, Steve – at last!

STEVE: Sorry to have been such a long time, darling. Have you seen Fabian?

TEMPLE: No. I've had a look in the restaurant. He's not there.

STEVE: He's probably in his office.

TEMPLE: Yes. Well, there's no hurry. I can see him later.
            Let's go into the cocktail bar.
STEVE: (*Suddenly*) Paul, there's the Inspector!
TEMPLE: Where?
STEVE: He's just coming out of the lift.
TEMPLE: By Timothy, yes! (*Pleasantly; raising his voice*) Good evening, Inspector!
KINGSTON: Hello, Mr Temple! What on earth are you doing here? Good evening, Mrs Temple!
STEVE: Good evening, Inspector.
TEMPLE: I rather suspect we're both here for the same reason.
KINGSTON: Fabian?
TEMPLE: Yes.
KINGSTON: (*Smiling*) Well, he's all yours, Mr Temple. I'm finished with him for the time being.
TEMPLE: Where is he?
KINGSTON: (*Rather pleased with himself*) He's in his office and somewhat the worse for wear.
TEMPLE: You sound as if you've been putting him through it.
KINGSTON: I've put him through it all right, but he's a pretty smooth customer. It would take a long time to get that gentleman down. He says the last time he saw Miss Ferguson she was with you – here – in the dining room.
TEMPLE: Well, she was certainly with us last night, but whether that was the last time he saw her or not remains to be seen.
KINGSTON: He apparently knew that Miss Ferguson was missing.
TEMPLE: Yes, I told him.
KINGSTON: When?
TEMPLE: This afternoon.

164

KINGSTON: Oh – so you saw him this afternoon, Mr Temple?

TEMPLE: Yes – we had a little chat.

KINGSTON: (*Not too pleased*) I see. You amateurs seem to get around one way and another.

STEVE: Does Fabian know that Miss Ferguson's been found?

KINGSTON: Yes, I told him.

STEVE: Was he surprised?

KINGSTON: Not unduly. Well, he's all yours, Mr Temple. Goodnight.

TEMPLE: Goodnight, Kingston.

KINGSTON: (*Turning*) Oh – there are two old friends of yours in the cocktail bar.

TEMPLE: Oh – who's that?

KINGSTON: Reynolds and Miss Wayne. I don't know whether they've been having a row or not, but things weren't too harmonious ten minutes ago.

TEMPLE: Did you speak to them?

KINGSTON: No, I was on my way upstairs – they didn't see me. Goodnight, Mrs Temple.

STEVE: Goodnight, Inspector. (*A pause*) You know, I don't know why Sir Graham keeps that man on. He's arrogant and self-opinionated and …

TEMPLE: (*Laughing*) Darling, he's nothing of the sort. He's an extremely clever man. Come along, let's go into the bar.

FADE SCENE.

FADE up the noise of cocktail bar chatter.
In the near background we can hear the dance orchestra.
FADE IN the voice of BETTY WAYNE: she is in a very bad mood and has obviously had a little too much to drink.

BETTY:	I don't know why you didn't complain about the glass. I told you it was filthy. I told you as soon as I saw it.
REYNOLDS:	(*Bored and irritated*) Betty, it wasn't filthy. It was just a spot – a minute spot. In any case, it's not important …
BETTY:	It may not be important to you but it is to me. I hate anything like that … I don't know what's come over this place, I really don't!
REYNOLDS:	Well, if you don't like it, you don't have to come.
BETTY:	Don't be naïve, Lance. Get me another drink.
REYNOLDS:	(*Quietly*) Don't you think you've had enough for one night?
BETTY:	If I thought I'd had enough I wouldn't ask for another one, would I, sweetie?
REYNOLDS:	Well, this has been a very pleasant evening, I must say!
BETTY:	Where's Fabian? I want to dance …
REYNOLDS:	It's perfectly obvious that Fabian isn't going to put in an appearance tonight, so if you want to dance you might as well dance with me.
BETTY:	I said dance, darling. Dance …
REYNOLDS:	(*Quietly; with authority*) Betty, pull yourself together … Here are the Temples …
BETTY:	Where? Oh … My God, what a wonderful dress! Now where did she get that from? She didn't buy it from me.
REYNOLDS:	Betty, please! Now remember …
BETTY:	(*Raising her voice*) Hello, there!
STEVE:	(*Crossing towards BETTY*) Oh, hello, Miss Wayne. Good evening, Mr Reynolds.
REYNOLDS:	Good evening, Mrs Temple. Hello, Temple – how are you?

TEMPLE:	I'm very well, thank you.
REYNOLDS:	I think you know Miss Wayne?
TEMPLE:	Yes, of course.
BETTY:	Darling, I'm waiting for my drink …
REYNOLDS:	(*Embarrassed*) Oh, I'm sorry, Betty. May I get you a drink, Mrs Temple?
STEVE:	Well – could I have a dry martini?
REYNOLDS:	Yes, of course. Temple?
TEMPLE:	I'll have a dry martini too – thank you.
BETTY:	Isn't this place deadly tonight? My God, it's like the Midland Hotel, Burslem …
REYNOLDS:	I'm afraid Betty's furious …
STEVE:	Really – why?
REYNOLDS:	She wants to dance and Fabian hasn't turned up yet.
STEVE:	Oh. I expect he'll put in an appearance later.
BETTY:	It's nearly twelve now – he ought to have been here hours ago. If Louis is not going to dance with customers they might just as well close the place down.
REYNOLDS:	(*Trying to turn the conversation*) What are you drinking, Betty?
BETTY:	I'm not drinking anything; I'm still waiting …
REYNOLDS:	Yes, I know, but –
BETTY:	Gin, dear. Gin. Pink gin – in a nice clean glass. (*To TEMPLE and STEVE*) Do you know I've just been given the fil-filth-iest …
TEMPLE:	Miss Wayne, I think you're just a little bit high if you ask me.
BETTY:	(*Offended*) What do you mean?
STEVE:	He means 'tiddly' …

BETTY: I can assure you I'm not in the least bit 'high'
                as you call it. I'm just annoyed because I
                can't dance.

STEVE: Well, my husband may not be Mr Fabian –
                but he's a good dancer.

TEMPLE: (*To BETTY*) Would you like to dance?

BETTY: (*Not too keen*) Well, I've already refused
                Lance …

REYNOLDS: (*From the background; at the bar*) Don't
                worry about me, go ahead …

TEMPLE: Come on, Miss Wayne. (*To STEVE: softly,
                aside*) I'll see you later, Steve. Don't move
                out of the cocktail bar.

STEVE: Yes, all right, Paul.

FADE DOWN the cocktail bar noises and conversation.
FADE COMPLETELY.

FADE UP the sound of the dance orchestra.
*The dance orchestra stops: there is a smattering of applause
from the dancers.*
The orchestra starts again.

TEMPLE: Do you want to carry on?

BETTY: (*A shrug*) Why not?

They continue to dance.
A pause.

BETTY: Your wife's right – you're a very good
                dancer, Mr Temple.

TEMPLE: Thank you.

BETTY: And thank goodness, a silent one. Lance talks
                all the time – he never stops.

TEMPLE: Really?

BETTY: It's infuriating.

A pause.

TEMPLE: Miss Wayne, you remember when Steve and I called the other night …

BETTY: Yes.

TEMPLE: I believe I told you we saw Wilfrid Stirling …

BETTY: You said you thought you'd seen him.

TEMPLE: We saw him all right; he'd just left your flat.

BETTY: (*Angrily; obviously telling the truth*) Mr Temple, I told you then – and I'm telling you now – I never saw Mr Stirling. He'd never been near my flat. How many times do I have to tell you that?

TEMPLE: (*Quietly*) Is that the truth?

BETTY: (*Wearily*) Yes – that's the truth.

TEMPLE: (*Smiling*) All right, Miss Wayne. I believe you.

BETTY: Well, that makes a nice change anyway.

A pause.

TEMPLE: That's a very nice dress you're wearing.

BETTY: What do you know about dresses?

TEMPLE: Judging from the number you've sold my wife I'm practically in the business.

BETTY laughs.

BETTY: Well, if you're in the business, Mr Temple, where did I get this from? (*A pause: amused*) Please …

TEMPLE: I never make a deduction without studying the evidence. I should say it's either Lachasse or Dior … correct?

BETTY doesn't answer: she is amused.

TEMPLE: There you are, you see. I'm an expert.

BETTY: Not on dresses, Mr Temple. I bought this in a shop straight off the peg.

TEMPLE: Oh – well, it looks like Dior – on you, anyway.

BETTY laughs.

A pause.

BETTY: Mr Temple …

TEMPLE: Yes?

169

BETTY:	(*After a moment*) Oh, nothing …
TEMPLE:	(*Quietly*) What were you going to say?
BETTY:	(*Hesitantly; seriously*) I was just going to say … Whatever happens … don't go down to Reading …
TEMPLE:	I've not the slightest intention of going down to Reading.
BETTY:	Yes, I know, but – well, don't, that's all.
TEMPLE:	Is this some kind of a warning or …
BETTY:	…Could be …
TEMPLE:	… just a friendly piece of advice?
BETTY:	You can call it that if you like. (*A change of mind, almost as if she is regretting what she has said*) Do you mind if we stop dancing now?
TEMPLE:	No, of course not. Am I talking too much?
BETTY:	No, it's not that. I – I want that drink.
TEMPLE:	Yes, all right.

The orchestra stops playing: there is a smattering of applause.

Gradually FADE DOWN the orchestra to the distant background.

FADE UP the cocktail bar background.

REYNOLDS:	Ah, here we are, Betty! Here's your drink.
BETTY:	Thank you.
REYNOLDS:	Temple – dry martini.
TEMPLE:	Oh, thank you.
BETTY:	Well – skoal! (*She empties the glass*)
STEVE:	(*Surprised*) My!
BETTY:	That was a pink gin that was! (*Puts down the glass*) You were right, Mrs Temple, your husband's a very good dancer.
STEVE:	I'm glad you gave satisfaction, darling.

170

REYNOLDS: Well, I'm afraid there won't be anyone else to dance with – Fabian's left.

BETTY: What do you mean?

REYNOLDS: It's quite a simple statement, Betty. Fabian's gone home. He left about two minutes ago.

BETTY: No, surely not …

REYNOLDS: Ask Mrs Temple …

TEMPLE: Did you see him?

STEVE: Yes, just for a moment.

REYNOLDS: He popped in and said goodnight. I didn't think he looked too good.

BETTY: Well, if Fabian's gone there's no point in staying. I'll see you in the hall, Lance.

REYNOLDS: Are we leaving?

BETTY: Yes.

REYNOLDS: Have another drink?

BETTY: No, I want to get off. (*To TEMPLE and STEVE*) Goodnight.

STEVE: Goodnight.

TEMPLE: Goodnight, Miss Wayne.

A slight pause.

REYNOLDS: Well, I suppose I'd better try and get hold of a cab. Unfortunately my car's in dock.

TEMPLE: Won't you have another drink before you go?

REYNOLDS: No, no, I don't think I will, thank you, Temple. (*Pause*) Oh, by the way, there's a rumour that Howard Gilbert's going to be reprieved. I believe it's in the stop press of the newspapers.

TEMPLE: I haven't heard anything.

REYNOLDS: I see. Have you seen the Home Secretary?

TEMPLE: No, it's not my job to see the Home Secretary. I understand Sir Graham's seen him.

REYNOLDS:	Mr Temple, what do you think the chances are?
TEMPLE:	I don't know, Reynolds. We shall just have to see.
REYNOLDS:	(*Thoughtfully*) Yes. Well, I mustn't keep Betty waiting – that would be disastrous. Goodnight.
TEMPLE:	Goodnight.
STEVE:	Goodnight, Mr Reynolds.

A pause.

TEMPLE:	Was Reynolds right – did Fabian look under the weather?
STEVE:	He certainly did. If you want my opinion he's desperately worried about something.
TEMPLE:	It sounds as if the Inspector really did lay into him.
STEVE:	Yes.
TEMPLE:	(*Quickly; urgently*) Finish your drink, Steve. I want to get off!
STEVE:	Why – are we going home?
TEMPLE:	No …
STEVE:	Well – where are we going?
TEMPLE:	We're going to Reigate House.
STEVE:	But that's where Miss Wayne lives.

START FADE.

| TEMPLE: | Yes, I know. I'll see you in the front, Steve, I'm going to get the car … |

COMPLETE FADE.

FADE IN of DAN PRIESTLEY: he is a North country man in his late fifties.

| PRIESTLEY: | Good evening, sir. Did you ring? |
| TEMPLE: | Yes. Are you the Head Porter? |

PRIESTLEY:	Supervisor, Head Porter, Messenger Boy, and chief cook and bottle washer as you might say …
TEMPLE:	Well, you're the man I want, Mr – ?
PRIESTLEY:	Priestley, sir.
TEMPLE:	Well, Mr Priestley, I'm making a few inquiries. I think perhaps you can help me.
PRIESTLEY:	What sort of inquiries? There isn't a flat going if that's what you're thinking …
TEMPLE:	No, no, it's just that I'm rather interested in one of the tenants here.
PRIESTLEY:	(*Suspiciously*) Oh – are you from the police?
TEMPLE:	No, it's purely a private inquiry.
PRIESTLEY:	Well, what is it you want to know?
TEMPLE:	Who occupies the flat immediately above Miss Wayne's?
PRIESTLEY:	(*Surprised*) Above Miss Wayne? Now let me see … That'll be 23 … Oh, that's Mr Williams.
TEMPLE:	Is Mr Williams a man of about fifty two or three, grey hair, got rather a bad limp, walks with a stick?
PRIESTLEY:	That's right.
STEVE:	Why, Paul! That's Stirling …
TEMPLE:	(*Quietly*) That's all right, Steve … (*To PRIESTLEY*) How long has he been here?
PRIESTLEY:	Now just a minute … If you've got any inquiries to make my advice to you …
TEMPLE:	Look, Mr Priestley – my name is Temple. Paul Temple. I'm making certain inquiries and I think you might be able to help me. Now how long have you known Mr Williams?

PRIESTLEY: Oh, about two weeks that's all. He's a new tenant: he's on a sublet. As a matter of fact, he only pops in occasionally.

STEVE: Has he a girlfriend?

PRIESTLEY: Well, I suppose he must have, but I haven't seen her. I was a bit worried about him at first. I mean him popping in and out two or three times a week. And I said to Mrs Priestley, he looks a respectable sort of fellow but I don't like it.

STEVE: And what did Mrs Priestley say?

PRIESTLEY: Oh, well – she's more free an' easy than I am. More broadminded you might say. She was on the stage.

TEMPLE: Oh.

PRIESTLEY: Are you representing Mrs Williams, sir?

TEMPLE: Well, er – naturally I can't divulge …

PRIESTLEY: I understand, sir.

TEMPLE: Well, you've been most helpful, Mr Priestley. I'm very grateful. (*Tipping PRIESTLEY*) Here we are …

PRIESTLEY: Oh, thank you, sir. Thank you very much, sir.

TEMPLE: (*Turning; an afterthought*) Oh, there's just one point. I don't suppose you've got the necessary authority, but if I wanted to see inside one of the flats at any time – No 23 for instance …

PRIESTLEY: Oh, I've got the authority, sir – and a pass key to inside all the flats.

TEMPLE: (*Very impressed*) Oh. Oh, I see. I didn't realise that.

PRIESTLEY: Oh, good gracious, yes, sir. I've got the authority all right. Would you like to see inside No 23?

TEMPLE:	Well, if it isn't putting you to too much trouble …
PRIESTLEY:	Not at all, sir. This way, Mr Temple …

FADE SCENE.

FADE UP the sound of a key being inserted in a lock. The key turns and the door opens.

TEMPLE, STEVE and PRIESTLEY enter the flat.

STEVE:	My word, it's a very nice flat, Paul.
PRIESTLEY:	This is the hall – the bathroom's over there – the lounge – two bedrooms …
TEMPLE:	Are all these flats built the same?
PRIESTLEY:	Yes, they're all the same. Except the top flat – one of the bedrooms is smaller.
TEMPLE:	Do you mind if I have a look in the lounge?
PRIESTLEY:	No, of course not.

TEMPLE, STEVE and PRIESTLEY enter the lounge.

STEVE:	I like the curtains, Paul …
TEMPLE:	Yes … Who does this flat really belong to?
PRIESTLEY:	A Mr and Mrs Svenson; they're a Danish couple. Very nice. They usually spend two or three months abroad every year.

A slight pause.

STEVE:	What are you doing, Paul?
PRIESTLEY:	Are you looking for something, Mr Temple?
TEMPLE:	(*Slowly; intrigued*) Yes, as a matter of fact I am. And, by Timothy, I think I've found it!

TEMPLE starts to pull a small case from behind the settee.

PRIESTLEY:	Be careful with the settee, sir.
TEMPLE:	There's something behind it. I … move that end away from the wall, Steve …
PRIESTLEY:	Here – what's the idea?
TEMPLE:	Give my wife a hand, Mr Priestley … That's right, Steve! (*Leaning over the settee*) There's

a small case down here, I … want … to … get … hold … of it … (*Lifting the case*) Here we are!

PRIESTLEY: What do you mean? What is it?

TEMPLE: What does it look like?

STEVE: It looks like a portable gramophone.

TEMPLE: Yes, but it isn't.

PRIESTLEY: Well, whatever it is it's a damn funny thing to put behind the settee.

TEMPLE: (*Laughing*) Yes, I agree. It was put there so no one should notice it.

PRIESTLEY: But what is it?

TEMPLE: Does anyone clean this flat?

PRIESTLEY: I think Mr Williams does it himself; if he got a daily I haven't seen her. Look 'ere, what is this, Mr Temple?

STEVE: Darling, what is it?

TEMPLE: I'll show you.

TEMPLE releases a clip and opens the portable case.

STEVE: (*Puzzled*) Well, what is it?

PRIESTLEY: (*Surprised*) Here, just a minute! I know what it is. I've seen one of them blinkin' things before …

TEMPLE: In the army, Mr Priestley?

PRIESTLEY: Yes, we used to have one at headquarters. They used it to interrogate the Jerries and then … Here, what's Mr Williams doing with it?

TEMPLE: I'll give you three guesses.

STEVE: He's been listening to what's been going on in the flat below.

TEMPLE: Yes …

PRIESTLEY: He'd only have to stick those blinkin' headphones in and he'd hear every word …

STEVE: (*Puzzled*) But why should Mr Stirling want to listen to Betty Wayne? I fail to see …

PRIESTLEY: (*Interrupting STEVE*) Just a sec! Stirling, did you say? Is that what they call this bloke – Stirling?

TEMPLE: Yes.

PRIESTLEY: Is he any relation to Brenda Stirling – the girl that was murdered?

STEVE: Yes, it's her father.

PRIESTLEY: But she worked at Conway and Racys.

TEMPLE: Well?

PRIESTLEY: (*Puzzled; excitedly*) Well, so does Miss Wayne.

TEMPLE: (*Quietly*) Yes, I know.

PRIESTLEY: (*After a moment*) You're not representing Mrs Williams, are you? There isn't a Mrs Williams.

TEMPLE: As a matter of fact I'm not representing anyone unless it's Howard Gilbert.

PRIESTLEY: You mean – you're investigating the Gilbert case?

TEMPLE: Yes.

PRIESTLEY: Why? Don't you think he did it?

TEMPLE: No, I don't, Mr Priestley.

PRIESTLEY: But he must 'ave done it! Why even my missis thinks … (*He stops: listens*)

A slight pause.

TEMPLE: What is it?

STEVE: There's someone down below …

PRIESTLEY: Yes, it's Miss Wayne. She's just come in … (*A moment*) There we are – she's just closing the front door …

TEMPLE: (*With authority*) Mr Priestley, I've taken you into my confidence over this business; now I

177

	don't want you to say anything to anybody about this man. You understand?
PRIESTLEY:	Yes, sir.
TEMPLE:	Now give me a hand with the settee. I want to put this thing back exactly as I found it.

TEMPLE closes the case and they move the settee back.

| PRIESTLEY: | It's all right, Mrs Temple. We can manage. |
| TEMPLE: | That's it … |

TEMPLE replaces the case behind the settee.

TEMPLE:	That's it, Mr Priestley … That's it. Thank you.
PRIESTLEY:	(*Hesitantly*) Mr Temple …
TEMPLE:	Yes?
PRIESTLEY:	This fellow Williams – or Stirling, rather … He always slips me ten bob every week.
TEMPLE:	Well?
PRIESTLEY:	Well, do I go on taking it? I mean – now I know he's up to no good, I shall feel a bit funny. I mean, it didn't matter so much when I thought it was just a bit of slap an' tickle – beggin' your pardon, Mrs Temple – but, well, if he's mixed up in a murder case …
TEMPLE:	If you want to help me, and incidentally help the police, you carry on just the same, Mr Priestley. Be pleasant to Mr Williams. Take the ten shillings – and forget all about tonight.
PRIESTLEY:	Okay, if that's the way you want it.
TEMPLE:	That's the way I want it. Come along, Steve. We'll go down and have a word with Miss Wayne. Oh, and Mr Priestley – not a word to your wife, you understand?
PRIESTLEY:	Do you think I'm crazy?

START FADE.

PRIESTLEY: She'd never stop nattering. (*Amused*) Besides, she doesn't know anything about the ten bob.

STEVE laughs.
COMPLETE FADE.

FADE UP the sound of a door bell ringing.
The bell stops and the door is opened.

BETTY: (*Tired; unfriendly; suffering from a hangover*) Oh, hello! What do you want?

TEMPLE: I want to talk to you, Miss Wayne. May we come in?

BETTY: It's very late. I'm tired. I want to go to bed.

TEMPLE: Yes, I know it is, but – there's something I want to tell you.

BETTY: It'll have to wait. I'll see you tomorrow. I've got a hangover. I don't want to talk.

TEMPLE: I'll soon cure your hangover. Now come along. I want to talk to you.

BETTY: All right. You can come in for five minutes. That's all, just f-five minutes.

STEVE: (*Quietly; to TEMPLE*) I'm afraid you won't get much out of her, darling.

TEMPLE: Don't worry, she'll sober up.

The door closes.

BETTY: What'll you drink? Mrs Temple?

STEVE: Nothing for me, thank you.

BETTY: Nonsense! You must have a drink.

TEMPLE: I'd like a glass of soda water.

BETTY: What? Just p-plain soda?

TEMPLE: That's all.

BETTY: (*A shrug*) Everybody to their taste.

BETTY picks up and uses a soda syphon.

TEMPLE: Fill it up. Right up … No, right up … That's it …

BETTY: Here we go … Careful you don't spill it.

TEMPLE: Thank you.

BETTY: Now I'll have a little gin and …

TEMPLE: (*Quietly; interrupting BETTY*) Miss Wayne …

BETTY: (*Turning*) Yes?

TEMPLE: Look at me …

BETTY: What?

TEMPLE: I said: look at me …

BETTY: I am looking at …

As BETTY speaks TEMPLE throws the contents of the glass straight into her face, there is a splash.

STEVE and BETTY stagger back gasping for breath.

BETTY: (*Intensely angry*) You fool! You stupid, ignorant fool! You've ruined this dress; you've completely ruined …

TEMPLE: (*With authority*) Sit down, Miss Wayne – and drop the act! You're as sober as a judge.

BETTY: Get out of here! Do you hear what I say – get out of here!

TEMPLE: Pass me that syphon, Steve.

STEVE: (*Taken aback*) What?

TEMPLE: You heard, darling. Pass the syphon …

BETTY: (*Furious*) You wouldn't have the nerve to squirt that at me!

TEMPLE: (*A definite threat*) Wouldn't I? (*A definite pause*) Miss Wayne … What did you mean when you said – "Whatever happens – don't go down to Reading" …

BETTY: I – I don't know what you're talking about.

TEMPLE: You know what I'm talking about. You made that statement while we were dancing. I think you meant it as some sort of a warning, but I'm not sure …

BETTY: (*Near to tears; a shade frightened*) I tell you I don't know what you're talking about! I don't remember dancing. I was tight. I don't remember what I said, I ... (*Despondently*) Mr Temple, leave me alone ... For God's sake, leave me alone ...

TEMPLE: (*Standing over BETTY; with authority*) Miss Wayne, in five days' time Howard Gilbert goes to the scaffold for the murder of Brenda Stirling. I don't think he committed that murder and I don't think you think so either.

BETTY: I don't know anything about it. I don't know why you're asking me these questions. Just because Brenda Stirling worked in my department it doesn't mean to say that I was a friend of hers or that I even knew what sort of a person she was.

TEMPLE: What sort of a person is Mr Reynolds?

BETTY: What do you mean?

TEMPLE: He's a friend of yours, isn't he? We've seen you with him often enough.

BETTY: (*Tensely*) What has Lance got to do with Brenda Stirling?

TEMPLE: He shared a flat with Howard Gilbert; he brought me a letter addressed to Gilbert from a gentleman named Fairfax.

BETTY: I don't know what you're talking about. (*Distressed*) Please, Mr Temple, leave me alone. I'm tired and terribly worried and I want to go to bed.

TEMPLE: What are you worried about?

BETTY: (*In tears*) Mr Temple, please!

STEVE: (*Softly; to TEMPLE*) Don't ask her any more questions, Paul. Darling, don't ...

TEMPLE: (*Quietly*) All right. Are you ready, Steve?

STEVE: Yes ...

TEMPLE: (*Turning*) Miss Wayne, earlier this evening when you said – "Whatever happens don't go down to Reading". I think you were trying to warn me against something. Now, for some reason or other, you've changed your mind. I'm going to give you a warning too, Miss Wayne. Be careful what you say in this flat.

BETTY: (*Puzzled*) What do you mean?

TEMPLE: Have you ever seen the gentleman who occupies the flat immediately above this?

BETTY: Mr Svenson?

STEVE: No, Mr and Mrs Svenson are away. They've let the flat to a man called Williams.

TEMPLE: And Mr Williams, for your information, happens to be Wilfrid Stirling.

BETTY: (*Tensely*) I don't believe it! You're lying! You're saying that because …

TEMPLE: Ask the porter! Ask him to describe Mr Williams.

BETTY: (*Frightened*) Is this true, Mrs Temple?

STEVE: Yes.

BETTY: (*Softly*) But I can hardly believe it, why – (*She pauses, then, tensely*) What did you mean just now when you said "Be careful what you say in this flat?"

TEMPLE: The flat's been wired. Stirling's been listening in to your conversations. (*Quietly; watching BETTY*) That's why he took the flat above you, Miss Wayne.

STEVE: (*Suddenly*) Paul, look out! Look out, she's fainted!

Dramatic FADE IN of music.

FADE DOWN of music.
FADE DOWN music completely.

STEVE: Have you finished in the bathroom, Paul?

TEMPLE: Yes.

STEVE: What time is it?

TEMPLE: It's about a quarter to two. Are you tired?

STEVE: Well, I'm tired, darling – but I don't feel sleepy.

TEMPLE: You'd better read for a little while.

STEVE: Yes. (*A moment*) Paul, do you think she'll be all right?

TEMPLE: Who – Miss Wayne?

STEVE: Yes. She seemed awfully pale when we left.

TEMPLE: She'll be all right. I'm putting my money on Miss Wayne.

The telephone begins to ring.

TEMPLE: I'm pretty sure that sooner or later she'll … Now who the devil is that?

STEVE: Shall I take it?

TEMPLE: No, it's all right, Steve – I'll take it. (*He lifts the receiver*) Hello?

STIRLING: (*On the other end of the line*) Hello – Paul Temple?

TEMPLE: Speaking …

STIRLING: (*A shade excited*) Oh, this is Wilfrid Stirling. I'm sorry to disturb you at this time of night, Mr Temple, but I've just had a reporter on the telephone. He told me there's a rumour that Howard's been granted a reprieve. Is that true?

TEMPLE: No … No, I don't think so.

STIRLING: (*Disappointed*) Oh. Then – there isn't any news?

TEMPLE: Not yet, Mr Stirling. There may be a stay of execution – we shall just have to wait and see.

STIRLING: I'm sorry to have bothered you, Mr Temple, only the fellow seemed pretty definite.

TEMPLE: That's all right. While you're on the phone, Mr Stirling, there's something I want to ask you. Did your daughter ever go to a club called La Martella?

STIRLING: I think you've asked me that once before, Mr Temple. She went out quite a bit, of course, but whether she went to this La Mar – what did you call it?

TEMPLE: La Martella.

STIRLING: I wouldn't know.

TEMPLE: I see. Well, goodnight, Mr Stirling.

STIRLING: Goodnight, sir. And again, I'm sorry to have disturbed you.

TEMPLE: That's all right.

TEMPLE replaces the receiver.

STEVE: Was that Stirling?

TEMPLE: (*Thoughtfully*) Yes.

STEVE: Well, what did he want?

TEMPLE: Apparently a reporter telephoned him; there's been a rumour that Gilbert's been reprieved.

STEVE: Do you think it's true?

TEMPLE: No. No, if it were true Sir Graham would know and he'd have contacted me. Besides, there isn't enough evidence to reprieve Gilbert, not yet at any rate.

STEVE: Paul …

TEMPLE: Yes? …

STEVE: I've been thinking about that story Lynn Ferguson told us. You know, it's rather curious that the person who asked her all those questions deliberately went out of his way to … (*She stops*)

TEMPLE: What is it?

STEVE: Didn't you hear anything?

TEMPLE: No.

STEVE: There's someone outside on the landing …

TEMPLE: Nonsense!

STEVE: Darling, there is, I …

There is a knock on the door.

STEVE: There we are – I told you!

TEMPLE: (*Calling*) Who is it?

CHARLIE: (*From outside the bedroom*) It's me, sir. Charlie.

TEMPLE: (*Calling*) Come in, Charlie!

The door opens.

STEVE: What is it, Charlie? What's the matter?

CHARLIE: There's a Mr Fabian to see you, sir.

TEMPLE: What – at this hour?

CHARLIE: Yes, sir. He says it's very important.

STEVE: But I never heard the front door bell, Charlie.

CHARLIE: It only rang once, madam. I went down to get a glass of milk just as he rang it.

TEMPLE: Where is he now?

CHARLIE: I put him in the drawing room, sir. He isn't 'alf in a tither about something. I wouldn't have asked him in, sir, only I knew you knew 'im and I didn't want 'im to think …

TEMPLE: That's all right, Charlie.

STEVE: You say he's rather het up about something?

CHARLIE: Blimey, not 'alf!

STEVE: Well, make some coffee and bring it into the drawing room.

CHARLIE: Oke – Yes, Mrs Temple.

START FADE.

TEMPLE: There's no need for you to come down, Steve.

STEVE: I know – but I'm coming.

CONTINUE FADE.

COMPLETE FADE.

FADE IN of LOUIS FABIAN; his manner is tense and slightly overwrought.

FABIAN: … I shall make a definite complaint to the Commissioner. He'd no right to ask me those questions. His manner was aggressive, his whole demeanour was most, most unpleasant.

TEMPLE: Yes, I appreciate that, Fabian, on the other hand the Inspector was only doing his duty.

FABIAN: Was it his duty to go on asking me the same questions over and over again when I'd already given him an answer? If you want my frank opinion the police want a scapegoat for the affair and they've picked on me.

TEMPLE: Nonsense!

FABIAN: Then why did he go on asking me those questions?

TEMPLE: Because the people who kidnapped Miss Ferguson appear to be chiefly interested in her reasons for visiting the club. Indeed, we suspect that's why she was abducted in the first place.

FABIAN: To find out why Scotland Yard were investigating La Martella?

TEMPLE: Yes.

FABIAN: But I'm the only person who would be curious about that, Temple.

TEMPLE: Exactly. Now you know why the Inspector asked you so many questions.

STEVE: Mr Fabian, was that your only reason for coming here at this hour of the morning – to complain about Inspector Kingston?

FABIAN: No. No, I saw your husband this afternoon, Mrs Temple. He asked me questions about a lady called Mrs Talbot.

STEVE: Go on …

FABIAN: I told him that I'd never seen Mrs Talbot and that as far as I knew she had never been to the Club.

TEMPLE: Well?

FABIAN: That was a lie. Mrs Talbot came to La Martella seven weeks ago. She had an appointment with Betty Wayne.

TEMPLE: (*Facing FABIAN*) Why didn't you admit that this afternoon?

FABIAN: I couldn't …

TEMPLE: Why not?

A pause.

FABIAN: (*Slowly*) A great many things have happened since this afternoon. May I – have a cigarette?

TEMPLE: Help yourself.

A pause.

FABIAN: Mr Temple, after I left the Club tonight, I made a call to an old associate of mine. (*A smile*) You'll note I used the word associate – not friend.

TEMPLE: Go on …

FABIAN: His name is Westerman. He was a friend of Mrs Talbot. In fact it was through Westerman that she visited La Martella …

TEMPLE: Go on …

FABIAN: For a consideration Westerman is prepared to tell you all about Mrs Talbot and her association with Betty Wayne. He might even be persuaded to tell you about other things, Mr Temple.

TEMPLE: What does your 'associate' call a consideration?

FABIAN: You'll have to discuss that with him yourself. I've taken the liberty of making an appointment for you.

TEMPLE: For when?

FABIAN: Tomorrow night, at ten o'clock. Is that convenient?

TEMPLE: Yes, that's convenient. At your flat, or La Martella?

FABIAN: I'm afraid you'll have to go out of town, Mr Temple. Down to Reading …

Dramatic FADE IN of closing music.

END OF EPISODE SIX

EPISODE SEVEN

THE NOTE

OPEN TO:

FABIAN: (*Slowly*) Mr Temple, after I left the Club tonight, I made a call to an old associate of mine. (*A smile*) You'll note I used the word associate – not friend.

TEMPLE: Go on …

FABIAN: His name is Westerman. He was a friend of Mrs Talbot. In fact it was through Westerman that she visited La Martella …

TEMPLE: Go on …

FABIAN: For a consideration Westerman is prepared to tell you all about Mrs Talbot and her association with Betty Wayne. He might even be persuaded to tell you about other things, Mr Temple.

TEMPLE: What does your 'associate' call a consideration?

FABIAN: You'll have to discuss that with him yourself. I've taken the liberty of making an appointment for you.

TEMPLE: For when?

FABIAN: Tomorrow night, at ten o'clock. Is that convenient?

TEMPLE: Yes, that's convenient. At your flat, or La Martella?

FABIAN: I'm afraid you'll have to go out of town, Mr Temple. Down to Reading …

TEMPLE: Why down to Reading – can't your friend manage to get up to London for an hour or so? Surely, it would be more convenient …

FABIAN: I suggested that, of course, but – he won't hear of it.

TEMPLE: All right – give me the address.

FABIAN: There's no necessity for that. I'll drive you down.

TEMPLE: All right; pick me up just before nine …

FABIAN: There's just one point, Mr Temple. Please don't say anything about this to anyone else, especially Sir Graham Forbes.

TEMPLE: Fabian, when I asked you about Mrs Talbot this afternoon you said you knew nothing about her, now you admit, quite frankly, that you were lying. Were you lying about Mr Hamilton?

FABIAN: (*Tensely*) No, I've told you, I've never heard of anyone called Hamilton.

TEMPLE: What about this Mr Westerman? Has he heard of him?

FABIAN: I don't know – you'll have to ask him that yourself.

STEVE: You described this man Westerman as an associate; do you mean he's in business with you?

FABIAN: He was; but I called him an associate, Mrs Temple, because – I don't want you to think that he's a friend of mine.

TEMPLE: (*Quietly*) Is Westerman blackmailing you?

FABIAN: (*A moment*) Yes …

TEMPLE: For money?

FABIAN: No … Three years ago I was in partnership with Westerman. We had, well – an agency business. One day we had a row and decided to split up. Eighteen months later I went into business on my own account and opened La Martella.

TEMPLE: Go on, Fabian …

FABIAN: About a year after the club opened I had a letter from Westerman asking me to go down to Reading. When I saw him he told me that he wanted to make certain of his friends memberships of La Martella. Two of them had

	actually applied for membership and I had turned them down.
STEVE:	Why?
FABIAN:	Because when you run a successful nightclub, Mrs Temple, you have to be very careful of your clientele. If you get the wrong people you can lose your business over night. Well – to cut a long story short, for certain reasons, I had to do what Westerman wanted. Mrs Talbot was made a member, so was Betty Wayne, so was Brenda Stirling and a girl called June Michael.
TEMPLE:	I see.
STEVE:	And what about Mr Reynolds?
FABIAN:	Reynolds?
STEVE:	Was he a friend of Westerman's?
FABIAN:	Oh, no. Lance Reynolds is one of our original members; I told you that the other night. In any case, one can't object to Reynolds, surely – he's a gent.
STEVE:	On what grounds would you object to Betty Wayne?
FABIAN:	Well, Miss Wayne drinks too much …
STEVE:	Isn't that good for business?
FABIAN:	Up to a point.
STEVE:	And Miss Wayne goes beyond that point?
FABIAN:	Sometimes.
TEMPLE:	Was Howard Gilbert one of your members?
FABIAN:	No, but he came to the club once or twice.
TEMPLE:	With Reynolds or Miss Stirling?
FABIAN:	I believe Reynolds – I'm not sure.
STEVE:	Mr Fabian, you don't think Westerman is using your club as a sort of headquarters? I mean, if he was mixed up with Mrs Talbot …

FABIAN: (*Interrupting STEVE; jumping at the idea*) That's exactly what I wondered, Mrs Temple. I also wondered whether Westerman was responsible for the abduction of Miss Ferguson.

TEMPLE: Who told you that Miss Ferguson was attached to Scotland Yard?

FABIAN: Westerman did. He telephoned me about a week ago. He said – "I don't know whether you know it, Louis, but the police have got their eye on your place. It's a youngster called Ferguson."

TEMPLE: And you believed him?

FABIAN: His information's usually pretty good, Mr Temple, especially where the police are concerned.

STEVE: Mr Fabian, what exactly was your business with Westerman?

FABIAN: I told you. We had an agency.

STEVE: Yes, but what kind of an agency?

FABIAN: We – bought and sold things.

STEVE: What sort of things?

FABIAN: Practically anything …

TEMPLE: I see.

FABIAN: (*Resentfully*) But there's nothing crooked about La Martella, Mr Temple. Believe me, that's a perfectly legitimate business.

TEMPLE: When you were mixed up with Westerman – did you deal in drugs at all?

FABIAN: (*Shocked*) Good God, no! Whatever makes you ask that?

TEMPLE: Because that's why Miss Ferguson was watching La Martella. Scotland Yard were under the impression that your club was being used as a distribution centre.

FABIAN: (*Amazed*) For drugs?

TEMPLE: Yes.

FABIAN: But that's absurd! Why on earth should they think that?

TEMPLE: I don't know, Mr Fabian. But they did. (*Dismissing FABIAN*) Well – it must be nearly two o'clock, so unless …

FABIAN: Yes, of course. I'm sorry. I didn't realise it was that late. I'll see you tonight, Mr Temple.

TEMPLE: Yes.

START FADE.

FABIAN: Nine o'clock.

TEMPLE: Nine o'clock.

FADE SCENE.

FADE IN of STEVE.

STEVE: Would you like some more coffee?

TEMPLE: Yes, I think I would. Thank you, Steve.

STEVE: It's funny, I don't feel a bit sleepy now.

TEMPLE: No, neither do I. I was just thinking, Steve. If I'd taken no notice of Stirling and we'd gone on that holiday we should probably have been in Paris by now.

STEVE: (*A sigh*) Yes …

TEMPLE: Or Dijon …

STEVE: Ah, Dijon!

TEMPLE: Now what should I remember about Dijon?

STEVE: (*Amused*) You remember – my nylons and the gentleman with a grey moustache.

TEMPLE: Oh, yes. He was mustard.

STEVE: Darling, please …

TEMPLE: Dijon, Steve. Mustard …

STEVE: Yes, dear – the old lady saw the joke.

TEMPLE laughs.

TEMPLE: By Timothy, this is jolly good coffee.

STEVE: (*Amused*) It was meant for Mr Fabian.

TEMPLE: Well, in that case I'm glad I got rid of him.

STEVE: (*After a moment*) Paul, did you believe that story of his?

TEMPLE: You mean – about Westerman?

STEVE: Yes.

TEMPLE: Did you?

STEVE: I'm – rather dubious.

TEMPLE: Rather dubious? (*Laughing*) What's happened to that good old intuition of yours?

STEVE: What do you mean?

TEMPLE: It was a pack of lies from start to finish. There isn't a Mr Westerman – there never has been a Mr Westerman.

STEVE: Are you sure?

TEMPLE: Of course I'm sure.

STEVE: Paul, I know you hate to be asked pointed questions, especially at this stage, but …

TEMPLE: You fire ahead, Steve. Ask me anything you like. I'm in a very good mood tonight.

STEVE: You certainly are. Well, do you think Fabian is the man we're looking for?

TEMPLE: (*Politely; pulling STEVE's leg*) The man you're looking for, darling, or the man I'm looking for?

STEVE: You know perfectly well what I mean! Is Fabian Mr Hamilton?

TEMPLE: Ah! That's a pretty pointed question.

STEVE: Well, I told you I was going to ask pointed questions!

TEMPLE: That's quite right, darling, you did.

STEVE: Look, Paul – who murdered Brenda Stirling? Was it Howard Gilbert or someone else?

TEMPLE: (*Quietly*) Someone else …

STEVE: Are you sure?

TEMPLE: (*Seriously*) Yes, I'm sure …

STEVE: Do you know who it was?

TEMPLE: (*After a moment*) Yes.

STEVE: Did the same person murder Mrs Talbot?

TEMPLE: Yes …

STEVE: (*Slowly; watching him*) That visit we made to the reference library was – quite a lucky break, wasn't it?

TEMPLE: Quite a lucky break. Pass the sugar, dear.

STEVE: (*Quietly; almost a shade frightened*) Paul … I think I know who it is …

TEMPLE: Do you, Steve?

STEVE: Yes …

TEMPLE: (*Slowly; watching STEVE*) Are you sure?

STEVE: Yes, I'm pretty sure.

TEMPLE: I wonder …

STEVE: (*Quietly*) What are you going to do next, darling?

TEMPLE: I'm not sure. But I know what I'm not going to do.

STEVE: What's that?

TEMPLE: I'm not going down to Reading.

FADE IN of music.

FADE DOWN of music.

FADE IN the sound of a typewriter.

A door opens and the typewriter stops.

STEVE: The Inspector's here, Paul. He wants to have a word with you.

TEMPLE: Yes, all right, Steve. Where's Charlie?

STEVE: He's in the kitchen – why?

TEMPLE: I want to see him for a moment. Oh, and Steve …

STEVE: Yes?

TEMPLE: I wonder if you'd do something for me, darling?

STEVE: What is it?

TEMPLE: I've written Miss Wayne a note. I want to make certain that she gets it some time today. Would you take it down to Conway and Racys?

STEVE: (*Surprised*) What – now?

TEMPLE: Yes, it's pretty urgent.

STEVE: Well, why can't Charlie take it?

TEMPLE: Because he doesn't know Miss Wayne and I want to be absolutely certain that it's handed to the right person.

STEVE: (*Puzzled*) Well – why don't you telephone her?

TEMPLE: Because I've written a note, darling. Here we are …

STEVE: (*Puzzled*) Yes, all right. I've got to do some shopping anyway.

TEMPLE: Don't wait for a reply, Steve – just say it's from me and that it's very urgent.

STEVE: All right. I'll be back sometime this afternoon … Probably about five …

TEMPLE: (*Stopping STEVE*) Oh, and Steve …

STEVE: (*Turning*) Yes?

TEMPLE: Keep out of the hat department.

STEVE laughs,
START FADE.

STEVE: (*Calling at the doorway*) Charlie! Charlie! Mr Temple wants you! He's in the study.

COMPLETE FADE.

FADE UP of a door opening and closing.

TEMPLE: Good morning, Inspector. Sorry to have kept you waiting.

KINGSTON: Oh, good morning, Mr Temple.

TEMPLE: Sit down, Inspector. Would you care for a drink?

KINGSTON: (*Sitting down*) No, thank you, sir. I've been having a talk with Miss Ferguson and there are one or two details I'd like to check, Mr Temple.

TEMPLE: For instance?

KINGSTON: Were you and Mrs Temple actually here when Miss Ferguson arrived?

TEMPLE: No, we turned up shortly afterwards. Charlie – my man – was going out and when he opened the door Miss Ferguson was on the doorstep.

KINGSTON: Did she say anything?

TEMPLE: Well – I believe she asked for me. She was in a pretty bad way you know.

KINGSTON: Yes, so I understand.

TEMPLE: How is she this morning, by the way?

KINGSTON: Oh, very much better. (*Irritated*) I need hardly tell you I take rather a dim view of this Ferguson episode, Mr Temple.

TEMPLE: Yes, I rather thought you would.

KINGSTON: If I'd known that Miss Ferguson had been instructed to watch La Martella I should never have gone near the place.

TEMPLE: Of course, it's no business of mine, Inspector, but Miss Ferguson's investigations had nothing whatever to do with the Gilbert case.

KINGSTON: How do you know?

TEMPLE: Sir Graham told me. Miss Ferguson was watching La Martella because the Special Branch were under the impression that the club was being used as a distribution centre for narcotics.

KINGSTON: And you think that's got nothing to do with the Gilbert case?

TEMPLE: Well, has it?

KINGSTON: In my opinion, yes.

TEMPLE: That's interesting, Inspector.

KINGSTON: Mr Temple, look – when Brenda Stirling was murdered her shoe was missing. Correct?

TEMPLE: Correct.

KINGSTON: When Mrs Talbot was murdered her shoe was missing too …

TEMPLE: Correct.

KINGSTON: Now in my opinion both these women were carrying a supply of narcotics. And, it's my bet …

TEMPLE: That the stuff was concealed in the shoe; probably in the heel?

KINGSTON: Yes …

TEMPLE: M'm. But, Inspector, I don't know whether Sir Graham told you what happened to Miss Ferguson.

KINGSTON: (*With sarcasm*) Yes, he did finally decide to confide in me.

TEMPLE: Well, Miss Ferguson was abducted and put through what was tantamount to a third degree. Her captors apparently were interested in why she was paying such frequent visits to La Martella. When she finally broke down and told them that she was investigating a possible drug smuggling organisation they completely lost interest in her and she was released.

KINGSTON: And what does that prove?

TEMPLE: Well, surely it proves that once they got the truth out of Miss Ferguson – that she was

	investigating the drug racket – they were no longer interested in her.
KINGSTON:	Couldn't that have been a blind?
TEMPLE:	What do you mean?
KINGSTON:	I mean – isn't it possible that you're thinking exactly what they want you to think? They question Miss Ferguson about her activities, they learn that she's investigating a possible traffic in drugs and they profess to be completely disinterested.
TEMPLE:	(*Thoughtfully*) Yes, I see what you mean …
KINGSTON:	It adds up, Mr Temple. They release the girl, knowing perfectly well that she's convinced that they have nothing whatever to do with the drug traffic and then ten to one …
TEMPLE:	She'll convince us …
KINGSTON:	Exactly.
TEMPLE:	(*Thoughtfully*) It's quite an idea, Inspector.
KINGSTON:	Oh, we do get ideas occasionally, Mr Temple.

TEMPLE laughs.

TEMPLE:	Well, let's take your theory a step further. How does Fabian fit into the picture?
KINGSTON:	Well, if I'm right Fabian's the head of the whole outfit.
TEMPLE:	And he murdered Brenda Stirling?
KINGSTON:	No, I wouldn't say that. After all, Gilbert was friendly with the Stirling girl – he was engaged to her – so it's possible he was also an associate of Fabian's.
TEMPLE:	And actually did commit the murder?
KINGSTON:	Yes.
TEMPLE:	Then how do you account for that statement – the one that Galino made?

KINGSTON: I can't account for it; on the other hand he now says that Mrs Talbot wasn't with him the night Brenda Stirling was murdered. I'm afraid which ever way you look at it he's a pretty unreliable witness.

TEMPLE: I don't know. He must have been considered a pretty important one otherwise he wouldn't have been beaten up.

KINGSTON: Yes, that's true. And it's only since he was beaten up that he's changed his mind.

TEMPLE: Exactly. (*Changing the subject; almost abruptly*) Inspector, forgive my asking, but – are you a married man by any chance?

KINGSTON: (*Smiling; a shade surprised*) Why, no, sir. I'm a bachelor. Why do you ask?

TEMPLE: (*Vaguely*) I – wondered, that's all.

KINGSTON: You must have had a reason for asking a question like that.

TEMPLE: Yes … I had a reason.

KINGSTON: Well?

TEMPLE: (*After a moment; facing KINGSTON*) I think it's possible that your life is in danger.

KINGSTON: Why do you say that – because of what happened to Miss Ferguson?

TEMPLE: Partly – and partly because of what happened to my wife and me in Darlington Street.

KINGSTON: Oh, yes – your car was shot to pieces.

TEMPLE: That's right.

KINGSTON: Well, if I'm in danger, it's all part of the job. There's nothing I can do about it.

TEMPLE: On the contrary …

KINGSTON: What do you mean?

TEMPLE: You can be on your guard, Inspector. Don't accept invitations, especially on the spur of the moment.

KINGSTON: (*Puzzled*) I'm afraid I don't understand you.

TEMPLE: Fabian came here last night and told me that a man called Westerman could give me vital information about Mrs Talbot and the murder of Brenda Stirling.

KINGSTON: Westerman? He's a new character. I've never heard of him.

TEMPLE: No, I don't expect you have. According to Fabian he lives at Reading. Fabian suggested that we went out there this evening. I accepted the invitation but I haven't the slightest intention of going.

KINGSTON: Why not?

TEMPLE: Because I'm convinced that Westerman doesn't exist, and the whole thing is a trap.

KINGSTON: Have you any reason for thinking that? Did someone warn you?

TEMPLE: Yes – and I'm warning you, Inspector. Don't accept any invitations – particularly from Louis Fabian.

KINGSTON: But if you don't keep the appointment, Mr Temple, he's hardly likely to come to me with precisely the same story.

TEMPLE: On the contrary, I think that's exactly what he'll do, and that's why I'm warning you. Don't you see, if he thinks I'm suspicious he daren't let the matter drop; he'll have to pursue it otherwise it would look more suspicious than ever.

The telephone rings.

KINGSTON: (*Thoughtfully*) Yes …

203

TEMPLE: Excuse me … (*Picking up the receiver; on the phone*) Hello? … Yes, Paul Temple speaking … (*Quietly; confidentially*) Oh, hello, Reynolds … Yes … Yes, he did as a matter of fact … Yes, last night, or rather this morning … No, of course I'm not … Yes … Thank you … Yes, I'll do that … Goodbye.

TEMPLE replaces the receiver.

KINGSTON: Was that Lance Reynolds?

TEMPLE: Yes.

KINGSTON: The fellow's a confounded nuisance; hardly a day passes without him ringing Scotland Yard. My secretary's fed up to the teeth with him.

TEMPLE: Yes, I'll bet she is. Still, if I'm ever accused of murder I hope I have a friend like Reynolds.

KINGSTON: What do you mean?

TEMPLE: Well, he's certainly standing by Howard Gilbert.

KINGSTON: Yes, but he doesn't think Gilbert did it.

TEMPLE: A lot of people don't, but they're not doing anything about it.

KINGSTON: By golly, I wouldn't say that! If you ask me there are too many people interfering in this case. Reynolds, Stirling, Miss Ferguson …

TEMPLE: Paul Temple …

KINGSTON: (*With a cold smile*) Well, you said it, sir. (*Relenting slightly*) No, I'm very grateful for any help you can give us, Mr Temple. I'm a little annoyed about Miss Ferguson because, quite frankly, I think Sir Graham ought to have taken me into his confidence before.

204

However, I suppose, strictly speaking, she wasn't working on the Gilbert case …

TEMPLE: No, of course she wasn't.

KINGSTON: (*Rising*) Well, I'll be making a move …

TEMPLE: Oh, by the way, Inspector. I meant to ask you. When you first described Lance Reynolds to me you said he was about forty-five or six, had private means, was interested in the ladies, and was a very keen photographer.

KINGSTON: Yes.

TEMPLE: How did you know he was a keen photographer?

KINGSTON: Have you ever been to his flat?

TEMPLE: No.

KINGSTON: He's got photographs all over the place. I should think he must have taken thousands of them …

TEMPLE: M'm. Does he develop them himself, do you know?

KINGSTON: I haven't the slightest idea. I should imagine so. Why do you ask?

TEMPLE: I wondered, that's all. Well, thanks for dropping in, Inspector. Let me know how Miss Ferguson gets on.

KINGSTON: Yes, I will indeed, sir.

START FADE.

TEMPLE: Oh – and if you do get an invitation from Mr Fabian …

KINGSTON: Don't worry. Forewarned is forearmed, sir.

COMPLETE FADE.

Slow FADE UP the noise of a typewriter.
The typewriter stops.

We hear the sound of TEMPLE taking a drink from a cup of tea.

A door opens.

CHARLIE: Did you ring, sir?

TEMPLE: Yes. I don't think much of this tea, Charlie. What did you put in it?

CHARLIE: Oh, just the usual, sir.

TEMPLE: M'm – well, it's not very good.

CHARLIE: (*A little hurt*) I usually make a nice cup of tea, sir.

TEMPLE: I'm glad you think so. Is Mrs Temple back yet?

CHARLIE: No, sir.

TEMPLE: She's very late.

CHARLIE: It's just after six, sir.

In the background we hear the sound of the front door opening and closing.

STEVE enters the house.

TEMPLE: Yes, I know, but she said she'd be back by … Oh, here she is!

The door opens.

TEMPLE: Hello, Steve! I was just beginning to wonder what on earth … (*He stops*) Darling, what is it? What's the matter?

STEVE: It's all right, Paul. I've been in a motor car accident, I – Oh, is that a cup of tea?

TEMPLE: Yes …

STEVE: Darling, lead me to it!

CHARLIE: It's okay, Mrs Temple, I'll see to it.

CHARLIE pours the tea during the following dialogue.

TEMPLE: Steve, are you all right?

STEVE: Yes, I'm all right, Paul. I've been pretty badly shaken, that's all.

TEMPLE: But what happened? Were you in a taxi?

STEVE:	No, I accepted a lift from someone and … (*Taking the tea*) Oh, thank you, Charlie. (*She drinks; a moment*) Oh, this is heaven!
CHARLIE:	Would you like something stronger, Mrs Temple – perhaps a drop of brandy or …
STEVE:	No, no, this is lovely, Charlie. (*Relaxing in a chair*) What a heavenly cup of tea.
CHARLIE:	(*Pleased*) Thank you, Mrs Temple.
STEVE:	(*Entranced*) You do make a wonderful cup of tea, Charlie.
CHARLIE:	(*Preening himself*) Well, I've always thought so, Mrs Temple. Still, it's nice to be told. (*To TEMPLE*) Would you care for another cup, sir?
TEMPLE:	No, thank you, Charlie. That'll be all …
CHARLIE:	Yes, sir.

CHARLIE goes out.

TEMPLE:	Are you feeling better now?
STEVE:	Yes.
TEMPLE:	What happened?
STEVE:	Well, I suppose I'd better start at the beginning.
TEMPLE:	(*Quickly; intensely curious*) No, no, you said you accepted a lift from someone.
STEVE:	Yes.
TEMPLE:	Who was it?
STEVE:	Mr Reynolds.
TEMPLE:	(*Surprised*) Reynolds?
STEVE:	Yes.
TEMPLE:	(*Quickly*) But what on earth made you accept a lift …
STEVE:	(*A little laugh*) Darling, don't you think I'd better start at the beginning?
TEMPLE:	All right. Go on, Steve.

STEVE:	Well, this morning, when I arrived at Conway and Racys, the first person I saw was Betty Wayne. She was just getting into the lift to go up to one of the executive offices on the top floor. I got into the lift and travelled up with her.
TEMPLE:	Go on …
STEVE:	I said I had an important message for her and gave her your note. She opened the note, read it, and then put it in her handbag.
TEMPLE:	Did she say anything?
STEVE:	No, she never said a word.
TEMPLE:	Did she show you the note – or tell you what was in it?
STEVE:	No, but whatever it was it certainly took her by surprise …
TEMPLE:	You mean she was shaken?
STEVE:	Yes, very badly shaken I would say. She dropped her handbag twice and got out of the lift without saying goodbye or good morning or anything. Anyway, after I'd delivered the note I went downstairs, through the hat department …
TEMPLE:	That was very restrained of you, darling …
STEVE:	… And into the lingerie …
TEMPLE:	Oh!
STEVE:	I stayed there until about half-past twelve and then I went into the restaurant. I left the restaurant at about a quarter to two and bumped, I mean literally bumped, into Lance Reynolds. We chatted for a few moments then I went up to the library and changed the library books. I suppose I must have stayed there until about half past two …

TEMPLE: Go on, Steve …
STEVE: Well, I had an appointment at half past two
                for a manicure so I took the lift and went up
                to the hairdressing department on the third
                floor. Getting out of the lift I bumped straight
                into Reynolds again.
TEMPLE: Was it deliberate? I mean, was he following
                you?
STEVE: No, I don't think so – not for a moment.
TEMPLE: Well, go on, Steve.
START FADE.
STEVE: They kept me waiting for the manicure and I
                didn't leave the hairdressing department until
                about half past three. I took the lift to the
                ground floor and the first person I saw when I
                got out of the lift was Lance Reynolds.
COMPLETE FADE.

FADE IN the sound of a descending lift.
*The lift stops and people pour out of it into the main hall of
the store.*
REYNOLDS: (*Laughing*) Hello, Mrs Temple! Are you
                following me or am I following you?
STEVE: It's beginning to look very suspicious!
REYNOLDS: I suppose if we'd arranged to meet we
                shouldn't have found each other.
STEVE: That's just about it.
REYNOLDS: Are you on your way home?
STEVE: Yes.
REYNOLDS: Can I offer you a lift?
STEVE: No, it's quite all right, I …
REYNOLDS: Have you got the car?
STEVE: (*Without thinking*) No, as a matter of fact I
                haven't.

REYNOLDS:	Well, you'll have the Dickens of a job getting a taxi at this time of the afternoon. Montepelier Square, isn't it?
STEVE:	Yes.
REYNOLDS:	I can drop you with the greatest of ease.
STEVE:	Well, if you're sure it's not taking you out of your way.
REYNOLDS:	No; it's a pleasure. I'm going out to Roehampton anyway. (*Excessively polite*) Let me take your parcels.
STEVE:	Oh – thank you.
REYNOLDS:	I'm rather glad we bumped into each other this afternoon, Mrs Temple.
STEVE:	Oh?
REYNOLDS:	Yes. The first time we met I had the feeling that we didn't quite – well, see eye to eye.
STEVE:	See eye to eye, Mr Reynolds? What about?
REYNOLDS:	Oh, nothing in particular. I just felt that you'd taken rather a dislike to me.
STEVE:	Well, that isn't quite the same thing. I frequently don't see 'eye to eye' with my husband but we certainly don't dislike each other.
REYNOLDS:	I'm afraid I've expressed myself rather badly, I – well, the fact of the matter is I was in rather a bad mood when I brought that letter to your house the other night. By the way, what happened about that letter – did your husband discuss it with Inspector Kingston?
STEVE:	Yes, I believe so.
REYNOLDS:	I know he discussed it with Howard Gilbert because I had a …
STEVE:	(*Quickly*) How do you know that?

REYNOLDS: (*Amused*) Because Howard wrote to me. We were very good friends you know, Mrs Temple. We still are.

STEVE: I see.

START FADE.

REYNOLDS: That letter seemed to me frightfully important. After all, the diary established the fact that Brenda did know someone called Fairfax.

STEVE: Yes.

REYNOLDS: Through here … My car's outside.

COMPLETE FADE.

FADE UP the sound of a car: it is travelling fairly slowly, in West End traffic.

During the following dialogue the car gets clear of the traffic and gathers speed.

STEVE: I think the traffic gets worse every day.

REYNOLDS: Yes. We'll soon be clear enough … Ah, here we are!

The car gathers speed and then settles down to a cruising speed.

STEVE: Did you see Miss Wayne this afternoon?

REYNOLDS: This morning. We had lunch together.

STEVE: Oh.

REYNOLDS: I gather you delivered a message to her from your husband.

STEVE: A note – yes.

REYNOLDS: Do you happen to know what was in that note?

STEVE: No, I'm afraid I don't. Didn't Miss Wayne tell you?

REYNOLDS: (*Amused*) Yes, as a matter of fact she did.

STEVE: Then why are you asking me?

REYNOLDS: (*Laughing*) I wasn't asking you; I simply wanted to know if you knew what was in the note.

STEVE: What was in it?

REYNOLDS: You'll have to ask your husband, Mrs Temple. (*Amused*) Incidentally, give him my regards when you see him and tell him I – gave you a lift home.

STEVE: (*Puzzled*) Yes, of course.

REYNOLDS: You know, it's curious how one can form a definite opinion of a person before meeting them. And then when you meet them you find that they're not – well, quite what you expected.

We hear the sound of an approaching car.

STEVE: Are you referring to my husband?

REYNOLDS: Yes. When I met your husband for the first time I was surprised to find that …

STEVE: (*Interrupting REYNOLDS*) There's a car passing you …

REYNOLDS: (*Casually*) Well, there's plenty of room … I was saying, when I met your husband for the first time …

STEVE: (*Quickly; frightened*) He's passing you on the inside! Look out!

REYNOLDS: (*Alarmed*) What?!

STEVE: Look out! He's passing you on the inside! Get over!!!

REYNOLDS: (*Angrily*) Why the stupid ass, he can't pass me on the inside! There isn't room!

STEVE: He is passing you!

REYNOLDS: Well, he shouldn't try to come on the inside like that, he'll force …

STEVE: Get over! Get over, Mr Reynolds! Quickly!!!

REYNOLDS: (*A shade frightened; almost losing control*) What on earth is he trying to do?

STEVE: Watch it! You're going for the kerb … Brake! For goodness sake brake! Brake!!!

There is the sudden screeching of brakes; the tearing noise of the car skidding on a dry road, the smashing of the radiator against a shop front; the crashing of glass; the excited voices and hysterical screams of pedestrians.

Against this can be heard the quick acceleration and departure of the other car.

REYNOLDS: (*Tensely; frightened*) Are you – all right, Mrs Temple?

STEVE: (*Breathless*) Yes, I think so …

REYNOLDS: I'm sorry about that, but – it wasn't … my … fault.

STEVE: No, of course it wasn't your fault. He tried to force you off the road …

REYNOLDS: What happened to the damn fool?

STEVE: He's disappeared. He made a pretty quick getaway.

REYNOLDS: Did you get his number?

STEVE: No, I'm afraid I didn't.

REYNOLDS: Was – it done deliberately, do you think?

STEVE: Well, it certainly looked very much like it.

FADE UP the background noises of general chatter and confusion.

REYNOLDS: Oh, Lord! Here's the strong arm of the law! Now for a confounded rigmarole. You'd better get out this side, Mrs Temple, it looks as if your door's jammed.

FADE UP the background noises and chatter.
FADE DOWN completely.

Slow FADE IN of STEVE talking to TEMPLE.

STEVE: After I'd made a statement I caught a cab and came straight back here.

TEMPLE: M'm.

STEVE: I must say Reynolds kept his temper awfully well; after all, the accident wasn't his fault.

TEMPLE: No; but from what you've told me I should imagine he could have avoided it.

STEVE: I don't know, Paul. I know he was talking at the time, but – well, quite frankly, I only spotted the car myself at the last minute.

TEMPLE: Did you see the driver?

STEVE: I saw him, but I certainly wouldn't recognise him again. It was an open car and he was wearing a scarf and a pair of sun glasses. Oddly enough I spotted the car at Hyde Park Corner but I didn't take any particular notice of it.

TEMPLE: He was probably tailing you.

STEVE: Yes, in view of what happened, I think he must have been. You know, I'm sure he did it deliberately, Paul, otherwise …

TEMPLE: He did it deliberately all right. Steve, you don't know how lucky you are!

The telephone starts ringing.

STEVE: I've got a pretty good idea. It was my side of the car that he very nearly … It's all right, I'll take it … (*She lifts the receiver*) It's probably Reynolds, he said he'd ring to see if I got home all right. (*On the phone*) Hello? …Yes … No, this is Mrs Temple speaking … (*Surprised*) Oh, hello, Miss Wayne … No, he's here now if you'd like to have a word with him.

STEVE hands over the phone to TEMPLE.

STEVE: It's Betty Wayne – she wants to talk to you. She sounds awfully het up about something …

TEMPLE: (*Smiling*) You surprise me. (*He takes the receiver; on the phone*) Hello, Miss Wayne … Yes … Yes, I know. I've just been hearing about it. My wife was with him … Didn't he tell you that? … No, just a coincidence … Yes, I think so too. The sooner the better … Do you want to come here or shall I … I see … All right, I'll be there in twenty minutes. Goodbye.

TEMPLE replaces the receiver.

TEMPLE: (*Quietly; delighted*) Apparently my note did the trick. I thought it would …

STEVE: (*Puzzled*) Paul, what's this all about? What was in that note?

TEMPLE: (*After a moment; looking at STEVE*) Would you like to see a copy of it?

STEVE: Yes.

TEMPLE: (*Opening a drawer*) Here we are …

A pause.

STEVE: (*After reading the note; staggered*) Why, Paul!

TEMPLE: (*Laughing*) Don't look so staggered, darling! (*Briskly*) Now I'm going to see Betty Wayne. Are you coming?

STEVE: Yes, all right. I won't be a moment …

TEMPLE: Don't be long dear, I want to get there as quickly as possible …

STEVE: Why? Is she going to talk?

TEMPLE: I hope so, Steve. I sincerely hope so.

FADE IN of music.

FADE DOWN of music.

FADE IN of BETTY WAYNE: she is slightly overwrought and obviously very worried.

BETTY: … But I don't understand how you knew the accident was going to happen, Mr Temple. When I

215

got your note I thought you were simply trying to convince me that ...

TEMPLE: (*Interrupting BETTY*) Miss Wayne, please! We've been here fifteen minutes and you haven't told me anything I don't already know. I don't want to be rude, but I'm a very busy man. If you don't intend to confide in me, please say so.

BETTY: (*Tensely*) What is it you want me to tell you?

TEMPLE: (*Quietly*) Don't you know?

STEVE: Who killed Brenda Stirling?

BETTY: (*Tensely; a shade frightened*) We can't talk here, you know perfectly well that ...

TEMPLE: Then why didn't you come to my house? I suggested it.

BETTY: (*A shade bewildered; distressed*) No, I didn't want to come to your house, I – I thought that if I did that I should only ... Oh, Mr Temple, I'm sorry to have dragged you here. I oughtn't to have telephoned you, I only did it because I thought ...

TEMPLE: You did it because you were desperate and you thought perhaps I could help you. Well, perhaps I can, Miss Wayne.

STEVE: You needn't worry about Stirling overhearing our conversation.

TEMPLE: He's not in his flat and I've told the porter to ring you the moment he arrives.

BETTY: I see. (*Suddenly; strained; tense*) All right ... All right, Mr Temple. Gilbert didn't murder Brenda Stirling. It's true that they went to the theatre that night; it's true that they had a row, but – that's not why she was murdered ...

TEMPLE: Go on ...

BETTY: It's a long story, I don't know where to begin, you see ... When Brenda Stirling first started to work

216

at Conway and Racys I … (*She starts to hesitate again*)

TEMPLE: Suppose we start with the Cordoba robbery, Miss Wayne?

BETTY: The Cordoba robbery?

TEMPLE: Yes …

BETTY: (*Surprised; softly*) Then – you know?

TEMPLE: I've suspected it for some little time, but I wasn't sure.

STEVE: (*Puzzled*) What do you mean, Paul – the Cordoba robbery?

TEMPLE: About a year ago a diamond pendant was stolen from a wealthy South American lady called Mrs Cordoba. You may remember the case; it was during Ascot week and she was staying at the Ritz. The pendant, which consisted of a cluster of rubies with three very large matching diamonds, was reputed to be worth nearly a quarter of a million dollars. The Yard investigated the case but the pendant was never recovered. Now you go on, Miss Wayne …

BETTY: Mrs Cordoba was a frequent visitor to Conway and Racys. I sold her literally dozens of dresses and on one occasion two mink coats …

STEVE: Two!

BETTY: (*Almost a smile*) Yes, I know it's unbelievable, Mrs Temple, but it's perfectly true. She used to think nothing of spending four or five hundred pounds on dresses, and I don't mean evening dresses – she used to buy those in Paris – I mean just summer frocks, cocktail dresses, accessories and that sort of thing. Well, one day she gave a party and she invited two or three of the girls from the store …

217

TEMPLE: Two or three?

BETTY: Brenda, June Michael and myself.

TEMPLE: Go on …

BETTY: We went to the party and thoroughly enjoyed ourselves. As a matter of fact, that's where I first met Louis Fabian and Lance Reynolds. (*Hesitantly*) It was also the first time I saw the pendant …

TEMPLE: (*Quietly*) Go on …

BETTY: The next morning, after the party, Brenda, June and I had a coffee together and naturally we talked about the party and the people we'd seen there. June said it was ridiculous that one person should have so much money and if someone decided to take Mrs Cordoba 'for a ride' – those were the exact words she used – she certainly wouldn't lose any sleep over it. Brenda and I laughed, naturally we thought it was just a joke …

STEVE: What sort of a person was June Michael?

BETTY: Well, she was an extremely good-looking girl and an excellent model, but she just had no idea of the value of money. Her salary was just over twelve pounds a week but …

STEVE: But she thought in terms of Goodwood and Ascot and Monte Carlo and St. Moritz …

BETTY: Yes, I'm afraid so, Mrs Temple. Well, about a week after the party at the Ritz, the Cordoba pendant was stolen. Naturally the papers were full of it; there was a great deal of fuss and we – that is Brenda, June and myself – were pretty excited. We felt that having actually met Mrs Cordoba and seen the pendant we were part of the whole thing. Then one day, I think it was about a fortnight after the robbery, June was taken ill. We never did

218

discover what was the matter with her but when she returned to the store she'd obviously lost weight and she looked as if she'd had a pretty bad time of it.

TEMPLE: (*Quietly*) Go on, Miss Wayne ...

BETTY: I asked her what had been the matter with her and she said that she'd caught a germ of some sort and that she'd also been very distressed by the sudden death of a close friend. This was obviously true because she looked like a person who had been crying a great deal. Brenda asked her who the friend was but she didn't tell us. Well, she began to get better and was soon her old self again. Well – I say she was herself; actually she looked a hundred per cent but she was inclined to be a little more independent than usual and there were times when she'd suddenly get quite impudent, arrogant almost. On one occasion I had no alternative but to report her to the General Manager.

TEMPLE: Go on ...

BETTY: Naturally, she was extremely annoyed about this and for several days we never spoke to each other. Then one evening about a week after this particular incident, June asked me round to her flat. We'd always been pretty good friends and I was rather glad that she'd decided to – well, bury the hatchet. When I arrived at the flat I was surprised to find that she'd prepared quite an elaborate dinner; there were cocktails and liqueurs and a man servant was busying himself in the kitchen. The whole set-up seemed to me strangely luxurious. June herself looked resplendent; she was wearing a heavenly dress. Anyway, it was perfectly obvious that she wanted to be friends;

she threw her arms round me and – well, we both agreed we'd been acting like a couple of silly school girls. After dinner – there were just the two of us, by the way – June made a brief reference to her friend.

TEMPLE: The one that had died?

BETTY: Yes. She said that he'd been a fairly wealthy stockbroker and that he'd left her three thousand pounds. I said three thousand pounds was a very nice windfall, on the other hand it would very soon disappear if she gave many expensive dinner parties. She just laughed and said, "Don't worry, Betty, there's plenty more where that came from …" …

TEMPLE: (*Quietly; watching her*) Go on, Miss Wayne …

BETTY: Well, we had quite a pleasant evening; we talked about the store and the people who worked there, and the customers – and the customers' husbands, and boyfriends, and, well, all the usual things women talk about. (*Hesitantly*) It was almost one o'clock when I left the flat …

TEMPLE: Go on …

BETTY: Just as I was leaving June went into her bedroom and brought out a small parcel. She gave it to me as we stood in the doorway. She said: - "This is for you, Betty. You've always been a very dear friend and I want you to know that I appreciate it. It's just a little present, darling." I took the parcel home, but I was so tired I didn't bother to open it – not until the next morning.

TEMPLE: (*Slowly*) Go on …

A moment.

BETTY: (*Hesitantly; tense*) You'll never guess what was inside that parcel, Mr Temple.

220

TEMPLE: (*Slowly; facing BETTY*) I know what was inside it. A pair of shoes …

FADE IN of closing music.

END OF EPISODE SEVEN

EPISODE EIGHT

THE GUILTY PARTY

OPEN TO:

BETTY: Well, we had quite a pleasant evening; we talked about the store and the people who worked there, and the customers – and the customers' husbands, and boyfriends, and, well, all the usual things women talk about. (*Hesitantly*) It was almost one o'clock when I left the flat …

TEMPLE: Go on …

BETTY: Just as I was leaving June went into her bedroom and brought out a small parcel. She gave it to me as we stood in the doorway. She said: - "This is for you, Betty. You've always been a very dear friend and I want you to know that I appreciate it. It's just a little present, darling." I took the parcel home, but I was so tired I didn't bother to open it – not until the next morning.

TEMPLE: (*Slowly*) Go on …

A moment.

BETTY: (*Hesitantly; tense*) You'll never guess what was inside that parcel, Mr Temple.

TEMPLE: (*Slowly; facing BETTY*) I know what was inside it. A pair of shoes …

STEVE: (*Amazed*) A pair of shoes!

TEMPLE: Yes … (*To BETTY*) Am I right, Miss Wayne?

BETTY: (*Puzzled*) Yes, but – how on earth did you know?

TEMPLE: Go on, finish your story …

BETTY: (*Hesitantly*) Well, there's not much to tell, I …

TEMPLE: I think there is. When did June give Brenda Stirling her present?

STEVE: What do you mean, Paul?

TEMPLE: (*To BETTY*) Didn't June give Brenda Stirling a pair of shoes as well?

BETTY: Yes, she did. I didn't know about this until almost a week later; then one morning, actually it was the day before Brenda's birthday, we were having coffee together and she told me that June had given her a present. I asked her what it was and she produced a pair of shoes.

STEVE: Were they the same as yours?

BETTY: Well, they were evening shoes, the same as mine, but they were really quite different. Both pairs were really quite beautiful though. (*To TEMPLE*) But how did you know that June had given Brenda a pair of shoes. Did she tell you?

TEMPLE: I never met Brenda Stirling.

BETTY: Oh, no, of course not, I was forgetting. (*Quietly; puzzled*) Well – how did you know?

TEMPLE: Miss Wayne, why do you think June Michael gave you those shoes? Why do you think she made a similar present to Brenda Stirling?

BETTY: I – I don't know.

TEMPLE: I think you do know, Miss Wayne, however – just in case you don't – I'll enlighten you. The Cordoba pendant was stolen by a gentleman called Larry Boardman; it was common knowledge that he'd stolen it but Boardman was a pretty shrewd bird and the police just couldn't pin it on him. Boardman also knew that the pendant would have to be kept in storage for a very long time; it was no good trying to get rid of it while the hue and cry was on. About six months after the pendant was stolen Mr Boardman developed an incurable disease and died. Before he died however he sent for a very dear friend of his …

STEVE: (*Quickly*) June Michael?

TEMPLE: Yes, Steve – June Michael. He told June that the pendant was worth at least £50,000 in the open market and he gave her information which would, at a later date, enable her to dispose of it. He did not, however, give her the pendant.

BETTY: Go on, Mr Temple …

TEMPLE: Instead he told June that the pendant must remain where it was for at least another two or three years. By that time it would, in his opinion, be safe to dispose of it.

STEVE: But if June didn't have the pendant …

TEMPLE: He gave June a small strip of microfilm; on that strip of film was inscribed the exact hiding place of the Cordoba pendant.

STEVE: (*Interested*) Go on, darling …

TEMPLE: (*To BETTY*) Am I right, Miss Wayne?

BETTY: Yes. At first June didn't know what to do with the film; she was naturally nervous and rather frightened of the whole business. Whether she ever considered handing it over to the police or not, I don't know. The fact remains however, she didn't. She kept the film for a short while and then one day her handbag was stolen and her flat ransacked. She realised then that other people were interested in the whereabouts of the Cordoba pendant. (*Hesitantly*) She decided to cut the film into three parts and …

TEMPLE: (*Quietly*) Go on …

BETTY: And she put each part in the heel of a shoe. I had one of the shoes, Brenda had one, and June kept the other one herself …

STEVE: Did you know about the film when she gave you the pair of shoes?

BETTY: (*Quickly; tensely*) No, no, I didn't. I swear I didn't! She told me the whole story – much later.

TEMPLE: (*With authority*) How much later?

BETTY: What – what do you mean?

TEMPLE: When did she tell you the whole story?

BETTY: Just after Brenda was murdered …

TEMPLE: (*Quietly*) I see …

STEVE: Miss Wayne, in view of what's happened, don't you think you've been rather fortunate?

BETTY: Fortunate?

STEVE: Yes. Brenda Stirling was murdered. June Michael committed suicide. Mrs Talbot …

BETTY: (*Quickly*) I don't know anything about Mrs Talbot.

STEVE: No? Well, Mrs Talbot was murdered and one of her shoes was stolen.

BETTY: Well, that can't have anything to do with this business. I – I know nothing about Mrs Talbot except that she was a witness in the Stirling case.

TEMPLE: Didn't you meet her one night – at La Martella?

BETTY: (*Tensely*) No … No, I didn't.

TEMPLE: I think you did, Miss Wayne. And shall I tell you what happened that night?

BETTY: Well?

TEMPLE: You sold her your part of the film. Am I right?

BETTY: Yes … Yes, but I still don't understand why she was murdered, unless … (*She stops speaking*)

TEMPLE: (*Quietly*) Unless – what?

BETTY: Nothing.

TEMPLE: Did you murder Mrs Talbot?

BETTY: (*Aghast*) Me?

TEMPLE: Yes.

BETTY: But why should I murder her?

TEMPLE: Well – having done a deal with her you might have decided to go back on it.

BETTY: But surely you don't believe that, why …

TEMPLE: (*With authority*) Miss Wayne – what happened between you and Mrs Talbot?

BETTY: I sold her my part of the film. She paid me a thousand pounds for it. I met her several times because I – Well, I was trying to get more money out of her. She first of all offered me five hundred pounds and I refused it.

TEMPLE: I see. Whose suggestion was it that you met at La Martella?

BETTY: I don't remember. I think, probably, it was mine.

TEMPLE: Did Mrs Talbot tell you whether she was buying the film for herself or …

BETTY: No, she said she was acting as a go-between, but she didn't say who for.

TEMPLE: I see. Miss Wayne, I think you've been a very stupid woman.

BETTY: Yes, I know.

TEMPLE: The moment you knew what was on that film you ought to have taken it to Scotland Yard.

BETTY: Yes, I realise that, Mr Temple, I realise that now more than ever, but – well – it seemed an easy way of making a thousand pounds. After all, I didn't steal the pendant, I didn't even take the film.

TEMPLE: But you knew what was on it.

BETTY: Yes, it's no good pretending I didn't because I did.

TEMPLE: (*After a moment*) Well, that's honest at any rate. (*Suddenly; almost a change of manner*) Miss Wayne, you did me a favour last night, and I haven't forgotten it.

BETTY: You mean?

TEMPLE: You know what I mean. You told me not to go
           down to Reading. Shortly after you warned me I
           received the invitation.

BETTY: From Fabian?

TEMPLE: Yes.

STEVE: What happened – did you overhear part of a
           conversation?

BETTY: Yes. I was in the ladies room, Mrs Temple, and
           Fabian was talking to someone outside. I –
           thought I'd better mention it to your husband.

TEMPLE: I'm glad you did, Miss Wayne.

BETTY: I'm afraid I didn't recognise the other person
           because – well, Fabian seemed to be doing most
           of the talking.

TEMPLE: I see. (*Suddenly*) Miss Wayne, I want you to do
           something for me. I want you to give a cocktail
           party.

BETTY: (*Surprised*) A cocktail party?

TEMPLE: Yes.

BETTY: When?

TEMPLE: Tomorrow night.

BETTY: You mean – here?

TEMPLE: Yes.

BETTY: But what an extraordinary request! Are you
           serious?

TEMPLE: Perfectly serious. Will you do it?

BETTY: Yes, of course – if you really want me to.

TEMPLE: (*Nodding*) I do.

BETTY: Well – who do you want me to invite?

TEMPLE: My wife and I. Sir Graham Forbes. Inspector
           Kingston. Lance Reynolds and Wilfrid Stirling.

BETTY: Yes, all right, Mr Temple. Shall we say, seven
           o'clock – tomorrow night?

TEMPLE: (*Nodding*) Seven o'clock. (*Suddenly; an afterthought*) Oh, and I think perhaps you'd better invite Mr Fabian.

FADE IN of music.

FADE DOWN of music.
Slow FADE UP of many voices: we are in BETTY WAYNE's flat.
TEMPLE, STEVE, SIR GRAHAM FORBES, LANCE REYNOLDS, LOUIS FABIAN and INSPECTOR KINGSTON are present.
FADE the voices down to the background.

BETTY: Won't you have another glass of sherry, Mrs Temple?

STEVE: No, thank you, Miss Wayne.

BETTY: Lance?

REYNOLDS: (*Abruptly*) I'm all right, thank you.

BETTY: Inspector? Oh, you've got a whisky and soda …

KINGSTON: I'd like just a spot more soda if I may?

BETTY: Yes, of course.

FABIAN: (*Handing KINGSTON the syphon*) Here we are, Inspector …

KINGSTON: Oh, thank you very much, sir.

BETTY: Are you all right, Mr Fabian?

FABIAN: (*Worried*) Yes, I'm quite all right, thank you.

BETTY: You don't look too happy with that glass of sherry.

FABIAN: No, no, please – it's very good sherry.

REYNOLDS: (*To BETTY WAYNE; aside*) Look, Betty, I've got an appointment at half past seven – how long is this thing going on?

BETTY: I don't know. It wasn't my idea.

REYNOLDS: What do you mean – it wasn't your idea?

231

The door bell rings.

BETTY: (*Quietly*) Don't be silly, Lance! Do you think
                I should have invited … Oh, excuse me –
                that's the door bell.

FADE DOWN the general conversation.

*BETTY WAYNE crosses into the hall and opens the front
door.*

BETTY: (*Pleasantly*) Oh, good evening, Mr Stirling.
                I'm so glad you could get here.

STIRLING: (*Apologetically*) I'm rather late I'm afraid.

BETTY: That's perfectly all right. Let me take your
                hat. Now come along, I'll introduce you to the
                others.

*FADE UP the noise of general conversation: it suddenly dies
down as BETTY re-enters the room with WILFRID
STIRLING.*

TEMPLE: (*Pleasantly*) Good evening, Mr Stirling.

STIRLING: (*Surprised*) Oh, good evening, sir. Er – how
                are you?

TEMPLE: I'm very well, thank you.

STIRLING: Good evening, Mrs Temple.

STEVE: Good evening.

BETTY: I think you've met Sir Graham Forbes and
                Inspector Kingston?

STIRLING: Yes – we've met before.

KINGSTON: Good evening, Mr Stirling.

FORBES: Good evening.

STIRLING: Good evening, sir.

TEMPLE: This is Mr Reynolds and Mr Fabian.

REYNOLDS: Good evening.

FABIAN: How do you do?

STIRLING: Good evening.

BETTY: Would you care for a glass of sherry, or
                perhaps – ?

232

STIRLING:	Have you a soft drink, Miss Wayne? I'm sorry to be rather a nuisance but …
BETTY:	Tomato juice?
STIRLING:	That would do nicely …
REYNOLDS:	(*Faintly irritated*) Temple, forgive me for asking but is this cocktail party your idea?
TEMPLE:	Yes.
REYNOLDS:	Well, don't you think it would be a very good idea if you came straight to the point?
TEMPLE:	What point?
REYNOLDS:	Look, Mr Temple, we're not exactly children. It's perfectly obvious why you invited us here this evening. Every person in this room – every single person – is connected, in some way or other, with the Gilbert case.
TEMPLE:	Well?
KINGSTON:	(*Quietly; yet with authority*) Well, what's this all about, Mr Temple?
REYNOLDS:	Exactly!
TEMPLE:	I'll tell you what it's all about, Inspector. Several weeks ago a girl called Brenda Stirling was murdered and her fiancé – a young man called Howard Gilbert – was arrested. You all know what happened. Gilbert was tried and eventually convicted.
REYNOLDS:	But he didn't commit the murder!
TEMPLE:	No, he didn't, Mr Reynolds …
FABIAN:	(*Tensely*) Then who did?
TEMPLE:	We're coming to that in a few moments, Mr Fabian. But first of all, let me draw your attention to a particular point which most of you seem to have overlooked. I'm referring to the motive for the murder. Now it was obviously true that Gilbert did have a row

with Brenda; Mr Stirling heard the row – or rather the beginning of it – and in any case Gilbert made no bones about it, he admitted, quite frankly, that they did have a row and that it was a pretty good one. But supposing Gilbert didn't murder his fiancée, then obviously the row was completely unimportant and …

FORBES: You had to find another motive.

TEMPLE: Exactly. Well, it took me some little time to find it, but eventually I succeeded. I found a photograph in June Michael's flat; it was the photograph of a friend of hers, a man who called himself Leonard Bradley. The man's features were vaguely familiar and I asked Sir Graham to check on it. We discovered that Bradley was none other than Larry Boardman, a notorious crook who – it was generally accepted – had been responsible for the disappearance of the Cordoba pendant. The pendant incidentally has never been recovered.

KINGSTON: But Boardman's dead: he died some little time ago.

TEMPLE: Yes, I know. And just before he died he gave June Michael a microfilm which indicated the exact whereabouts of the Cordoba pendant. Several attempts were made to get hold of the film and in desperation June split the film into three parts and hid each part in the heel of a shoe. She kept one shoe herself, the others …

STIRLING: Were given to Brenda and Mrs Talbot!

TEMPLE: To Brenda yes, Mr Stirling – but not to Mrs Talbot. Well, there's your motive.

234

REYNOLDS: Yes, but just a minute, Temple. You say Mrs Talbot didn't have one of the shoes – in other words she didn't have a portion of the film?

TEMPLE: I said it wasn't given to her by June Michael – in actual fact she had it, because she bought it from someone.

KINGSTON: From Miss Michael?

TEMPLE: No – from someone else.

FABIAN: Yes, but how does this fellow Hamilton fit into the picture? The night you came to La Martella you kept asking me whether I'd heard of anyone called Hamilton.

TEMPLE: Hamilton – or rather the gentleman who chooses to call himself Hamilton – knew that Boardman had given June Michael the microfilm and he was determined to get it. He murdered Brenda, faked the June Michael incident to look like suicide …

KINGSTON: (*Surprised*) You mean June Michael was murdered?

TEMPLE: I do, Inspector; and then he commissioned Mrs Talbot to buy the third and missing piece of microfilm. After a certain amount of bargaining she bought it for a thousand pounds. Having bought it however Mrs Talbot refused to hand it over to Hamilton except at a substantial profit. Hamilton agreed to meet her at Farnham; whilst this meeting was taking place he arranged for a confederate of his to search her flat in Soho Square.

STIRLING: And did Hamilton fake the evidence against Howard?

TEMPLE:	Of course. After he'd got Mrs Talbot to swear that she'd seen him leave the bombsite there wasn't a great deal of evidence to fake. Gilbert did have a row with Brenda and he did make a false statement to the police.
STIRLING:	I see.
FABIAN:	(*Irritatedly*) Yes, but you still haven't told us – Who is Mr Hamilton?
TEMPLE:	Don't you know, Mr Fabian?
STEVE:	(*Staggered*) Paul, you're not suggesting that Fabian …
TEMPLE:	(*Quickly*) Look out!!!
FABIAN:	(*Tensely*) Stand back! D'you hear me? Stand back!!!!
TEMPLE:	Steve, don't move!
FABIAN:	If anyone comes near me, I warn you – I'll shoot!
KINGSTON:	Put that gun down, Fabian!
FORBES:	Don't be a damn fool, man – put it down!
FABIAN:	(*Moving across the room*) I warn you, if anybody … (*Tensely*) Get away from that door! Get away from it!
TEMPLE:	(*To BETTY*) Get away from the door, Miss Wayne.
FABIAN:	(*Tensely; alert*) Now look, I'm going to walk across the room towards that door. I'm going to take the key and I'm going to lock it from the other side. If anybody rushes me – I'll shoot. (*Moving*) Now I warn you, stay where you are – all of you. And if you rush the door while I'm locking it I'll shoot through it from the other side. Is that clear? (*A moment*) All right … Now – just – stay – where – you – are …

236

There is a pause; there is the sound of a key being taken from a lock and then the door suddenly slams.

FORBES: Don't move! Don't move, Temple!

FABIAN: (*Shouting from the other side of the door*) I warn you, I'll shoot through the door if anybody comes near it!

There is the sound of a key being turned in a lock.

There is a moment's pause then TEMPLE, FORBES and KINGSTON rush towards the door.

TEMPLE: Force the door! Force it!!!!

FORBES: Be quick, Inspector!

KINGSTON is already holding the door handle and is trying to force the door.

TEMPLE: For goodness sake, break the lock, Inspector!

KINGSTON: Reynolds, reach me that thing in the fireplace! Be quick! Be quick, Reynolds!!!!

Dramatic FADE UP of music.

Slow FADE DOWN of music.

FADE UP of a bell ringing; the bell stops. A door is opened.

STEVE: (*Surprised*) Oh, good afternoon, Inspector!

KINGSTON: Hello, Mrs Temple. Is Mr Temple in?

STEVE: No, I'm afraid he isn't, but I'm expecting him back at any minute.

KINGSTON: Well, I won't stop, I've got an appointment at half past five.

STEVE: Yes, well –

KINGSTON: I was passing so I thought I'd drop in and have a word with him.

STEVE: Yes, of course. He'll be sorry he's missed you. Is there any news?

KINGSTON: I'm afraid not; but it's early days yet. We'll pick him up all right, don't worry.

STEVE: I expect you've had a pretty hectic twenty-four hours?

The telephone starts ringing in the background.

KINGSTON: Hectic! I never want to see another railway station or airport as long as I live.

STEVE: According to the newspapers the men of Scotland Yard … Oh, there's the telephone – will you excuse me?

KINGSTON: Yes, of course. I'll phone Mr Temple tomorrow morning.

STEVE: All right, Inspector! Goodbye!

KINGSTON: Goodbye, Mrs Temple.

FADE UP the sound of the telephone ringing.

The receiver is lifted.

STEVE: (*On the phone*) Hello?

FORBES: (*On the other end of the line*) Hello? Is that you, Steve?

STEVE: Oh, hello, Sir Graham! I'm afraid Paul's out.

FORBES: Oh, dear …

STEVE: I'm expecting him back at any moment though …

We hear the sound of the door opening and closing in the background.

FORBES: Did he leave any message?

STEVE: No, he simply said that if you telephoned I was to ask you … (*Hesitantly*) Wait a minute! I think he's just come in …

The door opens.

TEMPLE: (*Briskly*) Hello, darling! Is that for me?

STEVE: Yes, it's Sir Graham.

TEMPLE: Oh, good.

TEMPLE crosses and takes the receiver from STEVE.

TEMPLE: (*On the phone*) Hello, Sir Graham. Temple here …

238

FORBES: (*Briskly; a shade worried*) Well – what's happened?

TEMPLE: It's all right – there's no need to worry.

FORBES: Are you sure?

TEMPLE: Yes.

FORBES: (*Quietly*) Temple, I hope you know what you're doing …

TEMPLE: I know what I'm doing all right.

FORBES: Well, remember he's got the complete film, if he doesn't keep this appointment …

TEMPLE: He'll keep it all right. This is one appointment he will keep. Now don't forget, Sir Graham, I want the whole place surrounded …

FORBES: We're all ready, Temple. Everything is laid on. We're just waiting for the green light.

TEMPLE: Well – you'll get it tonight, Sir Graham.

FORBES: Good. Nine o'clock?

TEMPLE: Nine o'clock – at La Martella.

FADE IN of music.

FADE DOWN of music.

Slow FADE UP of a dance orchestra; the dance orchestra continues in the background.

We hear the sound of voices in the main hall of La Martella.

STEVE: I don't see any sign of Sir Graham.

TEMPLE: No … He might be on the balcony.

STEVE: Or in the cocktail bar.

TEMPLE: No, he's not in the cocktail bar, I had a look in there while you were in the powder room.

A pause.

STEVE: It's pretty crowded tonight.

TEMPLE: Yes. Let's walk through to the dining room, Steve.

239

FADE UP the dance orchestra; the noise of chatter and the people dancing.

STEVE: Well, if Fabian's here he's managing to keep well out of the way.

TEMPLE: Yes. (*Suddenly*) Hello – there's the Inspector!

STEVE: Where?

TEMPLE: On the balcony.

STEVE: I don't see him. Is Sir Graham with him?

TEMPLE: No, he's on his own. The end table, Steve – look!

STEVE: Oh, yes. I see him.

The dance orchestra stops playing: people start clapping.
After a moment the dancers leave the floor.
Slow FADE DOWN.

TEMPLE: Hello, Inspector!

KINGSTON: (*Surprised*) Why, hello, Mr Temple! What on earth are you doing here?

TEMPLE: I'll give you three guesses.

KINGSTON: Celebrating your silver wedding?

TEMPLE: No.

KINGSTON: Taking dancing lessons?

TEMPLE: No.

KINGSTON: Looking for Mr Fabian?

TEMPLE: Right!

KINGSTON: Well, I think you're going to be unlucky.

TEMPLE: Then what are you doing here?

KINGSTON: If you were given a choice: six hours watching Euston station or six hours at La Martella, which would you choose?

TEMPLE: Neither prospect would enthral me, but I see your point.

KINGSTON: Sit down – let me buy you a drink.

TEMPLE: Well – thank you.

KINGSTON: You know, Mr Temple, there are certain aspects of this case which, well – (*With a little laugh*) Look, let's put our cards on the table – whatever made you suspect Fabian? Fabian was way down on my list.

TEMPLE: Who was at the top of it?

KINGSTON: Why, Howard Gilbert, of course – that's why we arrested him.

TEMPLE: Yes, I know, but –

KINGSTON: You mean later – after the June Michael incident?

TEMPLE: Yes.

KINGSTON: Well, quite frankly, I suspected Lance Reynolds. I even began to suspect the girl's father – Wilfrid Stirling.

TEMPLE: Well, both Reynolds and Stirling were mixed up in this affair; don't have any illusions on that score.

KINGSTON: Yes, but it was Stirling who first brought you into the case.

TEMPLE: Yes.

KINGSTON: But why?

TEMPLE: Look, Kingston – let me begin at the beginning. The Cordoba pendant was stolen by Larry Boardman. He knew it was 'hot' so he hid it and made details on a piece of microfilm of its exact whereabouts. Boardman died and passed the film onto his girl friend June Michael. Now several people were after the Cordoba pendant and they guessed that June had the film.

KINGSTON: What do you mean, several people?

TEMPLE: Well, Reynolds for one. You see Reynolds was friendly with Betty Wayne and he also shared a flat with Howard Gilbert. Now Betty told him that she had part of the film and Reynolds realised that if he could get Howard Gilbert to get him the second part from Brenda Stirling …

KINGSTON: He'd be two thirds of the way home.

TEMPLE: Exactly. All he had to do was to buy – or steal – the final piece of film from June Michael. Gilbert however wasn't interested; he wouldn't play. So, in desperation, Reynolds decided to enlist the services of Wilfrid Stirling. He told him about the film and promised him a cut in the final proceeds. Before Stirling could get the film from Brenda – or rather, her part of it – she was murdered.

KINGSTON: By – ?

TEMPLE: By Hamilton. Now Hamilton was a mysterious individual who came into the picture on the death of Boardman. He knew that June Michael had the film and he was determined to get it. But June began to get very sure of herself; she was only interested in the Cordoba pendant. In short, although she met Hamilton several times at a pub called The Lord Fairfax she refused to do a deal with him. Hamilton was furious about this and turned his attentions towards Brenda Stirling. He met Brenda at The Lord Fairfax but she quite obviously didn't know what Hamilton was talking about; she'd never heard of the film. Unfortunately however she must have told him about June's so called inheritance and the gift of a pair of shoes both to herself and Betty Wayne. Hamilton saw the significance of this and made his first move …

KINGSTON: The murder of Brenda Stirling.

TEMPLE: Yes. Stirling of course was stunned by the murder and immediately suspected Reynolds. However, Reynolds had already heard of this mysterious Mr Hamilton and he finally convinced Stirling that Hamilton was the murderer. When Howard Gilbert was arrested they were horrified; both Stirling and Reynolds made up their minds to try and clear him. Stirling produced a diary of Brenda's which seemed to establish that she had previously made an appointment with a Mr Fairfax. Both Reynolds and Stirling believed that Fairfax was another name for Hamilton. In order to impress this point on me, Reynolds concocted a letter which was intended to establish the fact that Gilbert had been framed – which indeed he had.

KINGSTON: By Hamilton …

TEMPLE: By Hamilton.

KINGSTON: Well, how does Mrs Talbot fit into all this?

TEMPLE: Well, Mrs Talbot worked for Hamilton but I don't think she actually met him; at least not until that fatal appointment at Farnham. She was told by Hamilton to contact Betty Wayne and do a deal over Betty's portion of the microfilm. She was successful in this because Betty suddenly got cold feet and decided she didn't want anything more to do with the affair. Reynolds was furious when he heard that she'd sold her portion of the film to Mrs Talbot for a thousand pounds. He immediately …

KINGSTON: … Contacted Mrs Talbot and offered her fifteen hundred.

243

TEMPLE: I don't know what he offered her, but it certainly must have been pretty tempting because she decided to double-cross Hamilton and do a deal with Reynolds. That's why Reynolds telephoned her that day. He said: "Have you done what Hamilton wanted? Have you got the third shoe?" Meaning, have you done a deal with Betty Wayne.

KINGSTON: M'm – well, we know what happened to Mrs Talbot.

TEMPLE: Yes. We know, Inspector, Mrs Talbot was the sort of person you could very easily underrate.

KINGSTON: Why do you say that?

TEMPLE: Because I think even Hamilton underrated her. He must have paid her a fairly substantial sum to testify against Howard Gilbert.

KINGSTON: Unless he was blackmailing her.

TEMPLE: (*Amused*) Yes, that's a possibility of course. Although, quite frankly, it's my bet Mrs Talbot was about to blackmail Hamilton.

KINGSTON: But how could she do that if she didn't know who he was?

TEMPLE: She began to suspect; she started making inquiries; she even visited a reference library.

KINGSTON: What do you mean?

TEMPLE: She looked up the person she suspected in a reference book. I suppose she must have found out certain things about the mysterious Mr Hamilton and she wanted to check them against the biography of the person she suspected.

KINGSTON: How do you know that?

TEMPLE: Don't you remember what Peter Galino said: he said they met in a reference library. Well, I went to that reference library, Inspector. I

244

found out that Mrs Talbot asked for two books. One was a book called The Theory of the Photographic Process.

KINGSTON: But Reynolds is interested in photography; as a matter of fact that's his hobby.

TEMPLE: Yes, that's why Mrs Talbot asked for that particular book; just in case someone did happen to check up on her visit to the library. In actual fact it was the second book she was interested in.

KINGSTON: My word, she seems to have thought of everything – this Mrs Talbot.

TEMPLE: Not everything, Inspector – or she would never have gone down to Farnham.

KINGSTON: Yes, that's true. Temple, what do you think our chances are?

TEMPLE: Of what?

KINGSTON: (*Surprised by the question*) Of catching Fabian.

TEMPLE: I think they're excellent; but we don't particularly want to catch Mr Fabian.

KINGSTON: (*Tensely*) What do you mean?

A pause.

TEMPLE: (*Quietly*) Why don't you ask me the question, Inspector?

KINGSTON: What question?

TEMPLE: You're wondering about that book; the book that Mrs Talbot consulted. You want to know the title of it.

KINGSTON: Why should I? I – I don't know what you mean.

TEMPLE: The title of the book was Encyclopaedia of the Social Sciences. It contained biographical details of C.I.D. personnel.

KINGSTON: Well?

TEMPLE: The person Mrs Talbot suspected wasn't Mr Fabian – it was Detective-Inspector Kingston.

KINGSTON: (*Amazed*) What! You mean – she suspected me? She thought I was Hamilton?

TEMPLE: Yes.

KINGSTON: But, why? Why, for heaven's sake, should she think that?

TEMPLE: (*After a moment*) Because you are Mr Hamilton, Inspector – that's why!

KINGSTON: (*A moment: quietly, watching TEMPLE*) What do you mean?

TEMPLE: (*Slowly*) Shall I tell you why you came here this evening? (*A moment*) You had a note from Fabian asking you to meet him here. Fabian said that if you didn't meet him he'd put certain facts before Sir Graham Forbes.

KINGSTON: Go on …

The dance orchestra starts to play again: people take to the dance floor.

TEMPLE: You didn't want that to happen – not yet, at any rate. You were prepared to do a deal with Fabian because …

KINGSTON: Why should I be prepared to do a deal with Fabian?

TEMPLE: Because you've now got the complete film, Inspector, and you know perfectly well that your best bet is to let this business die down; then later, retire because of ill health, pick up the pendant, and quietly disappear.

KINGSTON: My dear Temple, what nonsense! If it's a question of your word against mine then I'm sure …

TEMPLE: (*Interrupting KINGSTON*) It isn't a question of anybody's word; it's a question of facts. I know

246

you received that note from Fabian because I told him to write it; I was present when he wrote it and I actually posted it myself. If you don't believe me, ask Mr Fabian.

KINGSTON: (*Puzzled*) what?

TEMPLE: He's standing behind you.

KINGSTON: (*Turning; surprised*) Fabian!

FABIAN: (*Amused*) Good evening, Inspector! Welcome to La Martella ...

KINGSTON: (*Intensely angry*) Why, you double-crossing little ...

TEMPLE: (*Quickly*) Fabian, look out!

KINGSTON strikes out and hits FABIAN on the jaw as TEMPLE moves forward.

FABIAN: (*Receiving the blow*) Ough!

The table is completely over-turned and KINGSTON makes a dash for it. TEMPLE utters an exclamation of annoyance.

A woman screams and from the dance floor there is a sudden babble of excited voices and confused conversations.

The dance orchestra almost stops playing then decides that the best thing to do is to continue.

In the background excited voices can be heard, shouting:

"There he is – he's on the balcony!"

"Stop that man!"

TEMPLE: (*Quickly; tensely*) Fabian, where does that passage lead to?

FABIAN: (*Dazed*) Oh, my jaw! What did you say?

TEMPLE: Where does that passage lead to?!

FABIAN: My office ...

TEMPLE: Anywhere else?

FABIAN: No ... No, I don't think so ...

FORBES and STEVE arrive.

FORBES: What happened?

STEVE: Darling, what happened?

247

TEMPLE: He hit Fabian, overturned the table, and made a dash for it.

FORBES: Well, he won't get far. I've got three men at the end of that passage.

TEMPLE: (*Quickly*) Is there anybody on the roof?

FORBES: Yes, don't worry, Temple – there isn't a loop-hole. I've got half the Flying Squad … Hello, here's Johnson! (*To JOHNSON*) Did you get him, Johnson?

JOHNSON: No, sir. He's locked himself in the office at the end of the corridor.

FORBES: Is that your office, Fabian?

FABIAN: Yes.

FORBES: Is there another entrance?

FABIAN: No …

FORBES: A window?

FABIAN: No.

FORBES: You're sure?

FABIAN: Yes, of course!

JOHNSON: No, there isn't a window, sir – we've checked on it. He'll have to come out the way he went in.

TEMPLE: Good! Come along, Sir Graham!

FADE SCENE.

FADE UP of TEMPLE banging on the door of FABIAN's office.

TEMPLE: Come on, Kingston! Don't be a fool! The game's up … Open the door!

STEVE: Don't stand in front of the door, Paul, in case he fires.

TEMPLE: Come on, Kingston – get this door open!

KINGSTON can be heard moving about inside the room: we hear the sound of furniture being moved.

JOHNSON: (*Puzzled*) What's he doing?

TEMPLE:	It sounds to me as if he's moving the furniture about …
JOHNSON:	Yes.
TEMPLE:	He's probably barricading the door.
FORBES:	Kingston, we'll give you ten seconds – if you don't open the door we'll blow the lock!

KINGSTON is obviously preparing something inside the room; tearing the curtains, moving the furniture.

TEMPLE:	(*Quickly*) Fabian, what's in this office?
FABIAN:	What do you mean?
TEMPLE:	Is there anything else, besides furniture?
FABIAN:	Well, the usual things, filing cabinets and …
STEVE:	(*Suddenly*) Paul!
FORBES:	What is it, Steve?
STEVE:	There's something burning!
TEMPLE:	What?
JOHNSON:	My God, she's right, sir!
FORBES:	Blow the lock, sergeant! Quickly!!!!
JOHNSON:	Stand back, Mrs Temple!

The Sergeant produces a revolver and fires at the lock of the door: he fires several times.

FORBES:	All right, now try it, sergeant!

JOHNSON tries the door; there is a heavy piece of furniture wedged against the door.

JOHNSON:	(*Trying, unsuccessfully, to force the door*) Mr Temple's right, sir – he's wedged the door …
TEMPLE:	(*Helping JOHNSON*) Yes, I think it's the desk … There's a strong smell of something; it's like petrol or …
FABIAN:	(*Softly*) Oh, my God!
FORBES:	What is it, Fabian?
FABIAN:	There's a drum of Veronex; it's in one of the cupboards.
TEMPLE:	Are you sure?

STEVE:	(*Coughing*) What's Veronex?
FORBES:	It's cleaning spirit, isn't it?
FABIAN:	Yes, I've been using it on the carpets, it was …
JOHNSON:	My God, that stuff's highly inflammable. If he's poured that over everything the whole place'll go up!
TEMPLE:	(*Quickly*) By Timothy, that's what he's been doing all right …
FORBES:	My God, he must be crazy to do a thing like that!
TEMPLE:	(*Tensely*) Fabian, listen! Go downstairs – tell the people there's a possibility of a fire breaking out. Don't waste any time … Get everybody outside as quickly as you can!
FABIAN:	Yes, all right, Mr Temple.
FORBES:	Steve, you go down with him …
STEVE:	No, I'd rather wait until …
TEMPLE:	Do what Sir Graham says! Please, darling!
STEVE:	Yes, all right.
FABIAN:	Come along, Mrs Temple!
TEMPLE:	Now the best thing we can do is get every available fire …

As TEMPLE speaks: from inside the room, there is the sound of an explosion as the drum of Veronex catches fire.

JOHNSON:	My God, now it's really started!
FORBES:	(*Calling*) Kingston, you fool – get the door open …
TEMPLE:	(*Calling*) Come out, Kingston … Don't be a damn fool!
FORBES:	My God, you can feel the heat now!
TEMPLE:	Yes, stand back, sergeant!

From inside the room: KINGSTON gives a low, stifled cry.

FORBES:	Do you hear that?
TEMPLE:	Yes. (*Quietly*) He's not going to come out …

JOHNSON: (*Coughing*) I … think … we can break … the door down … now.

TEMPLE: (*Gasping slightly*) No, stand back, sergeant …

FORBES and TEMPLE start to cough.

FADE UP the sound of the fire.

FADE DOWN the sound of the fire.

COMPLETE FADE.

FADE UP of street noises: crowds are gathering outside of the burning building.

We hear the sound of fire engines: firemen issuing instructions: the noise of water issuing from hoses; background noises of falling masonry, etc.

STEVE: Are you feeling all right, Paul?

TEMPLE: (*Very tired*) Yes, don't worry, darling.

STEVE: You've burnt your hand slightly …

TEMPLE: No, it's nothing – just a scratch. Now don't you go and catch cold, Steve.

FORBES: Here's Johnson!

JOHNSON: (*Tired; a little breathless*) They've found him, sir …

FORBES: Oh, good. There's no doubt, I suppose?

JOHNSON: No, I've seen him. It's Kingston all right.

TEMPLE: Was he identifiable?

JOHNSON: Yes – just about, sir.

FORBES: (*Softly*) My God, he must have been crazy to do a thing like that.

TEMPLE: Well, it's perhaps a good job he did, Sir Graham.

FORBES: Yes.

JOHNSON: I think they're just beginning to get the fire under control, sir.

FORBES: Oh, good. Well – that's not my department, thank the Lord!

JOHNSON:	Goodnight, sir.
FORBES:	Goodnight, sergeant.
JOHNSON:	Goodnight, Mrs Temple. Goodnight, sir.
TEMPLE:	Goodnight, sergeant.
STEVE:	Goodnight!

A long pause.

The fire and general noise continues.

STEVE:	Well – what are you thinking about, Sir Graham?
FORBES:	Oh … nothing in particular.
TEMPLE:	Kingston?
FORBES:	No. (*A little laugh*) If you must know, I was thinking about a very large cup of black coffee!
STEVE:	I know exactly the cup you mean, Sir Graham! Come along, darling! Come along, Sir Graham.

FADE DOWN the background noise of the fire etc.
FADE IN of music.

FADE DOWN of music.
FADE music completely.
TEMPLE, STEVE and SIR GRAHAM FORBES are having coffee in the drawing room at Montpelier Square.
TEMPLE is in very good form; care-free.

FORBES:	Steve, this is the most delicious coffee I've ever tasted!
TEMPLE:	Yes, you can't beat Charlie on coffee!
STEVE:	You beast – you know perfectly well I made it.

FORBES laughs.

FORBES:	Well, I suppose I'd better be making a move …
TEMPLE:	Nonsense, you can't go yet. Have some more coffee?
FORBES:	No, thank you. Four's my limit …

TEMPLE: (*Laughing*) Well, you can't go yet, Sir Graham. Steve's absolutely bursting with curiosity. I can see the questions simply popping out of her …

STEVE: Well, the thing I don't understand …

TEMPLE: By Timothy! There you are, Sir Graham!

FORBES: What is it you don't understand, Steve?

STEVE: Well, why did Kingston do all this? After all, he had a pretty good job …

FORBES: He also had a pretty nice collection of debts; apparently he'd been gambling very heavily and had lost nearly seven thousand pounds. After all, the Cordoba pendant was an easy way out. It was worth nearly £50,000 in the open market.

TEMPLE: Besides, don't forget Kingston was in a unique position; once he'd got hold of the pendant it was a simple job to make the necessary contacts.

STEVE: Yes, I can see that of course, but …

TEMPLE: And take Galino. Now Galino obviously knew something about Kingston, that's why he was beaten up. And don't forget Kingston was the only person who was allowed to see Galino at the hospital – except myself. Well, you know what Galino's reactions were. The poor devil changed his original statement – he was that terrified.

STEVE: Yes, of course Kingston admitted that he was at Farnham the afternoon that Mrs Talbot was murdered.

TEMPLE: Exactly. And don't forget he was at La Martella the night that Betty Wayne warned me against going down to Reading.

STEVE: But I thought she'd overheard a conversation between Reynolds and Fabian?

TEMPLE: No, darling, between Fabian and Kingston. And it was that conversation which enabled me to finally confirm my suspicions. I told Kingston that I'd been warned not to go down to Reading but I didn't tell him who had warned me, instead I got Charlie to go down to the phone box on the corner and telephone me. I pretended, in front of Kingston, that it was Reynolds on the phone and I gave him the impression that it was Reynolds who had overheard his conversation with Fabian. Well, you know what happened – or very nearly happened – to Mr Reynolds.

STEVE: I certainly do!

FORBES: But how on earth did you get Miss Wayne to talk?

TEMPLE: By simply frightening her. I told her that I knew who Hamilton was and that I had deliberately given him the impression that it was Reynolds who had warned me against going down to Reading. As soon as she heard about the car accident she knew that I was on the right track and she decided to talk.

FORBES: I see.

STEVE: Well, Paul – tell me: was Fabian working for Kingston?

TEMPLE: No, but Kingston was obviously beginning to make use of him.

FORBES: He must have started by doing Fabian one or two favours. For instance, he quite obviously found out about Lynn Ferguson and tipped him off about her.

TEMPLE: Yes.

STEVE: Then why was Lynn kidnapped?

FORBES: Because Kingston wanted us to concentrate on La Martella; he knew that by kidnapping Lynn he was throwing suspicion onto Fabian.

TEMPLE: Yes, that's why Galino made the statement about finding Hamilton at La Martella. Galino was told to make that statement – in fact he was warned that if he didn't make it the next time he wouldn't be just beaten up, he'd be murdered.

STEVE: (*Softly*) Oh, Paul …

TEMPLE: As soon as Fabian knew the whole story he offered to collaborate. Well – you know what happened.

FORBES: Incidentally, Temple – we picked up Mrs Stone this morning.

STEVE: Who's Mrs Stone?

FORBES: She was the woman you saw at Mrs Talbots; she was working for Kingston. She searched the flat and actually found the second piece of microfilm; the piece which Mrs Talbot bought from Betty Wayne.

STEVE: And she handed it over to Kingston?

TEMPLE: Yes. The real Mrs Talbot of course intended to blackmail Kingston and do a deal with Reynolds. After the Talbot murder Reynolds and Stirling contacted Mrs Stone, but it was too late. She'd already handed over the film. In any case, she knew what had happened to Mrs Talbot and she wasn't taking any chances.

STEVE: Just one more question, darling. Why did Stirling install that listening apparatus? Did he think Betty Wayne was working for Hamilton?

TEMPLE: I don't know whether he thought she was working for Hamilton or not, but he knew that Reynolds was friendly with Miss Wayne and he wanted to make sure that he wasn't being double-crossed.

STEVE: I see.

FORBES: (*Rising*) Well, that's the end of the Gilbert case.

TEMPLE: (*A sigh*) Yes, case number fourteen, Sir Graham …

FORBES: Fourteen? By Timothy!

They laugh.

STEVE: Surely it's not quite the end, Paul. What's going to happen to Howard Gilbert?

FORBES: It's already happened, Steve. He was released this afternoon …

STEVE: Oh, good! (*To TEMPLE*) Congratulations, darling!

TEMPLE: Thank you, Steve.

A slight pause.

FORBES: Well, I suppose I'd better be making a move. What are you going to do now, Temple? (*Quickly*) And no cracks about Sam Dodsworth and your feet on the mantelpiece!

TEMPLE and STEVE laugh.

FORBES: If I remember rightly you were off on a holiday when this business first started.

TEMPLE: Yes, we'd arranged a Continental tour. I'm afraid that's off, for the time being at any rate.

FORBES: Oh – why?

TEMPLE: Well, for one thing, thanks to Mr Hamilton the car's indisposed. Secondly, neither of us feel like a tour – we just want a jolly good rest.

FORBES: I can understand that.

STEVE: The trouble is I want to go to Venice and Paul wants to go to Monte Carlo.

TEMPLE: Oh, darling, we don't want to go to Venice. All that distance just for water and smells and ghastly gondolas.

STEVE: Venice doesn't smell! It's absolute heaven. In any case, what about Monte Carlo?

TEMPLE: Well – what about it?

STEVE: (*Lamely*) It's windy.

TEMPLE: (*Appalled*) Windy? Monte Carlo?

STEVE: Yes, darling. Monte Carlo.

TEMPLE: Nonsense, you're thinking of Eastbourne.

STEVE: Besides, it's the wrong time of the year for Monte Carlo.

TEMPLE: What do you mean, the wrong time of the year? It can't be the wrong time of the year if I want to go there.

STEVE: You know perfectly well I've set my heart on going to Venice!

TEMPLE: Nonsense! Originally we were going to go to Cannes so how on earth … (*Turning; sharply*) Yes, what is it. Charlie?

CHARLIE: Can I have a word with Mrs Temple, sir? It's about the laundry.

STEVE: Yes, all right, Charlie. (*To FORBES*) I shan't be a moment, Sir Graham – don't go.

The door closes.

A pause.

FORBES: (*Quietly*) Temple, it's none of my business of course, but – if you really want a rest I don't advise you to go to Italy. And certainly not Venice.

TEMPLE: Why?

FORBES: (*Tensely*) You haven't heard of the Rosario case?

TEMPLE: No.

FORBES: (*Glancing towards the door*) Well, a man called Rosario – A Venetian – has been accused of murdering his sister – Countess Tala, the wife of a prominent Italian diplomat. Rosario was tried and found guilty; he's due to be executed next Friday.

TEMPLE: (*Intrigued*) Go on …

FORBES: Now the most extraordinary thing is, several people claim to have seen Countess Tala since the murder – if it was murder – took place. A report came through from Roma two days ago that she'd been seen in the Larentzia Palleza; twenty-four hours later a prominent Italian journalist swore that he'd seen Countess Tala at a small café on the outskirts of Milan. And last night – and this is the most extraordinary thing, Temple – a report came through from the Vatican City that …

TEMPLE: Sh!

A moment.

The door opens.

STEVE re-enters.

TEMPLE: (*Brightly; very pleasant*) Ah, hello, darling. Everything all right?

STEVE: Yes, fine. What were you talking about?

TEMPLE: Oh – we were just talking, Steve.

STEVE: Well, I've been thinking. I think perhaps we will go to Monte Carlo after all.

TEMPLE: No, no, I wouldn't hear of it. If you've set your heart on Venice.

STEVE: No, Paul. You've had a very busy time, you deserve a rest.

TEMPLE: Well, I can rest in Venice, my sweet. You know me – easy come, easy go.

STEVE:	No, Paul – you wanted to go to Monte Carlo, so we'll go to Monte Carlo.
TEMPLE:	I'd just as soon go to Venice, Steve. As a matter of fact, I think I'd prefer to go to Venice.
STEVE:	But you said …
TEMPLE:	Yes, I know, darling, but Sir Graham says Venice is romantic, and he's perfectly right. It is romantic. And after all, Steve, we're not getting any younger, are we, darling? If we can snatch just a little romance out of the ordinary, commonplace, every day …
STEVE:	Come off that soapbox! You chiseller!
TEMPLE:	(*Astounded*) What!
STEVE:	Venice! I can just see us at Venice. Me on a gondola and you at police headquarters!
FORBES:	Steve!
TEMPLE:	By Timothy, you were listening!
STEVE:	Of course I was listening! (*Grimly; determined*) Monte Carlo – here we come!

SIR GRAHAM bursts out laughing: he is joined by TEMPLE and STEVE.

FADE IN of closing music.

THE END

Press Pack
Press cuttings about Paul Temple and the Gilbert Case ...

Paul Temple Returns
Radio's veteran sleuth, Paul Temple, who made his first appearance fifteen years ago, returns to the Light Programme for eight weeks on Monday, March 29th.

The title of the new series, by Francis Durbridge, again produced by Martyn C. Webster, who has produced every series since the first broadcast in 1938, is *The Gilbert Case*.

Latest and seventh in line of distinguished actors to play the title role is Peter Coke, an artist whose name is more usually associated with Shakespeare and serious roles. Paul Temple's wife is again inevitably Marjorie Westbury, who receives more fan mail for this programme than from any other broadcast she appears in. Others in the cast are Charles Leno, Richard Williams, Duncan McIntyre, Olaf Olsen, Grizelda Hervey, Peggy Hassard and Lester Mudditt.

The Gilbert Case opens when Wilfrid Stirling (Charles Leno) visits Paul Temple to tell him that he is convinced that Howard Gilbert (David Peel), despite the fact that he himself gave evidence against him, is innocent of his daughter's murder.

By Timothy! A New Paul Temple
Paul Temple, radio's original detective, is to change his identity when he comes back on air.

His radio character will remain the same – but another actor will project him into our homes.

The new Temple is Peter Coke, who looks younger than his forty years and whose most recent radio performances have been in plays of a very different sort – by Strindberg, Thomas Kyd and Anouilh in the Third Programme.

Paul Temple – whose adventures are a regular feature of *The Evening News* – is the creation of Francis Durbridge who has written every serial. The producer throughout has been Martyn C. Webster.

Radio Review by Joan Newton

Paul Temple and The Gilbert Case got away to a good start even though the first episode of this new radio thriller serial adhered closely to what Temple fans may now regard as the traditional opening formula.

A projected holiday, a murderer, a growing interest by the sleuth, holiday postponed and there we are … away on another adventure.

Peter Coke is an admirable choice as Temple and, with anybody else except Marjorie Westbury in the role, the part of Steve would lose its individual attractiveness.

A word of praise is overdue for a recurring favourite, Francis Durbridge's Paul Temple. The latest one, *Paul Temple and the Gilbert Case*, is as good entertainment as its predecessors.

The flaw in all such things, of course, is that one knows that Paul Temple will solve the mystery, and that neither he nor his wife will be killed in the process; and though I willingly make the effort to achieve "suspension of belief," I do sometimes long for a really outrageous and fantastic play in which the detective comes to a sticky end.

Perhaps those benefactors, who sometimes slip a little light relief into the Third Programme, might have a go at this?

Unknown publication

So Paul Temple is back and he hasn't changed a bit. And, what is lucky for him, his wife has not changed either.

What a paragon she is. After fifteen years of phone calls in the middle of the night, holidays always abandoned at the eleventh hour, flatfeet walking on her drawing room carpet and bodies turning up at most inconvenient moments, she just smiles and bears it.

Yes, a lucky dog Paul Temple.

Unknown publication

Listening to the strains of Coronation Scot, I thought as usual "Now we are off on another enjoyable trip with Paul and Steve." And I wondered as usual whether *The Gilbert Case* will prove yet another triumph for radio's best detective. And as usual the end of episode one found me sitting on the edge of my chair with my tongue hanging out panting for more. What is that special quality which hallmarks Francis Durbridge's whodunits just as definitely as that equally special quality which hallmarks the garments of *haute couture*? It is more than style, it is individual distinction, the planning which completes each episode like each new gown with the customer longing for more to come. Peter Coke, the new Paul Temple, impressed me very favourably, especially as being an admirer of Kim Peacock I was a little doubtful about a new interpretation. This, however, was an impeccable performance. Indeed, all the cast were very good, and one looks forward to hearing more of Mr Charles Leno as the plot develops.

And for the record, "a bit of a gammy leg" brought to an end *The Unlucky One*, the first part of *Paul Temple and the Gilbert Case*, in the Light Programme. Yes – he's back again, as masterful and ingratiating as ever, no doubt, to those addicts who have not gone over to space men and atomic sleuths.

Radio Roundabout by Robert Dennison

After keeping listening in varying degrees of suspense since the first episode on March 29th, *Paul Temple and the Gilbert*

Case comes to and end with the eighth episode on Monday when we shall learn whether Howard Gilbert was guilty of murder.

Given a cold-blooded diagnosis, these Paul Temple serials are composed of little substance and lots of situations which lend themselves to suspense but for all that this radio detective has a large following. Why? Perhaps it is because it is Peter Coke who plays the part of Temple and Marjorie Westbury the part of Steve, his wife, who always manages to inveigle herself into the unravelling of these entertaining mysteries.

Paul Temple and the Gilbert Case will be missed: I for one am looking forward to the next story.

Wrong Villain? By **Brian Vaughton** (contains spoilers)
Paul Temple broadcast plays, written by Francis Durbridge, invariably make entertaining listening. The last mystery, *Paul Temple and the Gilbert Case*, which ended on Monday night, was no exception.

However, I do protest at Mr Durbridge's choice of villain in this instance. Usually they are characters who thoroughly deserve their sticky end in the final episode. But surely making a police detective-inspector the master-crook in this play is entirely wrong in principle.

Are we not brought up to aid and respect our police and to "ask a policeman" if in doubt? Or does the BBC consider these standards as old stuff now when they allow a broadcast, with a peak listening figure, to upset our confidence and arouse suspicions about the integrity of the strong arm of the law?

Overworking Them?
One wonders if there is a tendency as there was in earlier years – remember the many calls that were made on the First

Lady of Radio, Gladys Young? – to overwork some of the voices or, in other words, to make excessive demands on them. Take as an instance, Marjorie Westbury, who listeners at home and in Paris know, is ready to tackle any role in drama. She is one of the soloists in the new opera next Sunday, and I hear, is also delighting basic Home Service listeners as the young adventuress, Margaret Catchpole, in a serial of that title taking the story by Cobbold, which Jonquil Antony has adapted.

A Paul Temple thriller would not be the same without the Worcestershire-born actress, who was brought up in Birmingham, so tonight we shall find Miss Westbury in the new serial Mr Francis Durbridge has written around radio's veteran detective and which the Midland author has called *The Gilbert Case*. You will hear it in eight weekly parts.

If some of her admirers think Miss Westbury is in danger of being overworked they must recognise that it is a tribute to her versatility, which has rarely been equalled in the whole range of broadcasting's repertory.

Mimicry is no unimportant part of her gifts. I well remember when Mr Louis MacNeice wanted someone to imitate some parrot calls in one of his shows he thought at once of Miss Westbury. She had to repeat several times piercing parrot squawks, followed by a cracked "and that is over, how d'you do!" It was her gift of mimicry that gave Miss Westbury her first opportunity in radio a little over twenty years ago.

Those Telephone Calls by **W.C. Taylor**
Here comes another "Disgusted!"

Isn't it 'sickening, sir,' that in radio productions nearly every time people answer a telephone they say "Hello" (both Paul Temple and his 'wife' were guilty recently) before giving their name and number.

This is a very bad example, for children particularly. Can't our scriptwriters get out of this awful habit?

York Man Lost Teeth – Call Paul Temple

Paul Temple was said at last night's meeting of the York Executive Council of the National Health Service, to have been the cause of a man losing his lower denture.

The man, it was stated, rushed from the kitchen, where he had been washing himself, to switch on the wireless to follow the latest developments in the Paul Temple serial.

When the radio programme was over, he found the teeth were missing.

He thought his daughter had mistakenly thrown the denture, with some soap wrappings, on the fire.

Laughter followed a suggestion by Mr J. Saville, vice-chairman on the committee, that Paul Temple might be called in to locate the missing denture.

The committee found that the need for replacing the denture was due to a certain amount of lack of care, but in view of the financial circumstances of the man, who had applied for replacement, the charge for it was to be made on National Health Service funds.